The

RENT
COLLECTOR

a novel

CAMRON WRIGHT

SHADOW
MOUNTAIN

Visit us at shadowmountain.com

First published in hardbound 2012.
First published in paperbound 2013.

Library of Congress Cataloging-in-Publication Data
Wright, Camron Steve, author.
    The rent collector / Camron Wright.
        pages cm
    Summary: Sang Ly struggles to survive by picking through garbage in Cambodia's largest mu-
nicipal dump. Under threat of eviction by an embittered old drunk who is charged with collecting
rents from the poor of Stung Meanchey, Sang Ly embarks on a desperate journey to save her ailing
son from a life of ignorance and poverty.
    ISBN 978-1-60907-122-6 (hardbound : alk. paper)
    ISBN 978-1-60907-705-1 (paperbound)
    1. Ragpickers—Cambodia—Fiction. 2. Cambodia—Fiction. I. Title.
    PS3623.R53R46 2012
    813'.6—dc23   2012017499

Printed in the United States of America
PubLitho

20   19

To the Provider of hopes, dreams, and second chances

"*When you realize how perfect everything is*

you will tilt your head back and laugh at the sky."

—BUDDHA

CHAPTER
ONE

I once believed that heroes existed only in old men's fables, that evil in the world had triumphed over good, and that love—a true, unselfish, and abiding love—could only be found in a little girl's imagination. I was certain the gods were deaf, that Buddha was forgotten, and that I would never again see the natural beauty of my home province.

It was a time when I learned about shape-shifters, shadows, and redemption; when I finally grasped the meaning of a Chinese proverb whose venerable words still rattle about in my head: *The most difficult battles in life are those we fight within.*

It was also the year that I came to truly know the Rent Collector.

Beep beep beep.

The steady rumble of uninvited trucks tries to pry into the safety of my dream, a dream in which I am still a child prancing along the trail toward the rice fields where my family works in the Prey Veng province of Cambodia's countryside. It is a cheerful morning as I pull at my grandfather's bony fingers, tugging him along while he struggles to keep up.

"Hurry, *Ancient Snail*," I say with a smug yet spirited bounce.

"If I am a snail," he quips, "you are *salt,* and you'll soon have to drag my dead and lifeless body back home and explain to the village what you have done!"

I pay him no mind and instead pounce like a frog, jumping from rock to rock along the path.

"Perfect," I answer, not letting my determination waver. "Everyone in the village loves snail. Tonight, we'll eat like kings."

I catch the slightest smile before he heaves a sigh—but then he shuffles to a stop. His gaze sharpens, his head tilts, his attention shifts to the distant countryside. Then we both feel the ground beneath us tremble.

He bends close, squints his eyes at mine, and peeks into my thoughts as though he were the village fortune-teller. I find it unnerving and so I glance down at my bare and dirty toes. He won't allow it. With a touch from his calloused finger to my chin he raises my gaze. He speaks assuredly, but still with enough grandfatherly giggle trailing in his voice to make certain my little-girl ears pay attention to every smiling syllable.

"Life will not always be so hard or cruel. Our difficulties are but a moment."

I stare back, trying to make sense of his words, for my life is neither *hard* nor *cruel.* I am still too young to recognize that we are poor— that in spite of the grandeur of the province and the hours my family toils each day, we don't own the land on which we work. I haven't yet grasped that earning enough money to buy food on the very day we eat it isn't an adventure embraced by the world.

The rumble grows louder, and Grandfather rocks forward on his toes.

"Remember, Sang Ly. When you find your purpose—*and you will find your purpose*—never let go. Peace is a product of both patience and persistence."

How can a child pretend to make sense of such a puzzling phrase?

"Sang Ly," he repeats, as if he finds eminent joy in the sound of my name, "it starts today. Today is going to be a very lucky day."

I am tired of the games, tired of his words zipping past like dizzy fireflies. I reach out and latch on to his cheeks, pinching them tightly together. "What are you saying, Grandfather? You don't make any sense."

"Sang Ly, the trucks are coming. It is time to go." His lips continue to move but his voice grows younger, stronger. "Sang Ly, wake up. The trucks are here. It's time for me to go."

As my husband, Ki Lim, rocks me awake, it isn't my grandfather who is sucked away from the safety of a child's dream. Rather, it is me.

The touch of my husband, the stir of our child, the relentless beeping of the snaking trucks confirm that I am no longer a girl of seven at home in the distant province but a grown woman of twenty-nine living at Stung Meanchey.

"I'm sorry," I whisper to the dark shape of the man standing over me. "I overslept. I dreamed that I was . . ."

I rub at my eyes. My dreams don't matter. I was supposed to pack last night's rice into Ki's carry tin for today's lunch. He needed to get an early start, as we must earn an extra 12,000 *riel* today to have enough to pay the Cow.

"I am sorry," I say again, seeking his understanding with all the softness and sincerity that a dazed and drowsy wife can muster. "Hurry. Go now, and I will bring your lunch."

Like Grandfather in my dream, Ki also sighs deeply.

"If you come, please be careful. Watch for needles and stay back, far away from the trucks. You know what happened to Prak Sim."

I nod, still groggy, but awake enough to wonder if I can lie back down after he leaves, close my eyes, and coax Grandfather's dreams back into my head—but then the baby cries.

With careful hands, Ki picks up our son, Nisay, from the floor near the foot of our mat where he sleeps and passes him to me. At nearly sixteen months, the child is still small enough that I can carry him in one arm with ease. He should be talking, watching our lips, listening to us repeat his name, mimicking our words with baby laughs and giggles. Instead, when he's not fussing, his gaze is hollow and distant. His hair is thin and patchy, his little naked belly protrudes below his skinny ribs as though he's swallowed a ball, and I feel like a neglectful mother every time I take him out onto the city's streets.

It's not that we aren't trying to feed the boy; we beg him to eat. When he does, however, it mostly races through him, flowing out the other end as a never-ending bout of nighttime diarrhea that I scrub off the floor each morning.

"Do we give him the medicine this early?" Ki asks.

"Later, after he eats. It will be easier for him to keep it down."

"Let's hope he's feeling better." Ki says, before turning toward the sound of the trucks.

"I'm certain of it," I reply, wanting to tell him about my dream. Instead I wrap our naked baby in a towel and gently rock him in my arms, hoping to settle his cries.

"Please be careful," Ki repeats as he steps to the canvas curtain that serves as our front door to pull on his boots.

I lift the baby's broom-handle arm and attempt to wave good-bye to Daddy, but Ki Lim has already stepped outside and is trudging off into the early-morning darkness, answering the incessant siren call of the burping trucks.

"I dreamed again about Grandfather," I finally whisper to the only one possibly listening, a child now quietly suckling against my chest in the darkness. "Only today it was different."

I listen to his labored breathing, imagine him tilting back his head and asking, *"How? How was the dream about Grandfather different today, Mother?"*

I pause instinctively before I answer, waiting just long enough to heighten his interest. "Today was different, Nisay, because before he left, Grandfather promised that it would be a *very lucky day*."

When people ask where we live, I tell them we reside alongside the bank of a beautiful river called *Stung Meanchey*. After all, the name does mean *River of Victory*. If they know the place at all, they hesitate, smile quizzically, and then we both break out into tremendous laughter, for in spite of being named *river,* Stung Meanchey is the largest municipal waste dump in Phnom Penh—indeed, in all of Cambodia.

The place is mountainous, covering over 100 acres. Piles of putrid rubbish tower hundreds of feet high, surrounded by constantly shifting valleys that weave and connect like the web of a jungle spider. Navigating its changing paths can be tricky.

I tie my hair behind my head and step outside the structure that we call home: a three-walled shed of sorts that was once used to protect bags of concrete from the rain. It sits atop a small mound at the dump's northeastern perimeter, slightly elevated above the shacks that lie distant on each side.

Since there are no structures allowed within the center of the dump itself, my view of the place is unobstructed and occasionally quite spectacular, especially after a hard rain has banished the constant haze. In fact, if anyone tries to build a permanent shelter within the dump proper, it is torn down by government workers (hired thugs). As such, the massive kingdom of Stung Meanchey is an encircled fortress, guarded by tin and cardboard castle walls on every perimeter.

I don't intend to portray the place as miserable or entirely without joy. On the contrary—in spite of its hardships, there are slivers of time when life at the dump feels normal, almost beautiful. Pigs forage in the dirt lanes, children pick teams and play soccer, mothers and fathers banter about their day, babies are born, life presses on.

It is the beautiful times I cherish.

This morning I stand outside and survey my surroundings, hoping to divine what might be in store. The smoke is tolerable, subdued by a brief thundershower last night, and I nod at my distant neighbors already busily about their daily activities. I brush the swarming flies away from our cistern, scoop a pan of water, and then hurry back to clean up our bed mat where Nisay sleeps. He has not been well and so, for many weeks, my first morning job has been to wash away his diarrhea. It may sound disgusting, but in a place of swirling odors, we hardly notice. Frankly, cleaning up his mess is the least of our problems.

I tease that we live by a river, but there is truth to my jest. When the rains come, they leach through the rotting trash, causing foul liquids to ooze, mix, and trickle into noxious streams. The waters splash and then dry, leaving ugly, black stains that won't go away for days. They cause our skin to rash. Mostly they just stink.

Even though it is not wise to touch such polluted waters, they're difficult to avoid. You see, we haven't yet figured out a way to move around this place without touching the ground.

But toxic water is not our greatest danger. That would be the fires.

As I said, today the smoke is tolerable. Other days, it hangs thick in spots, making it impossible to see beyond the first rise of garbage. There is both smoke and fire because as the mountains of garbage around us decompose, they form and trap methane gas. Beneath the weight of the piles, the temperatures rise until the gas ignites and burns. Stung Meanchey is literally always on fire, and it is almost impossible to put out the flames. Monstrous government bulldozers will push the garbage around, hoping to reduce the hazard, but ironically, they don't care who they run over and bury in the process.

We finally get extended relief from the smoke when the rainy season begins—but then the brown rivers form and . . . well, it is perplexing to live at Stung Meanchey.

We never know whether or not to hope for rain.

The Cow knocks on our door early.

We don't call her *Cow* to her face, though I hardly think she would notice or care. She might even wear the title as a badge of honor. Her real name is Sopeap Sin, which means *the kind and pretty one.* Her parents were delusional and blind.

Sopeap is an abrupt, bitter, angry woman who has lived at Stung Meanchey longer than anyone can remember. There is a story told by some—perhaps myth, perhaps not—that claims she was the illegitimate child of Vadavamukha, a sky god with the body of a man and the head of a horse. (Having a horse-headed father would explain a lot.) The myth says that for years he hid his daughter in a trash can to conceal the evidence of his escapades from his wife, Reak Ksaksar Devy, the blood goddess. One day, however, when Reak became suspicious, Vadavamukha hurled the can from the sky. It landed at Stung Meanchey with Sopeap inside—and she has been here ever since.

Of course, I don't really believe the myth. A sky god, horse head or not, would never waste a completely good garbage can on Sopeap Sin.

On a rare occasion, the woman will salvage trash like the rest of us. Most days, however, her time is spent sleeping, swearing, or drinking cheap rice wine. Yet at the first of every month—the only time Sopeap seems to be remotely sober—she also collects rent for several landowners from the poor families who live in the huts that circle Stung Meanchey. Besides *the Cow,* we also call her *the Rent Collector.*

Sopeap wastes no time.

"You have my money?" she demands, sounding like an angry schoolmaster, the kind who long ago silently smothered patience and concern.

I reach into my pocket and pull out our entire fortune, all the money we have to our name, and hand it over (except for just enough that I have kept out to buy today's dinner).

She knows better than to waste time counting.

"This is not enough. I need the rest!"

My hesitation betrays a feeble excuse poised on my tongue. She doesn't wait for my fibs but instead begins to berate me.

"Lazy child! Sang Ly, I have people begging me for this space."

It would be funny if it weren't true—not the first part, as Ki and I are anything but lazy, but the fact that others wait to get into Stung Meanchey. It's a notion that causes me to grin.

"What do you smile at?" she bellows. "If you can't pay, I will have no choice but to move others into this spot. You foolish girl!"

I want to kick this cow in the udder, but instead I clasp my hands together in a gesture of mercy, a simple plea for understanding.

"We had the money, but Nisay has not been well. We had to buy him medicine this week, American medicine, to see if it would help."

"Foolishness!" she hisses.

When I'm in a cheerful mood, I will often count the number of times Sopeap uses the word *foolish*. This morning, however, she is especially irritated, and so I try to be serious.

"We will have our rent today, I assure you. Ki Lim is already out working the trucks. He will gather more than enough." I straighten and stand tall, attempting to project confidence.

"In a single day? Impossible!" she declares. I nod, but in a circular motion, so as to neither agree nor disagree. She watches my head circle, takes a drink from her bottle, and then swallows hard.

"Sang Ly," she exclaims irritably, "the landowners expect their money and I have my own obligations." She turns in disgust, then calls back to me, "I will be back tonight."

At the dump we don't take fashion too seriously, but as she waddles away, I clench my teeth to stifle my laughter. No matter the time of year, even in the hottest weather, the woman never removes the hideous brown socks that sag ridiculously around her already thick ankles.

Somehow she senses my amusement because, without turning around, she reinforces her threat.

"Tonight!"

CHAPTER
TWO

The sun at Stung Meanchey shows no prejudice. It scorches the old and young, the fat and skinny, the humble and proud. Ki once said he noticed that it only shines on the poor in this particular spot of Cambodia, and he's right—but only because nobody rich lives at the dump. The sun's heat is especially hard on the pickers—those who sort through the garbage—since most wear long-sleeved shirts and full-length pants, tucked into heavy rubber boots, to protect themselves from the flies, filth, and smoldering fires.

The work is grueling in this place where Phnom Penh's poorest families struggle to build a life from what others throw away—a life where the hope of tomorrow is traded to satisfy the hunger of today.

To make it through the long hours, many will rest in the early afternoon while they eat lunch beneath makeshift lean-tos. The shelters are temporary and consist of a cardboard floor (cardboard is plentiful at the dump), bamboo poles or tree branches tied together to form a skeletal shell, and a cloth or canvas canopy stretched across the top to provide shade.

Though most of the shelters are rudimentary and crude, some are elaborate, even works of art. And a shelter that has required effort to build sometimes becomes more than just a temporary place to rest; it becomes an oasis in the filth, a gathering place.

I have noticed this phenomenon especially among the female pickers. Perhaps it's a subconscious nesting competition. Jorani Kahn will use a floral sheet instead of dirty canvas. Dara Neak will layer many pieces of cardboard on the ground to offer a softer place to sit. Sida Son will carry in a larger pot of water for those she invites to join her. Even at Stung Meanchey—perhaps *especially* at Stung Meanchey—people still long for social acceptance.

In spite of these efforts, attempts at permanence are fleeting.

The drivers of the monster bulldozers that push the trash into piles at night will sometimes work around the shelters, leaving them intact for several days. Other times, a beautiful shelter, painstakingly crafted during the better part of a morning, may be nothing but a mix of flattened hope and moldering trash a day later. It's a lesson that is learned early at Stung Meanchey—and yet, it's a lesson not of discouragement but rather of persistence. Just as ants do when their nest is disturbed, we return, survey the damage, and then without hesitation immediately get to work rebuilding.

Though many of the shelters are inviting, even charming, no clear-thinking person would ever dare to stay the night—unless waking up beneath a mountain of smoldering, stinking, smothering trash sounds like a fun way to die. Ki says his friend's cousin's brother was killed in this manner, but I think he's just teasing me, trying to scare me into being extra careful as I travel the dump's paths. Whenever I ask him to point out the friend or the cousin, he promises he will, but he never does.

As I arrive with my child at the area where the shelters have been built, on a plateau of trash above the dumping trucks, I try to spot Ki. It's just after noon, too early for most of the pickers to have taken their first break, so the trucks are still swarmed. Though I recognize some of the pickers, there are many I don't know. Faces at the dump constantly change.

I have packed Ki's rice into his lunch tin, except for a little I mashed up to feed Nisay, and when I finally see my husband, I wave the pail in the air with my free hand to get his attention. He motions that he'll come momentarily. With Nisay's weight putting my left hip to sleep, and my right hip about to follow suit, we look for a place to sit.

"Hey, Sang Ly! Over here!"

It's Lucky Fat. When the boy sees us, he hollers for us to join him. He's built a rather crude shelter, but I humbly accept his offer and lay Nisay on the cardboard in the shade beneath the canopy. My baby fusses when I put him down, but I let him be, hoping the heat of the day will soon coax him back to sleep.

"Are you bringin' Ki lunch?" Lucky asks, with more animation than any human being living in a dump should be able to display.

"Surely. Do you have lunch yourself?"

He nods, looking pleased that I would ask.

I don't know Lucky's real name, but I have no doubt that he popped out of the womb both plump and happy. Unfortunately, since he's an abandoned child, no parents are around to ask. He's called *Lucky* because he has an uncanny knack for finding money lost amongst the garbage. He's called *Fat* because . . . well, he's fat. Many say that Lucky looks just like a grinning Chinese Buddha (not the Cambodian Buddha, who is quite skinny). Lucky takes the comparison kindly and, for the past year, has been collecting Buddha statues he finds amongst the trash. Now, a dozen months later, his hut is so brimming with broken Buddhas that a newcomer might conclude the child is religious, obsessive, or desirous to become a monk.

In spite of his nickname, Lucky's life has not been easy. He was left at the dump at just seven years of age, shortly after we arrived. Although I could never imagine abandoning my own child, I have seen enough desperation in my life to understand the mind-set of those who do. However, what is unfathomable to me is that with an array of choices available for leaving a child—orphanages, monasteries, foreign medical clinics—how could any mother choose to leave her child at the dump, a place where useless things are thrown away?

Still, Lucky has survived admirably.

He was taught how to sort trash by Prak Sim, another boy orphan four years older. Even with the difference in their ages, the two became fast friends, working together, living as brothers. Eight months ago, however, Prak Sim was run over and killed by a garbage truck. If it were me and I had lost my family in such a tragic manner, in a place so desperate and bleak, I would have chased after the truck and thrown myself beneath the massive and heartless tires as well. Not Lucky. To this day, he remains cheerful.

As Ki approaches, struggling to carry his bag, Lucky's grin is wider than normal.

"Either my husband has resorted to gathering rocks, or it's been a very good day," I say to Lucky, as I wait for Ki to fill in with his explanation. He wastes no time.

"It was the second truck this morning. It carried a load of bent pipe connectors. We could all hear them clanking against the sides as they came out, and the pile was swarmed; I was right there and gathered up a good number of them."

Lucky is nodding ferociously, as if he's known all along, and it's only then I realize he is also sitting against a bag full of metal.

"Do you know what this means?" Ki asks.

"We get to eat tonight?" I say wryly.

"We will actually have enough to pay the Cow. She's going to bust an udder."

Lucky laughs like a jackal, and it catches us so off guard we can't help but follow suit—and then Nisay stirs.

"Oh, and I almost forgot," Ki adds as he reaches for his bag. He searches in the sack and removes a book. "It's old, but I think Nisay will like it."

He hands it over, and I thumb its dirty pages. The edges are worn and the back cover is water stained, but the illustrations inside remain vibrant, crisp, and colorful. Though I can't read the words, I can see that it is certainly a book for children—and a perfect gift.

"Did you buy this?" I ask.

"No. I found it just before the pipe truck arrived. Meng reached for it at the same time, actually grabbed it first, but when I reminded him that Nisay's been sick, he handed it over."

"That was nice," I say.

"Now, take what money I have," he continues, "and go buy pork and papaya for dinner, and some of the good rice. I'll be home later to celebrate. Who knows what else I'll find?"

As I make my way down the trail of trampled garbage, Grandfather's words ring in my head.

"It's going to be a very lucky day."

In spite of the sun's glare, I raise my chin and step confidently across the matted path of flattened trash.

"I can hardly wait to see the look on Sopeap's face," I tell Nisay, who only grunts at my rambling as I carry him home. "I will say nothing at first, as she demands her money, but will instead bow my head to the ground and linger patiently for her fury to build. It will be like when we watch the storm clouds thicken, churn, and complain as they rumble over the dump in their tantrums of thunder."

I stop for Nisay to acknowledge me and agree that his mother is crafting a brilliant plan. Though he says nothing, I won't let his lack of enthusiasm silence me. "It will be all I can do not to grin," I tell him. "I'm going to stand there until she calls me foolish at least a half dozen times. Then I will lift my chin and ask her if she is finished. She will be so taken aback by my manner and confidence that she will pause with utter shock. Then, after she exhales a long, stale breath, and just at the moment she is about to lash out again, I will roll open my fingers and present her with the rest of this month's rent and most of next month's. If she doesn't snatch it up right away, I'll press the money into her hand and then wave her toward the door as I declare, 'Sopeap, our business is finished!'"

I've painted such a vivid description, I want to clap. Of course, that's difficult with a child in one arm and my child's book in the other.

"Your mother, Nisay," I say instead, "will have stood up with pride to the Rent Collector of Stung Meanchey."

Only then do I finally hear my son gurgle and laugh.

Nisay is sitting up on the floor between my straddled legs. He is feeling better, so we take the opportunity to inspect his gift—his first book. I point to a picture and then wait for him to notice, as if his mother reads to him every night before bed. Instead, he reaches for the pages with an effort that says, *If I can just get hold of that, it's going straight into my mouth.*

I keep the book distant, but he remains undeterred.

"Nisay," I announce, "I'm going to read you a story," as if my explanation will change his mind about chewing on the edges of the delicious pages.

An illustration of a majestic grove of trees adorns the opening spread. Beneath the trees stands a young Cambodian mother cradling her son. The wind must be blowing because the leaves swirl around them both as they watch in awed wonder. I have no clue what the words beneath the image say, so I point instead to the characters and make up a story of my own.

"This mother cares very much for her son, just like I care for you."

In spite of its being true, it's a ridiculous way for any story to begin, and I'm certain that Nisay understands his mother is a fraud. I turn the page to see that the same woman and her son have climbed a great mountain. I skip to the next and notice they stand by a deep blue ocean. How, I wonder, do this mother and child get around so quickly? If I were writing this story, I would surely do things differently.

I am about to try again, devising a reasonable plot in my head, when I hear Ki approach. He will be surprised to see us reading. When he doesn't step in right away and I hear the sound of slurred words, I realize it is Sopeap, still drunk and returning for the rent.

"Coming," I announce, not wanting the woman to enter my house without permission. I leave Nisay on the floor but set his book out of reach, at least temporarily, while I go and tend to Sopeap.

The sun is just setting, and when I pull back the tarp, it takes a minute for my eyes to adjust properly. My heart drops. It is not Sopeap. It is Ki. He has fallen to the ground and is crawling toward the house. His shirt is stained crimson from blood oozing from behind his right ear. He tries to speak but can only spit red.

I don't understand his words, but I know exactly what has happened. There are gangs that roam the dump—Ki has been robbed.

There are no more dreams, no visits from Grandfather, no more *luck*. Instead, by early morning, dark circles on the mat beneath Ki's head form what look like halos in various shades of red and brown. He has slept through the night with a rag held to his wound. But in spite of the hours that have passed, when he sits up, fresh ruby droplets spider down the back of his neck, racing each other across his patchy, jaundiced skin.

"Ki, you're still bleeding," I say, in a hushed tone that I hope won't wake the baby. I reach out and press the rag against his matted hair. "We must get you to a doctor."

His reply seeps with disappointment. "We have no money."

"I have a little left from yesterday," I say, "and we can borrow more from Mother."

"Sang Ly, she's barely making it herself."

He is right. "Then take what little we have," I tell him. "At least try. We will go with you." As I reach for Nisay, Ki Lim waves me away.

"Stay with the baby!" His voice is instantly stern and hard, now lacking yesterday's confidence.

"You can't go alone," I tell him. "Not like this."

"Sang Ly!" he answers, in a tone that demands I listen. "I said *I'll be fine!*"

I argue no further, but press the last of our money into his hand and then tie a clean rag around his wound. He pushes on his sandals.

I want to follow him out of the dump to at least make sure he gets to the paved streets, but then Nisay's whimper reminds me that the child still needs to be cleaned. Instead I watch from the curtain as Ki stumbles away from the house and toward the path that connects to the city.

I loved my grandfather and I remember him fondly. After all, he virtually raised me. Still, I gaze heavenward and finish our conversation. I imagine I've grasped grandfather's cheeks once again in my hands to look him in the eyes. Mine are no longer little girl hands, but those of a grown woman—and my declaration is simple.

"*Good* luck, Grandfather. We needed *good* luck!"

By late afternoon, I have scrubbed away the blood from our floor and I'm fussing about, repeating mundane tasks while trying to amuse Nisay.

Ki has not returned.

Then a voice calls out. "Sang Ly?"

I recognize the tone, and it is not my husband. Sopeap has returned. I freeze, but she calls out again more loudly.

"Sang Ly!"

I consider staying quiet, but in a one-room home there is nowhere to hide. All she'd need to do is pull back the curtain to find us. Then Nisay whimpers, giving us away. "Traitor," I mutter.

I step to the tarp and reach for the corner. Even before throwing it open, I smell liquor mixed with disdain. There is no greeting between us.

"Do you have the rest of my money?"

My head hangs as planned, but I am not pretending.

I shouldn't have schemed such a cruel plan to berate her, imagining I could present our rent so arrogantly. It was my pride that brought this evil upon our family. The ancestors are punishing me for sure. My heart wants to explain but my head knows it is useless.

"No. I am sorry."

Sopeap has always been an ugly barking dog, an animal that annoys but doesn't bite. Today she shows teeth. Her snarl is deep and growling. Her stare is grey and cold. "Be gone by tomorrow!"

At first I step back. Then I plead forgiveness. "Please, no! Ki was robbed last night, his head was cut open, everything was taken."

She grunts her disbelief. "Always an excuse. Be gone by morning or I will send the police!"

Nisay must sense my desperation because his whimper turns into a cry. As Sopeap glances at the child, she spies his book spread open on the floor.

And then, Sopeap freezes. Her shoulders slump, her breathing halts, her gaze drops. The ferocious storm of anger and lightning that encircled us only moments before dissipates. She takes a step forward, inside of our home, as if she can hardly believe what she is seeing. She takes a second step and her lips open, then quiver, but no words escape. For what feels like several minutes, but is probably only moments, she says nothing.

I try to read her eyes through the silence. I struggle to grasp what is happening, but, like the child in my grandfather's dream, I lack understanding. She shuffles another step closer to my son. I'm so confused that my instincts take over and I rush in front and snatch Nisay from the floor.

Sopeap pays no attention.

The sound starts low at first. As it mixes with Nisay's fussing, I'm not sure where it is coming from. It could be the muted howl of a wounded dog, but it's far away—and then I realize it's coming from Sopeap.

It grows louder—a painful, sorrowing lament, as if all the earth's darkness were conspiring to snuff out her existence. As she moans, she stoops down, almost sitting, but with no chair. It's as if she is afraid to touch the book at first. Then, after her fingers brush its surface, she lets them wrap about the cover to pull it close, handling it as though it were a king's treasure.

It's a beautiful book, but it's still old and tattered. With her stained hands, she opens the cover and turns a single page, hesitates, and then turns another. Her eyes lock onto each new picture, as if every colorful drawing confirms to her brain what her eyes see and her fingers touch: *It's real. It's not a dream.*

Her groaning grows, and I understand that the woman—a person I believed to be beyond feeling—is so awash in anguish and torment that I don't know what to do. I reach out and touch her shoulder, thinking it will help, but she doesn't respond. Instead, still crouched, she begins to rock ever so gently, forward and back, forward and back. I step away, sensing that though I stand in my own home, I don't belong, even as a spectator, to so much personal grief and suffering.

I find myself wishing, hoping, praying that Ki Lim will arrive and rescue me, help me to know what to do, how to help. But he doesn't, and for what feels like an eternity, Sopeap doesn't move from her crouched spot on the floor. And then gradually, with each exhaled breath, the moaning subsides, the heaving softens, the rocking slows.

Without speaking a word, Sopeap rises, then stumbles across the room, around our drape of a door, and out to the front of my house.

I follow.

She is three steps away when, for the first time, she realizes that I am watching. She glances first at the book in her hand, then back toward me and Nisay. When she focuses on the book for a second time, I sense what she is thinking, and I both nod with my head and gesture with my hands, as if to say, "Please, keep the book."

She doesn't acknowledge but she must understand because she turns away and flees, soon swallowed by the dump's concealing smoke and haze.

I return Nisay to the mat inside, unable to process what I have witnessed. I continue my duties—fuss with Nisay, clean up his mess, straighten our bed mat—but I also replay the scene of Sopeap and the book over and over in my head. It's like watching a movie in the city that you've seen a hundred times, knowing how it always ends—but then one day, it ends differently.

How can a woman so empty and beyond feeling become so over-come with emotion that she can't speak? But there is more to the picture. In my mind, as I watch her study again each page of Nisay's book, it finally hits me.

"That's it!" I exclaim aloud.

I pause to let my head absorb, process, and ponder my discovery.

It was Sopeap's eyes, the way they darted at every picture, the timing of each turn of the page, the soft movement of her lips. Is it possible? Yes, I'm certain of it. Sopeap Sin, the woman we call *the Cow*—she can read!

It is late when Ki returns. I light a lamp so that the flame's glow will let him see to get into bed. He is grinning. The white tape and sterile gauze that wrap his bandaged head contrast with his bronze skin, which has finally returned to a healthy color.

"Thank goodness you're back. I've been so worried."

"I'm fine," he replies casually—too casually.

"What did the doctor say?"

"Parlez-vous Français?"

"What?"

"I have no idea either. She was speaking French. She stitched me up, gave me a shot, and right now—*I feel really good.*"

The anger in his face is gone. Instead his pupils are unusually wide and his speech curiously slow.

"Do we owe them money?" I ask, hating to broach the subject. Oddly, it doesn't bother him.

"It was free. I went to the charity clinic, near the Russian hospital, off Khemarak Boulevard. You know, the clinic the French run."

I wrinkle my brow. "But they only treat pregnant women—and babies." I know this because I took Nisay there just a few weeks earlier.

Ki's dilated eyes twinkle. "Yeah, but I passed out on their waiting room floor. What could they do? I was bleeding all over their tile."

When he giggles, I can't help but join him, laughing more at his intoxication than his story. "What did they give you, anyway?"

"I'm not sure, but it really helps!"

"Then you still have the money?"

Despite the relaxing effects of the drugs, he turns serious for the first time since his return. He shakes his head back and forth as his fists tighten—not in an angry manner, just matter-of-fact.

"Sang Ly, you have no more worry about the gangs robbing us."

"Why not?" I ask.

Ki sucks in a heavy breath and then pulls up one leg of his pants. In the flickering light of our single oil lamp, I can see, strapped to his ankle, the unmistakable outline of a long, silver, razor knife.

In the morning I remove Ki's bandage and inspect his wound. In spite of his wincing, the stitching is admirable, the bleeding has stopped, and I can tell that Ki is going to live for at least another day. I break the news. "Doctor, I think the patient will survive!"

He's not half as amused as I. After I replace his bandage, he rolls back down to the floor. The happy drugs are now a distant memory.

Without offering an explanation, I pull on my pants, long socks, and boots, and then reach for my gloves and straw hat. "I'll be in the garden," I announce, trying to be cheerful.

Considering that we are out of rice, I see no other option. Since Ki is in no shape to pick, I will go today instead. He cracks open a stare, certain that I've lost my mind. When he doesn't utter a word, I try again. "I'm leaving the cave to hunt. I'll be back with food."

Perhaps drugs dull one's senses. Perhaps I'm just not that funny. Either way, I decide directness is now my only option. "Watch the baby, Ki. I'm going to pick."

I grab an empty canvas sack, wave my good-bye, and then trek out to greet a new day at the dump. As I do, there's one thought on my mind: *Stay away, Grandfather. I don't have the time or patience for any more of your luck.*

I have been told that there is a specialized college degree that stud-ies civilizations by sifting through the layers of their trash. If this is true, if there really is a degree called *Somran Vichea,* or garbology, as Dara Neak claims, I should be the teacher. It also brings up another fascinating question: If people realized someone would be sorting through their trash, would they be more careful in what they throw away?

One of the first things I've learned, as a student of the dump, is that people hoping to make a decent living here are delusional. If they still insist on trying, it's important to explain three widely used picking techniques from which to choose.

The most risky is a method that Ki seldom tries, its danger still evidenced by a scar he bears on his left ankle. There are times at night when the mountainous garbage burns so intently and is so fully consumed that even the bulldozers won't try to squelch the flames. By morning, anything combustible or toxic has burned away, leaving behind a layer of purified ash that pillows pieces of red-hot scrap metal ripe for plucking. This method of gathering is treacherous because if you march through the ash too soon, hidden scrap will burn through your rubber boots in seconds. Some resort to braving the ash at night, reasoning that the metal's glow lets them see where not to step. While it's true that a few of the very skilled (or stupid) make a reasonable living this way, many ultimately burn and scar their bodies so badly that they end up crippled and begging for food on the streets of Phnom Penh—a life worse than picking garbage in Stung Meanchey.

A better alternative, and the most popular picking method (the one Ki prefers), is working alongside the trucks as they purge their loads. Of course, working around trucks, whose drivers appear eager to run you over just for sport, means you must always be alert and watchful. This method is also competitive and furious. People crowd together, everyone flinging their sticks fashioned with a sharp metal hook at the end, ready to tear open the tumbling bags of garbage. They pick, prod, and pry at the sacks of trash, searching for any scrap of discarded metal, glass, or plastic worth selling to the buyers.

The last picking method, and the one I prefer, is working away from the trucks, in open areas that have been stirred up by passing bulldozers. It's a method that is less hectic, less dangerous, and unfortunately also the least fruitful. It's a method that requires not quick thinking but rather methodical diligence. If you are persistent and patient, it can still prove worthwhile. This method is followed mostly by the elderly, the children, and anyone recovering from injury. I prefer it because it lets my eyes and hands disengage from my brain, working like a robotic machine, thus giving me time to think. As I see it, with no money, no rice, a sick child, and a husband with a line of fresh stitches still throbbing in his head, I have a considerable amount to think about.

I always tell Ki that it's a dangerous thing sending me to work the dump, not because I'll get run over by a truck, burn my legs and feet, or fall into a pool of toxic sludge—though all those are possibilities. It's dangerous because my thoughts get away from themselves. Mixed with emotion, they pile up like the garbage that surrounds me. They stack layer upon layer, deeper and deeper, month after month—crushing, festering, smoldering. One day something is certain to combust.

Where did Sopeap learn to read? What would cause a woman so hard and brutal to break down into a well of tears? Does Ki really think his knife will protect him from the gangs of thugs? What if the unspeakable happens? Could Nisay and I survive alone at Stung Meanchey?

It's late in the day when I finish. I have filled a canvas bag half full of discarded plastic and metal cans that I balance on my shoulders. I carry it to the buyers, where it is sorted and weighed. They offer less than I expect, but I am too tired to barter. I take my money, then go to the home of the rice vendor, where I purchase two kilos of rice and some vegetables. She tells me that I seem quiet today, not my normal self. I shrug politely, take my food, and head for home, hoping that all has been well.

I have been quiet today because fear in my heart has been fighting with frustration in my brain, leaving little energy for my mouth. Halfway through the day, my brain declared itself the winner and started to work out a plan. Grandfather loved luck, but I am tired and can no longer wait around for its arrival. I haven't spoken to Grandfather all day because I know he'll be angry when I tell him that his luck is . . . well . . . lacking. It won't stop by, it doesn't call, and I must conclude that we've been abandoned. It's like the friend who gets a job in the city, begins to earn decent money, and then no longer visits. Luck has also moved on to better times, and it's not coming back.

Seriously, what does one do when the ancestors no longer listen? To my dismay, Grandfather's words echo in my ears. *Crafting a plan is easy. Taking action will always prove to be the more difficult path.*

And the question remains, will my plan work? Will everyone, including Ki Lim, think I've banged my head against a garbage truck? While he will undoubtedly be surprised, it won't be my husband who is the most astonished. The person most likely to think the toxic smell of the dump has finally rotted away my brain will be a woman whom I still struggle to understand—Sopeap Sin.

៣

CHAPTER THREE

"Hello?"

The voice outside the flap is so hoarse that at first I don't recognize it. When I pull back the canvas, Sopeap waits. She does not look well.

"May I speak with you?" she asks.

Now I am worried. Not because of her ragged appearance but because she *never* asks for permission to speak. "Absolutely," I say.

"Is your husband . . . Ki Lim . . . is Ki okay? I heard he was . . . injured." She stumbles around her words, as if they are drunk with her.

I am not certain what she is asking. Sopeap has never cared about Ki—or anyone—bleeding or not. Before I can answer, she mumbles the real reason for the visit.

"May I buy this book?"

She is holding Nisay's book, raising it toward me, as if I may have forgotten what happened on the night she stumbled away with it clutched in her hand.

"The book is yours. I told you that when you were . . . " I don't know how to finish without offending. Her interruption saves my awkwardness.

"How much?"

"No. Sopeap, I *gave you* the book."

It's as though I am speaking a strange language and she can't comprehend my meaning. Seconds pass before she processes the notion.

"Thank you." The phrase *thank you* coming from Sopeap Sin is about as common as fresh air at Stung Meanchey. What she says next only compounds my puzzlement.

"I will mark your rent for this month as paid in full."

I choke, stumble, and then grab at my ears. Sopeap Sin, the Rent Collector, the greediest person I have ever known, has never been concerned about our well-being, and she has certainly never forgiven any rent.

And then I realize I must be dreaming. I bite my lip—it hurts. I glance around the room—it's our home at the dump. Surely, if I were dreaming, I'd be living in a place nicer than this.

"That is kind," I finally reply. "It will help us out a great deal."

She lingers, as if she has more that needs to be said. "The other night . . . I was . . . I had been drinking. I don't remember much . . ."

It is my turn to interrupt. "Sopeap, there is no need to explain." My words lie. I desperately wish to understand. More important, I wonder if now is the right time to pose my question. I take so long debating with myself that she assumes we are finished and turns to leave. She is three steps away when I call out.

"Sopeap?"

She pauses, pivots, waits. "Yes?"

"Will you teach me how to read?"

"I don't like it, Sang Ly. It's just not right."

I had expected Ki Lim to be excited. Can't he see that if I learn to read, I can teach Nisay, and then, perhaps, our son can follow in better footsteps? Our only other hope is to enroll him in one of the NGO charity schools when he gets older, but there are thousands of destitute Cambodian children and very few openings. As a mother, I need a greater hope than that.

"Fine. If not me, then she can teach you," I say.

This irritates Ki further. "Don't be foolish. I dig through stinking garbage every day just so we can eat!"

"I'm sorry. I didn't mean it like that. I just . . ." How do I explain? "Ki, if we don't give Nisay every possible chance to do better . . ."

Ki sighs, and I can't tell if it's a sign of disgust or surrender. "I just don't like our son being around Sopeap Sin," he adds. "She's a witch, and I don't trust her."

I wait to tell Ki about Sopeap's conditions. He would never understand. I'm not sure I understand. After he leaves, I revisit in my head the conversation I had with Sopeap.

"Why? Why do you want to read?" she had asked, obviously a bit unsettled by my request.

I should have been prepared with a quick reply, but I wasn't. And to make matters worse, Nisay, who was sound asleep on the floor, awoke with a start and began to holler. Then I realized he was my cue.

"I need to be able to teach my son to read stories, like the book you hold in your hand . . . for his sake."

"Is that why you gave me the book? So I would teach you to read?" With every word, her tone hardened and I questioned my judgment in asking.

"No, I . . . well, yes, yes, I did. I saw how much the book meant to you and I hoped that you'd see how important reading will be to my son. Sopeap, I need to teach Nisay to read so that he can find a way out of this dump and into a better life."

"What's wrong with the dump?" she asked, as if we lived in paradise.

Was she serious? Could she not glance around? Were her eyes blind from the smoke? Was her nose dead from the smell? I couldn't say for certain why this set me off, but it did, and my reply was not kind.

"Are you out of your drunken mind?" I asked with disgust. I expected Sopeap to bolt. Instead, she paused, as if I were finally speaking her language. She rolled her thick lips inward but said nothing. I took the pause as an opportunity.

"The only way my son will get better is if I get him out of Stung Meanchey."

"What is wrong with him?" she asked.

"He's not well. He has never been well. You've seen him. We have tried folk remedies, taken him to doctors—French, Cambodian, and American. They give us medicine, but as soon as it runs out, his diarrhea and fever return. I need to do something more to help him. I need to do something *now*."

As Sopeap's shoulders rose, her features wrinkled. "And you think that something is teaching him to read? Why, if medicines don't work, do you believe reading will help?"

How could I explain the illogical feelings swirling and swelling inside, forcing my action? "Sopeap," I said, "I'm not replacing one with another. I don't expect reading to make his body well. But I hope reading will give him something to look forward to, a reason to fight. I want to believe reading will fill him with courage."

I picked Nisay up from the floor and held him over my arm to calm his cries. Sopeap's gaze shifted to the child, and for a moment it appeared as though perhaps my arguments were working. Her head bobbed as she watched him, as if memories pulled from her brain were causing it to lose balance.

I continued, "I'll keep taking him to doctors. I'll keep searching for answers. I just don't think anything will change until he has the desire to get better. I can't rely on Grandfather's luck any longer. So yes, as naive as it may sound, I believe reading will help Nisay. I want to think that reading will offer him hope."

In spite of my poorly phrased argument, my plea had at least been heartfelt—and for that I deserved some respect. I received none. The interest I thought I read in Sopeap's face faded, and instead of showing sympathy, her response was swift and biting.

"If you're looking for hope," she said, sarcasm hardening her voice, "you should know that it died at Stung Meanchey."

She didn't flinch. I couldn't tell if she was serious. There was no hint of amusement, no wry grin, and as her eyes stabbed deeply into mine, I realized how much I despised the woman. The longer we sat with our eyes locked in a silent battle, the harder I could feel my teeth grind.

I blinked first. "Perhaps hope did die at Stung Meanchey," I answered, as I scooted closer to be sure that she wouldn't miss my point. "Or . . ." I gestured toward her with my finger, while lowering my head, as if a new idea had just arrived. I let the moment hang as I sharpened my remaining words. ". . . it could be that what died at Stung Meanchey was *you!*"

I took a step back. I was furious and expected fury in return.

Instead Sopeap paused—and then she laughed. Not a chuckle, as though I'd said something funny. Nor was it a snicker, as if I'd done something stupid. Instead, it came from deep within her chest, and as it spilled out, it surprised her more than it did me. Her eyes then darted back and forth, as though she were watching a dog chase its tail. As I waited just inside my little three-walled shack with a tarp nailed on the front, I thought I also heard the ancestors laughing.

And then everyone was silent.

Sopeap turned to face me, as if she wanted to be sure there would be no misunderstanding.

"I have conditions," she announced.

"I beg your pardon?"

"I said, I have conditions."

"Anything."

"Don't you want to hear what they are first, before you agree so quickly?"

I nodded. "Yes, of course."

"First, every Friday, without fail, you will bring me a bottle of Bourey rice wine."

"Okay. I can do that." Ki Lim was not going to be happy. "Anything else?"

"Yes. Did you not listen? *Conditions* is plural. Two . . ."

To keep the word *Cow* from creeping into my brain, I began to calculate the price of Bourey rice wine in my head. No, Ki Lim was not going to like this at all.

"You will always do your homework," she said.

"Home work?"

"No, not *home—work*. It is one word, *homework*. Say it again."

The classes had apparently already begun. "Homework," I repeated.

"Good. Now, have you ever done homework?"

There was a school in the province where I grew up, but I had attended for only two years as a child before giving up to help Mother in the rice fields. I didn't remember anything called *homework*.

"I have never done homework," I admitted.

"You will begin now—and you must try your hardest. I can tell you are bright, but it will still be difficult. I will not have you waste my time. Do you understand?"

"Yes."

"Lastly, you will need some pencils, paper, and something hard to write on. Can you get these things?"

"I believe so."

"*Believing* is not enough, Sang Ly. If you want to resurrect hope, *doing* is the most important. Can you *do* these things?"

"Yes."

"Okay."

She was about to walk away when I stopped her by asking, "But, Sopeap, when do we start?"

"We will start . . . on Friday!"

CHAPTER
FOUR

I was right about Ki Lim. He wasn't happy at all.

"You can't be serious! We have to buy the drunken hag *Bourey* rice wine? Regular rice wine isn't good enough? Who does she think she is?"

Before I can answer, he asks a more probing question. "How do you know for sure that she can even read?"

"I watched her eyes the night she was here; she was reading Nisay's book."

"You watched her eyes?" he asks.

"Well, yes, and she—" I stop. It is a reasonable question, and in less than a breath, I realize I am not absolutely certain. He may actually be right.

He continues, "Let's assume, just for a minute, that she *does* read, even a few words. That doesn't mean she knows enough to teach you—or anyone."

"Well . . ."

"And how much time will it take? Who will watch Nisay?"

With each question, I grow more concerned. Perhaps I should have given my brain more time when planning my strategy in the dump.

It hasn't rained for several days and the heat is stifling. Before bed, I pull back our canvas tarp to provide some air. Now, hours later, with the moonlight finally breaking through the haze, it reflects off the hands of our wall clock that reads ten minutes after two. Naturally, since we have no electricity and the clock's insides have been taken out, its time never changes. Ki found it in the dump several months ago, and I hung it on our wall because I liked the printed flowers that adorn its face. I tell Ki often that it's right twice a day, and at the moment, if I had to guess, I'd say that it's pretty close.

In spite of the stench of burning trash, neither my husband nor my son has stirred for hours. I reach over again to touch the three used pencils that lie beside our mat, as if one may have tried to sneak away in the darkness. Like me, they remain prostrate, waiting for morning to come.

Lucky Fat helped me find them, and, to my surprise, Ki sharpened them for me with his knife. They sit on top of their own sleeping mat, several sheets of various and assorted papers. The papers aren't new. Every sheet has words or markings on the opposite side. No matter—I will still have sufficient space to write my letters. Next to the pencils and paper rests a bottle of premium rice wine—the expensive brand that Sopeap demanded. Ki had protested, but I reminded him that we only had enough money to buy it because Sopeap hadn't made us pay this month's rent.

In the stillness of the morning, Ki's breathing also reminds me that his concerns about the Rent Collector are valid. I don't know for sure if Sopeap *can* read.

I pretend the clock is ticking softly in the darkness, counting down the hours, the minutes, the seconds. I told Ki I wanted to hang the clock on our wall because I liked its flowered face—but that's not exactly true. There is more. It helps me to remember that even though something is broken, it can still serve a purpose. Someday, if we ever have the money, I want to take it to a clock maker and have it repaired. It's silly, I know, because buying a new clock would be less expensive.

Sometimes broken things deserve to be repaired.

My thoughts ramble. *Will I learn to read?* I implore the ancestors to just give me a chance. I'm wrong about a lot of things, but I believe that Sopeap really can read and that she'll teach me. Like my clock and its telling of time, I hope this will be one of the moments, even if it's only twice a day, that I'm right.

I rush outside in the early-morning light and scan the hazy horizon, trying to spot Sopeap. The smoke is heavy and it's difficult to make out silhouettes. After several minutes of study, I am certain that none of the shadows is my new instructor. I carry in more water and scrub the floor again where Nisay slept, to make sure it is spotless should Sopeap decide to sit there while she teaches. I pat the area dry, at least as much as possible, and then return to the path in the front of the house. No teacher.

Our canvas wall is loose on the far end, and, using the rock that Ki keeps by the side of the house, I hammer the nails along the tarp's top edge until all are tight. Then I hear someone coming and glance across my shoulder. *Never mind.* It is a neighbor who is just passing by.

The massive cistern that holds our water at the side of our house is tipping slightly. I turn and twist the pot until it appears level and stable, and then I get on my knees and scrape up and pack enough dirt around the base to ensure it remains so. I imagine Sopeap will arrive when I least expect and interrupt me, perhaps even compliment me on being such a good worker. She doesn't.

Inside I organize my papers, sorting them again, this time by shape rather than by how much open space remains on the back of each page where I will write. I pick up one of my pencils and hold it to a paper as if I'm about to write something very important, though I can't imagine what.

With each accomplished task, my throat tightens, my breathing deepens, my focus shortens, and my hope fades like a morning moon. When Ki arrives at noon to see how my first day of learning is progressing, he finds me sitting alone on our mat, my knees pulled tight to my chest. I am not crying—I refuse. But as he enters, I neither move nor speak, afraid any discussion of the obvious topic will demolish my resolve.

I expect him to say, "I told you so." He doesn't, though a heavy sigh handles the job just as admirably.

"Where is Nisay?" he asks instead.

"Mother wanted to work today, so Narin is watching him. Let me fix you something to eat, and then I will go and pick him up."

I have a cousin, Narin Sok, who also came to the dump from the province. On occasion, when special circumstances arise, we will watch each other's children. Because I didn't know what time Sopeap would show up, I left with Nisay before dawn, just after Ki Lim headed out for the day.

Now, after preparing Ki's rice, I reach for my sandals—and then we both hear a commotion at the front door, near where our curtain is pulled back. We look up at the same time. It is Sopeap Sin and she can hardly stand.

"Where have you been?" Ki asks, before Sopeap enters and before I can say a word. He seems to be forgetting that she is still the Rent Collector, a woman with the power to kick us out of our home at any time.

She ignores his tone, looks past him as if he weren't there, and instead directs her question to me. "Do you have my rice wine?"

Ki steps sideways to block her view. "You get nothing until you carry out your part of the bargain."

"Out of my way!" She threatens—at least as threatening as a staggering, drunken woman sounds to a larger, stronger man. She attempts to move around him, but Ki Lim will have none of it.

"Don't you dare!"

I don't know if he's defending me or begrudging her. I assume it's the former and I step to his side.

"Ki, it's okay." I interrupt with words, coupled with a soft touch to his shoulder. "It's not worth it," I whisper. "She is still the Rent Collector."

Then, with Sopeap watching, I reach out and place a twice-polished bottle of Bourey's finest distilled rice wine into her hands. "You need this worse than we do."

She is about to stumble away when I stop her.

"Sopeap, you forgot these." I force her fingers around my three pencils and hold her clasped hand tightly. Then, before she has a chance to see the moisture forming in my eyes, I thank her for coming and retreat behind the safety of our curtain.

CHAPTER
FIVE

As I pour a spot of menthol oil into my hands, its pungent odor wafts around the room and Nisay immediately begins to wail.

"Oh please, child, I haven't even touched you yet."

He doesn't care and I hear his objection loud and clear. "*True, you haven't, but you're sure as certain about to!*"

And he is right, but I have no choice. It is a remedy practiced by my mother and father, and by their mother and father, and I'm certain by a line of waiting parent ancestors that stretches past heaven. It is as old as Cambodia itself. It is called *Koah Kchol,* a name that means *to scrape air.*

It starts with oil distilled from leaves of the *Mentha arvensis,* a menthol plant that grows wild in the jungle. Once the oil is rubbed thoroughly onto the skin and it's had a chance to soak in, a coin or other piece of round metal, held sideways, is used to scrape the recipient's back, chest, and arms, using long parallel strokes.

The skin is scraped to bring toxic air to the body's surface and restore the natural balance of hot and cold, keeping these universal elements in harmony. As a side effect, it also causes blood vessels just beneath the surface to rupture, resulting in maroon, zebra-like lines that remain for two or three days before they fade.

Once, several weeks before, after one of Nisay's treatments, an American doctor arrived at Stung Meanchey on behalf of Charity House, a Christian service organization that had come to offer free medical assistance for the day to children at the dump. Naturally, I took advantage, hoping it would finally be a time for answers. When the doctor noticed Nisay's lines, through a translator, he called my treatment *superstitious nonsense* and *a complete waste of energy*. He said I should instead trust modern medicine and administer a course of antibiotics, which he then provided.

I will try anything to help my child and so I followed his instructions implicitly. However, ten days later, when the medicine ran out, Nisay's symptoms returned. I would like to find that doctor and explain to him the difference between superstition and intuition, and to let him know that his solution proved to be *nonsense* and *a complete waste of energy*. He didn't leave a forwarding address.

And so I continue to search for answers, and as I scrape my son's skin today, I console with words meant to soften his cries—words that I suppose are meant for me. "Child, we only want you to get well. Understand that while it's painful, it's for your own good. If we do nothing, your illness will worsen. I promise that in spite of your complaints, one day you will thank me. Be brave, my little son, and when you are a father and you pour oil into your own hands and your own sick child begins to sob, remember."

We don't have running water—unless you count my pouring it out of a cup. Instead, we purchase our water from a vendor several huts to the west, who in turn buys rights from the government (read *bribe*) for the flow of water that comes from one of several pipes that feed into the dump. About once a week, I carry water to our home in two large jugs that hang from a stick draped across my shoulders. It's an arduous, three-trip effort that, by necessity, requires I stare down at the path as I walk so as to not lose balance, trip, and spill my precious load.

This morning I left Nisay with Teva Mao, my neighbor two houses down the hill, and when I am finished, I will watch her two youngest children while she repeats the effort for her own home.

On my second trip back, I almost run over Sopeap, who has squatted squarely in the middle of the trail to wait. As I jolt to a stop, some of my water sloshes out. If she notices that I'm annoyed, it doesn't show. She sets down her bag alongside her drooping socks so that she can gesture with her hands as she speaks. "Friday turned out to be a difficult day," she announces.

I want to blurt out, *"Oh, really?"* I don't.

"I'm sorry," I offer instead. "You didn't look well." What I mean is that she acted like a drunken pig, but I hold my tongue.

"Are you ready?" she asks.

I turn. "For what?"

"Are we going to hold lessons? Don't you still want to learn how to read?"

"I . . . uh . . . yes . . . I suppose, but I have Nisay . . . and then I need to watch Teva's children while she gets—"

She interrupts. "I can make arrangements. Do you trust Teva Mao to watch Nisay?"

"I do . . . yes . . . certainly."

"I will speak with her. Carry back your water and I will meet you at your house."

I don't know what to say but finally mutter, "Okay," and then I add, "Ki will be surprised. He doesn't think you—" I pause mid-sentence, regretting that my excitement has only highlighted my stupidity. I hope that she doesn't notice, but I feel a guilty blush creep across my face as she turns.

"He doesn't think I can *read?*"

"Well, um, he wasn't sure. He thought you could be . . . pretending."

I wonder if she'll be angry, but instead the notion brings her obvious pleasure. "Sang Ly," she answers, "I have been called many names in my life. Some call me *Sopeap Sin*. Here at Stung Meanchey many call me the *Rent Collector*. Still others simply call me *Cow*. But my most cherished title, the one I most revere, was a long time ago in the Department of Literature at the Royal University of Phnom Penh. There, for nine wonderful years, the most cherished of my life, my students called me *Teacher*."

CHAPTER
SIX

I already know the basic sounds of the Khmer (Cambodian) alphabet. I mean, other than being illiterate, I do *speak* the language. I've been told (mostly by those who don't read or write either) that, with the speaking part out of the way, learning to match sounds to letters will be easy. *Surprise!*

Perhaps ever more naively, I expect Sopeap to be understanding.

"Sang Ly, pay attention! I won't repeat myself."

I can't help but admire the glossy pencil I hold in my hand, one taken from the stack she has extracted from her oversized bag. I touch its tip to the crisp, unused sheet of starched paper that lies on the varnished board in my lap—all supplies she has brought. I'm ready to take notes on every word—but of course, I can't yet write. Still, even pretending feels sensational.

I look up with such eager anticipation that she softens.

"Please, put down the pencil, Sang Ly, and listen."

While I am crouched on the floor, Sopeap stands beside a small portable easel. I'm glad she has brought it with her because it makes our tiny home feel like a real school. The easel lets her write with a piece of chalk and then she wipes it away with ease. What a wondrous invention!

She continues. "We've already talked about consonants and vowels. Now, Khmer consonants are divided into two series. The sound each vowel makes will depend on the series to which the consonants belong. I know it seems complicated, but it's not. It's these sounds that we're going to learn first. Do you understand?"

I nod *yes,* not understanding.

"Good. Now, go ahead and pick up your pencil."

For the better part of the afternoon, Sopeap repeats a letter, writes it on the board, then announces the sound the letter makes. I copy it down exactly as she has written it. To help me remember the sounds, she has agreed to let me draw a small picture beside each letter. If the letter makes the *b* sound, for example, I will draw a picture of a bird beside it, since both the word and the letter sound the same.

"For your homework assignment," Sopeap announces, "three days from today, I want you to have memorized all the letters we have written—both names and sounds. Can you do it?"

"That quick?"

"Yes. Can you do it?"

"I will try."

"Trying is not good enough. Will you *do* it?"

It has become a familiar question. "Yes. I will do it."

It appears she is satisfied because her head nods with mine. "That is good. Now, keep writing the letters we have learned."

I am on my fourth page when Ki pulls back the tarp and enters the room. We are both surprised.

"What are you doing home?" I ask, perhaps sounding as though he isn't welcome. "I thought you took your lunch with you today."

"Lunch? Sang Ly, I'm home for dinner."

"But it's not . . ."

Sopeap gathers her supplies. "It has been nearly six hours, Sang Ly," she says. "You need to go and pick up your son, and I desperately need a drink."

"What is she like?" Lucky Fat asks, eyes as round as his cheeks. No one, including the boy, can picture Sopeap Sin actually teaching.

"She is stern, but she is also smart. I mean, who would have guessed?"

"Does she hit you?"

I can't help but giggle. "Hit me? No, of course not—at least not yet."

It's his next question that catches me off guard. He glances down first at his feet, shuffles them in the garbage. "Sang Ly, after you learn . . . once you can read and write on your own . . . would it be all right . . . "

"What is it? Just ask."

"Could you teach me how to write my name?"

I put down my sack and picture myself standing in front of a chalkboard, the same as Sopeap, showing Lucky how to carefully draw each perfect line. I take a deep breath, not caring that the air is particularly smoky, and then I try to remember if I've ever been asked a more satisfying question. I can't think of what it might have been.

It is several moments before Lucky interrupts. "Are you okay?" he finally asks.

I turn my head, not wanting him to see my eyes, certain that I look completely ridiculous. I clear my throat, pretending to cough, wanting to be sure my voice won't crack when I answer. "Why, yes," I say to Lucky. "It will be my pleasure."

"Are you listening to anything I'm saying?" Ki asks as I scrub out the pots from dinner.

"I'm sorry. I was thinking about Sopeap."

"The Cow?"

"Don't call her that."

"You are right. She's more of a bull."

"Ki, please."

"What should I call her, *Princess?* Perhaps *Her Majesty?*"

"How about *Teacher?*"

"If she is such a wonder teacher, why is she living at the dump? Why isn't she at a school or a university?"

It's a valid question and when I don't answer, Ki fills in the blank for me. "I'll tell you with two simple words—*rice wine.* The woman is a hapless drunk."

"Perhaps," I say. "She does drink a lot, but there's something more."

"And what's that?"

"I don't know, but I intend to find out."

CHAPTER
SEVEN

In Cambodia, when parents get old, they move in with their children, who offer shelter, food, and happy grandchildren. It's the perfect retirement plan—as long as your children don't live at the city's municipal dump.

Instead of being angry, Lena, my mother, relishes her situation. She showed up at Stung Meanchey two months after we'd left the province. She stayed with us just one night and by the next afternoon had arranged to live with her distant cousin, Dara Neak, about a ten-minute walk across the dump. Although I'm supposed to be the one helping Mother, she instead watches Nisay on the days she doesn't pick. Her biggest fault—perplexing to this day—is that Mother *loves* to pick trash.

"It's an adventure," she says. "You never know what surprises you'll find."

I remind her that *surprises* usually mean human body parts.

"True, but the people who work here are nice," she adds, "except perhaps Sida Son, whose shelters are just pitiful. The poor, angry woman is so jealous."

I forgot to mention, Mother builds some of the best day shelters Stung Meanchey has ever seen.

Sopeap was tolerable during our first lesson, but today she is madder than a constipated water buffalo. Some drunks are embarrassing, constantly making fools of themselves. Other drunks are friendly, bowing to everyone they meet. Sopeap is pure vinegar, and though she isn't too drunk to teach, she's too drunk and angry to show any patience.

"Foolish girl! Listen to me!"

"I'm trying, but I don't understand what you're saying."

She pounds the chalkboard in rhythm to her words. "Syllables begin with one of these consonant clusters . . ."

"It's so confusing."

She puts down her chalk. "I don't know how else to explain. We are finished for today. We will try again tomorrow."

As she gathers her things, I blurt out the more applicable question of the day. "Why do you drink so much?"

She jerks toward me. "Why do you ask so many stupid questions?"

And then her face twists and wrinkles as she draws both hands toward her stomach. She bends forward, as if she's about to crumble to the ground. Before I can ask if she is okay, she straightens, lurches out through our open canvas door, falls onto her hands and knees just beyond the house, and vomits up her morning liquor.

I am speechless.

After several moments, when she apparently feels well enough, she stands, turns toward me, and then, as if nothing unusual has happened, announces, "I will see you tomorrow."

I should learn my lesson and bite my lip. I don't. Sopeap is drinking way too much. It has to stop. "Will you be sober?"

She answers so casually, after having just puked in my yard, one may have thought she'd been asked about the upcoming storm or the best time to catch the sun setting over the dump's horizon. "Tomorrow? Yes, I'll be sober tomorrow, but the day after—no, I'll be drunk as a soldier."

And then she shuffles away.

It's a few minutes later when I go out to gather some cardboard to cover her mess, until a good rain can properly wash it away, that I notice something disturbing. On the ground where she has vomited, I also see blood.

"Nisay's finally asleep," Ki says. "Come to bed."

"I told you, I must finish my homework."

"Or what? She'll sit on you?"

"No, but she may throw up on me."

When I continue drawing my letters, he presses. "Aren't you coming?"

"I told you, in a bit."

I am working by the light of a small oil lamp. We usually save it for emergencies—when Nisay is sick, for example. How can I make Ki understand that having my homework done for Sopeap is unquestionably an emergency?

He rolls over in disgust.

After I've drawn several additional letters, I relent. "Let me finish three more."

He doesn't answer and I'm not sure if he's already asleep or just ignoring me. I write each one as precisely and cleanly as possible. Not only will I turn this sheet in to Sopeap, but she will then make me repeat each letter and its sounds, both dependent and independent. Who knew reading and writing were so complicated?

When I finally put out the light and crawl beside Ki, I snuggle close and wrap my arm around him. He doesn't respond. It's too dark now to see him, but the pace of his breathing and the tightness of his chest tell me he is awake.

"What are you thinking?" I whisper.

Seconds pass. When he does answer, I'm surprised to hear worry rather than frustration. "What will happen once you know how to read?"

"What do you mean?"

"How will it change things?"

I have been so focused on my learning that I haven't noticed his apprehension.

"I hope it changes many things," I answer softly. "I hope it will somehow get us out of the dump—and if not us, that it provides a path out for Nisay. Don't you want those things too?"

It is a long time before he replies. "I know that we don't have a lot here," he says cautiously. "But at least we know where we stand."

"Where we stand? What do you mean?"

Silence. Worry in the dark can make it even darker.

"Ki? Tell me what you're thinking."

"Life here *is* hard," he finally says, "but it is constant. New trash always arrives—every single day. It will never end. When we are hungry, I go out and pick a bag of plastic or metal or glass, sell it for a few *riel,* and we buy our food. We generally have enough to eat. We have a roof overhead to protect us from the rain. Life isn't complicated here."

His affinity for the dump is unexpected. For three years, we have talked about the day we'll make enough for a better life.

"But the gangs almost killed you . . ."

And then, like a slap, it hits me. I should have picked it up sooner but I am tired from the study.

"Food and shelter—yes, we have those here," I say, in a muted tone, "but I don't think that's what you are worrying about."

He rolls to face me, though without light we can see only murky shapes.

"Living at Stung Meanchey," he says, "forces us to work things out, to need each other. If you learn to read—"

I don't wait for him to finish. "Ki, listen . . ." In the darkness of our tiny room, his concern is clear. "It doesn't matter if I learn to read, or where we live, or how we earn a living—no matter what, I will need you."

He listens, then asks another question. "But do I make you happy?"

How can a woman raising her child in a place choking with trash answer that question and have her reply make any sense? Both at the dump and in my home tonight, I'm careful where I step. "Ki, you are the part of my life that I would never change. But offering our son opportunity, working with you to improve our life together—that kind of change is good, don't you think?"

He hesitates, thinking but also listening, and so I continue. "I just need to get Nisay better."

"Do you think he's sick just because of where we live?" he asks.

The answer is so apparent it nearly screams, and Ki must hear it also because before I can reply, he responds to his own question. "Of course, we *do* live in the dump."

There is a silent moment, until we both break out in laughter. We hold each other in the darkness for a very long time and then, with Nisay gently stirring at the foot of our mat, Ki helps me pull off my clothes.

On the days Mother can't watch Nisay, if he is not too fussy, I lay him on the ground beneath a makeshift cardboard lean-to and pick garbage nearby in the afternoon. Lately, I have surprised Ki with my eagerness to pick, even on the days when I'm learning letters in the morning with Sopeap. What I haven't told him is that I pick every day because it provides the perfect opportunity to study. It's a game I've devised where I look for paper when gathering—more specifically, paper with printing on it—and choose at random a letter from a word. I have five seconds to say the letter's name and sound aloud. Each time I get ten in a row, I pretend to win exotic prizes—furniture, bags of rice, clothing, and packaged food.

I begin today with a torn green flyer, with pictures of an expensive home on the back, and I randomly select the letter *a*. I speak to Nisay, who is now sleeping, repeating the letter's name first and then pronouncing its sound, as if the child lying nearby were even remotely interested.

"Nisay, this is the letter ិ (*i*). It makes the *I* sound. Did you hear me?"

If someone were watching, they'd think I'd completely lost my mind—certainly a justifiable conclusion. I pick through layers of garbage, looking for recyclable trash, until I stuff two smashed aluminum cans and an empty perfume bottle into my canvas bag. I then snatch another loose piece of printed paper that looks to be from a magazine and randomly pick out my next letter. I know this one easily.

"This is the letter ន (*noo*) and it makes the *N* sound."

I'm about to dig for more stray cans when I decide to cheat and sneak in another letter in between my searching. I snatch a light yellow wrapper that I recognize as packaging from one of the fast-food chains so popular with tourists in the city. It's not the vivid artist's rendering of an American hamburger on the front that catches my attention but the bright orange letters printed beneath. They are shadowed in blue and seem to float above the paper. As I admire the charm of the design, I arbitrarily pick the first letter of the last word.

"Nisay, this is the letter ស (*saa*). It makes the *S* sound."

I am about to toss the wrapper and resume working when my eyes roll across each of the letters that follow. I have been repeating the tones of individual letters for so many days that my head doesn't realize it should quit. As my brain stitches the sounds together, my tongue and mouth work in unison to pronounce them. It's a short word, and in an instant, I understand that the letters grouped together spell the word *samnang*—meaning *luck*.

I am so astonished, I speak it aloud a second time, emphasizing each sound as my eyes pass over the letters, forcing my mind to confirm what my lips have already declared. "Sam—na—ng."

Without any help from Sopeap, I have read my very first word!

I glance around for someone with whom I can share this amazing moment. Ki is picking. Nisay sleeps. Other gatherers work at a distance. I alone am aware of the miracle that has just occurred.

I have read my first word!

My brain must finally be grasping the depth of my accomplishment because it's now telling my body to jump up and down and scream as loud as humanly possible—to let everyone know that I, Sang Ly, an illiterate, foolish girl from the province, living in Phnom Penh's largest waste dump, have just read *MY FIRST WORD*.

I try to dance as best I can in rubber boots, and I'm about to shout in celebration, but my body doesn't listen. Instead, my legs buckle and I slump down onto the trash that so generously provided my reading material. I pull my knees to my chest, bury my head in my lap, and cry the most personal and satisfying cry that I've had in a very long time.

Thank you, Grandfather, for helping me to read my first word.

When I am finished, I carefully fold the wrapper, place it in my pocket, throw my recycle sack over one shoulder and Nisay over the other, and then skip in my heavy boots toward home.

By the time Ki arrives, I am unstoppable. I have deciphered the entire slogan and the wrapper now hangs on the wall below our clock. I pull it down to demonstrate my astounding newfound ability.

Even though I have already memorized every word, I point to each one for Ki as I read them aloud. "It's from Lucky Burger. See, this is their name right here." I motion to the words above the picture, in case he has any doubt.

He glances first at the lettering and then at me, I hope understanding that now is not a good time to be funny. I continue. "The slogan underneath, right here, says *Roal Thngai-mean samnang—Where Every Day Is Lucky.*

Ki can't help himself. "Does this mean we have to eat hamburgers?"

I leap toward him, wrap my arms around his waist, pull his body close against mine, and hold tightly. We embrace for a long time, but the best part of the evening—the moment I will remember more than any other—is that Ki hugs back.

CHAPTER EIGHT

Kim Pan plants rice.
Then Kim rides on the wat-er buff-a-lo.
Kim calls to Bora Chan.

The pictures on each page are simple sketches; I don't care. It's my concentration on the words that opens up a more colorful and moving visual picture in my head.

Yes, I stumble at first on such words as *buffalo,* but after I've read them two or three times, if I falter it's only because I don't want to make a mistake and disappoint the teacher. It's as if my head knows their meaning but my mouth wants to take it extra slow, just to be sure. At times I think I can hear my brain screaming, "*I am reading here, so please, all other body parts, do your best to keep up!*"

"I should have brought harder books," Sopeap says, as I finish one page and move to the next. I bite my lip and remember what happened last time I was prideful. "I will drop off some harder books tomorrow before I leave."

"You are leaving?"

"I have an appointment that will keep me away for a few days. I want you to practice reading at least four hours a day until I return."

"Ki says if I practice much more, my head will explode."

"Your head will not explode, I assure you. Just work hard, raise your reading level, and next time, we will discuss grammar."

"Grammar?"

"Yes, the policeman of writing. But don't worry, there is not much written grammar in our language. Besides, you already understand most of it from speaking. After that, we will finish."

"But I don't want our lessons to end."

"Why not? You are reading sentences. You need to become more proficient, but with practice, it will come."

"There are more things I want to learn."

"Things? What things?"

"I want to learn about *literature.*"

"Literature?" Sopeap halts, turns. "What do you know about literature?"

"Only that you said you taught literature at the university."

"Sang Ly, you've just learned how to read. I think it's a bit early to jump into stories."

"I don't," I plead. "I think it would be the perfect way for me to practice." I can't tell if Sopeap is annoyed or flattered that I would even ask.

"Tell me what you think literature is," she finally questions, shuffling a step back.

"It's reading, I guess—important reading—from books."

"Reading, yes, but there's more . . . well . . . how do I explain?"

Her eyes are perplexed, her mouth open. "To be honest," she says, "I am tired. I haven't been feeling well and I just don't think I will ever have enough energy to teach you literature."

"But you have enough energy to collect rent—and to drink. That can't be good for your body."

Why can't I just keep my big mouth shut? I regret my words as, for just a second, it looks as though Sopeap will berate me—but she stops.

She doesn't answer right away, and when she does, she speaks to herself. "It's not my body I soothe. How do I explain it to the child?"

When she looks up, I shrug. She continues: "Teaching someone to read, Sang Ly, is very mechanical. It is like picking trash—straightforward, simple rules—you just follow the motions instinctively as your brain directs."

"Okay, I understand that."

"But literature is unique. To understand literature, you read it with your head, but you interpret it with your heart. The two are forced to work together—and, quite frankly, they often don't get along."

"Can't you teach me with both?"

"That's what I'm trying to explain to you. My heart wouldn't be in it. It would be like preparing you a wonderful dessert, meant to be savored and enjoyed, but making it with salt instead of cane sugar. It would leave a terrible taste in your mouth. I have given up on literature, and in those weak moments when I imagine otherwise, rice wine comes to my rescue."

"You could quit drinking."

"And you could let a poor woman rest. Besides, you are not ready," she says flatly.

"Ready? What do you mean?"

"You're anxious to jump into the river, but you haven't checked to see if the water is deep enough."

I don't bother pretending. "Sopeap, you speak in riddles. What are you saying?"

"I'm saying that life at the dump has limitations, but it serves a plate of predictability. Stung Meanchey offers boundaries. There are dangers, but they are understood, accepted, and managed. When we step out of that world, we enter an area of unknown. I'm questioning if you are ready. Everyone loves adventure, Sang Ly, when they know how the story ends. In life, however, our own endings are never as perfect."

"I'm just talking about literature," I say.

"And so am I."

We're both getting irritated.

"Explain it to me, then," I say in frustration. "Why is someone like you even here at the dump? Are you hiding from someone?"

"Hiding? Yes, Sang Ly. I'm hiding at Stung Meanchey—beneath the scorching sun, and even when it shuts its dreary eyes, still my shadow mocks."

"There are times when you speak like my grandfather."

"I don't know what that means."

"It means I need to understand . . . won't you give me a chance?"

"You're asking me to remember what I've spent years trying to forget."

She shakes her head side to side, stretches her weighted shoulders, and winces, as if a pain is bothering her back—and she keeps glancing toward me, as if wishing will make me go away. When it doesn't, she closes her eyes.

So I wait.

She is now silent and stony. I imagine she is trying to turn herself into a stone statue, like those at Angkor Wat, simply because she wants to be rid of me, and it's all I can do to resist the urge to push her over. I poke out my finger to touch her, but her mouth opens first and she begins to speak. "Our next reading lesson will be the last."

My heart drops, but she continues. "However, I will agree to the following: Work hard while I'm gone. You will need to improve your reading substantially between now and then, and that will take a tremendous amount of study and practice. On that day, bring me an example of literature that we can discuss. Then, we shall see if we are both ready for more lessons."

"What kind of example?"

"That is your decision."

She ignores my confusion and instead returns her chalk to the holder below the board, stacks books into her bag, and turns away.

"Wait! I'll need books, won't I? Should I go into the city to find them?"

Sopeap pauses long enough to reach out with her wrinkled and blemished fingers to grasp my cheeks, oddly the same as I would do to Grandfather. Only now that I am on the receiving end, I don't like it.

"You foolish child," she declares. "You don't need to go to the city. Even at Stung Meanchey, the dirtiest place in all of Cambodia, we are awash in literature."

"But where?" I ask.

Hiding behind a chilling stare, the old woman smirks. I wait for her answer. She offers none, but instead twists away.

"That's it?" I call out.

She shuffles to a stop one final time. "You will know when you find it. Literature should be discovered. I must go now. Good luck, Sang Ly."

She has forgotten her bottle. "Wait!" I call out. "You didn't take your rice wine."

She doesn't turn around. "Save it for me," she answers. "I'm certain that I'll need two next time."

59

I am anxious to discuss my assignment with Ki so that he can be on the lookout as he sorts through garbage from the trucks. But when he arrives home, he is distant.

"What is the matter?" I finally ask, after he has eaten his rice and boiled eggs in utter silence. "Are you angry?"

"At what?"

"I don't know—*me?* You haven't said two words all through dinner."

"I'm sorry, I was thinking."

"About what?"

His hand brushes against his ankle, confirming his knife is there. "I saw them today."

"Saw who?"

"The gang who robbed me."

I crouch beside him. "Where? What happened?"

"Nothing happened. They walked through the dump in the middle of the day, as though they were daring somebody to do something. Nobody did. Everyone just turned away and kept working with their backs toward them."

"Did you find the police?"

Ki laughs aloud. "You think they care? You know they won't come into the dump—not for us, anyway."

"How many were there?"

"Half a dozen—all walking together, like a pack of dirty animals."

"Did they see you?"

"No, they were far enough away. But I saw them. Even through the haze I could tell who they were—especially the tall one."

I'm concerned at Ki's methodical tone, his intent gaze. I don't want him planning anything crazy. "Ki, you need to stay clear of them. Let this be."

He turns to meet my stare. "They robbed us, Sang Ly. They could have killed me. They took what wasn't theirs. It's not right."

"Ki, I understand, but nothing good can come of this. Promise me you'll keep your distance."

Ki lifts his head, offers a noncommittal shrug. "Like the other cowards? Then I'm no better."

"Those thugs are not worth dying for."

"You are right—but you are. If protecting my family isn't a cause worth dying for, then what's left?"

He taps the weapon's rigid handle. "Now, if you don't mind," he adds, "I need to get some rest."

Sopeap was wrong. My head really is about to explode. I have been reading aloud for so long from the books she left me that Ki has threatened to stuff garbage into his ears. It's not that my reading isn't liked. In fact, it actually settles Nisay down. However, Ki says that too much sugarcane will rot even the strongest teeth. I'm sure he means it as a compliment.

I take a break from the books and thumb through a few of the glossy fashion magazines that I had Ki pull from the trash. I used to muse over the pictures, envy the beautiful women, and wonder about their lives. Now that I can actually read the words, I am amused. The teasers splashed across the covers say it all.

Seduce Your Man in the Kitchen. I picture our one-room home and giggle.

Eat at Home and Save a Bundle. I'll keep that in mind.

Wear Your Best Dress to Work. Not a good idea at Stung Meanchey.

And my all-time favorite: *Will Eating Starchy Rice Make You Fat?* I glance down at my thin frame. Can they be serious?

I don't think any of this is the literature that Sopeap had in mind. I'll keep searching.

Choob khyol or *cupping* is an ancient remedy that means to *suck the wind*. I don't know if it will work any better than scraping, but I must try. Mother says that cupping will not only improve Nisay's circulation and appetite but restore his balance. My plea is that it stops his diarrhea.

We take Nisay to a practitioner in the city, a man who learned the art from his father. We are greeted on the street by his female assistant and escorted down a narrow alley to his treatment room. It is small but clean. The man inside is young, but he carries himself with confidence, as though he's performed the treatment a million times. He bows his head in greeting as we enter, but then continues to prepare a tray of glass, globe-shaped cups that stand in rows like soldiers. They are translucent, perhaps blown from melted soda bottles, each about the size of a round lime. He lights the end of a small torch, then sets it aside on a stand that keeps it upright.

"We are ready," he announces. "Take off his little shirt and we will begin."

He instructs Ki to lay Nisay facedown on a blanket that is spread across a narrow wooden exam table. The instant Ki complies, Nisay begins to fuss and then squeal. Ki holds his feet so he won't roll over. I pat his legs for comfort.

"Oh, you whiny child," I protest, knowing that he's perfectly fine.

I know from experience that though the cups will feel warm to

62

his skin, they won't be painful. Nisay doesn't care. He has been to the doctor too many times to believe differently.

The man picks up the torch and his first cup and then pushes the burning end into the round globe. Just when it looks as though the flame might smother and go out, he pulls away the torch and places the open end of the cup's rim directly onto Nisay's back. My child screams louder.

As quickly as the man can pick up and heat each cup, he repeats the process, lining the glass globes on my baby's body in almost perfect symmetry. As the glass cools, I can see my son's skin pull upward into the opening, as the excess energy or *wind* is drawn out of his thin body. By the time the man is finished, my child's back is covered with eight clinking cups, and he actually looks quite ridiculous. An adult receiving the same treatment may have up to three or four times the number, with cups also being placed on the arms, legs, chest, and even forehead. If it were Ki receiving treatment today, I'd be teasing him to no end. With Nisay, I refrain. My son's arms and legs are so skinny that the cups won't stick there, so we decide that his back will be sufficient. True to form, and in spite of my encouragement otherwise, Nisay never quits bawling. Though he kicks constantly for ten minutes (which feel like thirty), the cups hold fast. Then the man pushes his finger against each cup's rim to pop them off, and as quickly as they were placed, he returns them to the waiting tray—and the treatment is over.

I pick up Nisay from the table and hold his bare, polka-dotted body over my shoulder. "It's over," I tell him. "Quit crying now." Surprisingly, he does.

The man is paid, tears are dried, and we head home. It is on our walk back, after we enter the dump, that we pass Lucky Fat.

"I just came from your house and you guys weren't there," he says.

"No, we weren't," I reply, confirming the obvious. He doesn't ask where we've been or why Nisay's bare little body is spotted with perfect circles.

"Well, I found a book and left it for you. I'll keep looking for more. Oh, and while I was there, Sopeap came by."

"She's back?"

"Yeah, and she left a message. She said for you to plan on Friday, that you'd know what that means."

"It means," I say, "that my time is running out."

ع

CHAPTER
NINE

Sopeap said it was all around us, that we were swimming in it. Perhaps literature is easier to find in the dump if you're a drunk. I have read wrappers, cans, magazines, notes on napkins, directions, bills, packaging, bottle labels, even tattoos on men picking trash. Nothing feels like literature. I have let friends know to keep their eyes open for books—surely, I must be looking for books. Still, the one that Lucky left yesterday only showed how to fix a moto. While it may be literature to a mechanic or anyone who owns a moto, I am neither. I only need a single example. If I show up with nothing, our lessons will end.

It is after dinner, after dark, after Nisay has finally fallen asleep, and after we are lying down that Ki casually says, "Oh, I forgot to tell you. Your cousin was here looking for you."

"Narin? When? What did she want?"

"It was when you were still out—*working*." He emphasizes the word and I can't tell if he's making fun of me for looking for literature in a dump or if he is resentful that I'm not gathering my share of recyclables. When he pokes me and begins to laugh, I'm relieved it's the former.

"You didn't say what she wanted."

"She said she found something, but didn't say what."

I take a generous breath, try not to sound excited. "But she didn't leave anything?"

"Not with me. She mentioned that she was watching Nisay on Friday and would give it to you then."

That would be the day Sopeap is coming, the day of our lesson, and that means one thing is certain—waiting until Friday to see Narin is not an option.

"I'm not really tired yet," I say as I roll over and stand up in the darkness. "Perhaps I'll go out for some fresh air."

Ki laughs so loud that Nisay stirs. I guess it is pretty funny, when one associates *fresh air* with the aroma and haze of the dump that permeate our home at night.

"Take the light," he says, not bothering to ask where I'm going or how long I'll be gone. "And take the path in front of the homes, around the perimeter. It's longer, but it's safe. Don't even think about cutting across the dump."

I kiss him quickly, then grab the light that he'll sometimes use to pick in the dark when we have enough to pay for a charged battery. I don't bother clicking it on inside, as I'm afraid it won't work and he'll insist I stay home. The moon is out anyway, and there is sufficient light to see my way just fine.

When I arrive at Narin's, I strain, hoping to see a glow coming from inside. There isn't one. Should I turn around and go home empty-handed?

"Narin?" I call out through an open window.

Nothing. I try again. "Narin?"

The door to the home opens and my cousin steps out. "Sang Ly? What's wrong?" she asks, her voice ringing with worry.

"Everything is fine. It's just that Ki said you came by. I would have come earlier, but he just told me. Did you find something? Did you find a book?"

"No, I'm sorry, no book. What I have may be nothing. I was reminded of a simple poem that I learned in the province, one Mother taught me. She would whisper when I was restless and couldn't sleep."

"I'm not sure if a poem is what I need. Sopeap did not say if poems were literature, but I'd love to see it."

Narin glances down in the moonlight. "I have nothing written. I don't read. Instead I remember it. Like I said, I don't know if it's what you want, I just—"

"Narin, I'd love to *hear* it."

She points to the step and we sit, so as to not disturb her children, who are already trying to sleep. She scoots close, and as she begins, I can almost hear my aunt's raspy voice.

Laugh with me, monkey. Bring impish tricks and mischievous heart. Help sorrow waft and cheer restore before the sun sets red.

Run with me, tiger, with imposing stripes of orange and deafening growl. Cause enemies to cower and bring my spirit courage.

Pull with me, water buffalo. Turn furrowed fields to golden rice that's sweet. Show true resolve and the strength of a determined mind.

Rest with me, turtle, with emerald shield and wisdom old

as time. Teach me to value a strong home that will protect against the rain.

Swim with me, fish, through renewing waters that are broad and deep and blue. Cleanse my body and keep it cool from the sun's hot rays.

Sing with me, bird. Trill nature's song and carry tired limbs through indigo sky. Open my eyes to the world's expanse and Nature's wonder.

Scurry with me, beetle. Remind of life's short days and of precious time. Tap your violet legs about to keep me alert and prepared.

Scurry, beetle—sing, bird—swim, fish—rest, turtle—pull, water buffalo—run, tiger—laugh, monkey. Play together in my dreams. Dance across nature's sky. It's now time that I must sleep.

We sit quietly with our thoughts that drift and mingle with the nighttime sounds of the dump. We remember our lives in the province—but mostly we remember Aunty.

"I miss Mother," Narin finally says aloud.

"I know. I miss her too." I put my arm on my cousin's shoulder, hoping to offer comfort.

Narin's mother, my aunt, passed away just two months after Narin arrived at the dump. Back then, since the family didn't have a way to contact her, nearly three weeks passed before the news could be delivered from the province.

"Is it literature?" she finally asks. "Is it what you are looking for?"

"I don't know for certain, but I think it feels like literature," I reply.

She seems pleased as I continue. "I am going to need to write it down. If I come back in the morning with a pencil and paper, do you think you could repeat it again slowly?"

"Yes. But when you return, can I ask a favor?"

"Certainly."

"Would you mind writing a second copy, one that I can have?"

They are words she knows by heart and yet she wants something in hand—this must surely be literature. I squeeze Narin's arm. "Thank you."

"For what?" she asks.

"For helping me find my first piece of literature. Now, there is just one more problem."

"What's that?"

"I hope Sopeap agrees."

As my teacher arrives, she stumbles, and I presume she has been drinking, but I smell no alcohol.

"Did you have a successful trip?" I ask.

"It was more trying than I expected. But I am here and on time, so let's get started."

For the first hour, Sopeap bluntly details the use of grammar. As she promised, it is clear and straightforward, usage that I grasp from speaking the language. While I prod her along, wanting to move the discussion forward, she purposely drags on as if to spite me.

"Do you have any questions?" she finally asks. "If not, we can end." She hesitates, waits, watches—and I consider that she may be toying with me.

"I did my homework," I tell her.

"I thought you might have," she answers. "Are you going to show me or just sit there grinning like a monkey?"

I take out two copies of Narin's poem and pass one to her.

"Before we read it," Sopeap says, "tell me its history."

I narrate Narin's circumstance, her life in the province, the passing of her mother. I don't know how much information Sopeap is asking for and so, after I ramble for longer than I should, I apologize and then wait for instructions.

"Read it and I'll follow along," she says.

While I want to be methodical and not mispronounce any of the words, I do my best to deliver them with the verse's natural rhythm— to read it as Narin shared it. The sounds flow smoothly from my lips, and when I finish, Sopeap is quiet, even pensive.

"Did you know," she says, without revealing whether she likes it or not, "that poetry predates literacy?"

"What does that mean?"

"People recited poems before they could even read or write. They would repeat them aloud, hand them down orally in songs, legends, and stories—and this poem you have read was apparently passed along in the very same manner. You, Sang Ly, are likely the first person to ever write it down."

I consider the notion, touch my fingers to the page, and let them follow my scribbles, which now feel somehow special. Sopeap has not yet finished her inspection. As she reads it again, I watch the whisper of her lips, the moving of her eyes, and the rhythmic nodding of her head. Her fingers curl around the pages, embracing them, and I promise to read more diligently and with more passion from this moment forward.

"Do you see it?" she asks.

"See what?"

"Look at the words, their order. Can you see the pattern in their structure? The last stanza repeats the subject order, but in reverse."

I hadn't noticed. I feel like a blind baboon.

She continues, "And this was recited at bedtime, clearly."

"Yes, that's what Narin said."

"Notice the last line; it caught my eye. It says 'Dance across nature's sky.' Do you see why?"

I stare at the poem, read the lines again. "No, I don't."

"Every stanza lists a color. See them? Red, then orange, then golden, which I presume is yellow, and they continue. Do you see each color?"

"Yes." Now that she's pointed them out.

"The poem is painting the colors of the rainbow," she says, "colors that *dance across a sky.* Fascinating."

Reading is too new. She couldn't possibly have expected me to notice such things, and yet I feel as though I've failed my first test—and perhaps my last.

"Now, I have a question for you, Sang Ly. Why would you call this literature?" In but a moment, her tone firms and a sudden hardness seeps through.

"You just finished saying, there are words and patterns that repeat—"

She interrupts, even more demanding and stern. "Words and patterns are meaningless."

"But you're the one who noticed them. You're the teacher and you said—"

"Stop!" she demands, cutting me off midsentence. "We aren't talking about the teacher; I am asking *you.* Besides, if you ask half a dozen teachers about literature, they will give you twice the number of answers. Now, listen to my question, Sang Ly. WHY IS THIS LITERATURE TO YOU? WHY SHOULD I CARE?"

She raises her voice at me and I don't understand why. I don't know what she expects of me. While my nature is to fight back, today I'm not ready for her sudden blows—as if she's found a hole in my armor and has forced her angry self inside.

"It's just a poem. Why are you mad at me?" I ask, sounding now like a hurt child.

I must look pitiful because she turns away, slaps her hands to her side, and stomps her foot in frustration against the bamboo slats of my floor. She mumbles, but it's to herself and I can't tell what she is saying. I wipe at my face and swallow hard, attempting to gather my composure as I wait for her to turn around and face me. She does.

She speaks now with words so soft and low it doesn't seem possible they come from the same woman. "I am not angry with you. I am frustrated at a lost and tired old woman who is just too weary. Now, do you have an answer for me?"

If I pretend an understanding with her staring straight into my heart, she will know I'm a fraud. I answer truthfully and remove all doubt. "I don't know what literature is. I don't understand it. Is that the answer you were hoping to hear? If so, you can go now."

"That is the problem today that vexes me," she explains. "As I once told but a small handful of my students, so long ago—*you do know, child.* You just don't realize it yet."

Sopeap turns the battered watch on her wrist around so that she can see the time. "I had no intention of continuing our classes," she says, "but I believe I have changed my mind."

"You have?"

"Over the next several days," she continues, "I will do my best to remember a few of the literature lessons that I once taught at the university. But we will need to go through them quickly."

"Okay, but why quickly?"

Sopeap hesitates. Her eyes fidget as her focus darts around to everything in the room but me.

"I wasn't going to . . . I mean . . . I wasn't prepared to say anything yet," she replies cautiously, "but I'm making plans to leave Stung Meanchey."

90

CHAPTER
TEN

I am kneeling on the floor in the corner to clean the ashes out of my cooking stove when our canvas flap lifts open and Lucky Fat scrambles inside. I am about to scold the boy for not calling out first, as I may have been undressed, but the fright in his eyes waves away my concern. He glances back before speaking, all while sucking in panting breaths.

"Please, Sang Ly . . . I need your help . . . Come quickly!"

"What is it?"

"My friend is hurt . . . bleeding. I don't know what to do."

Lucky's voice cracks as his urgency pulls me to my feet. I brush off my hands and reach for Nisay's shirt. While dressing my child, I pepper Lucky with questions.

"Where?"

"At my place."

"What happened?"

"I'm not sure."

"You said he's bleeding?"

"Yes."

"Let's get Teva. She can—"

"No!" Lucky blurts out. "You must come alone!"

I don't understand the boy's fear and it makes me nervous, but I nod my agreement, gather Nisay in my arms, and head out the door.

I insist we stop briefly at Teva's, but just to see if she can watch Nisay. All the while Lucky waits, terrified, as though I may slip, share the news, and cause disaster. I say nothing.

Lucky lives directly across the dump, on the far perimeter, and currently there are two paths that lead to his home. The longer one weaves around the base of the trash, making a wide circle that is flat and easy to navigate. The shorter path switches up two separate mountains of garbage, across a dipping plateau, and down the opposite side. Lucky doesn't hesitate as he climbs up the hill. Though the boy is known for being fat and happy—not fast—today I must scramble to keep up.

Like nearly everyone at the dump, Lucky lives in a small hut fashioned from an array of bamboo poles, weathered boards, cardboard, and tin. His place is smaller than most, but for a boy living alone, it suits him fine.

He stops in front of the hut, hesitates, scans around yet again, and then motions for me to step inside. I pull open the door cautiously, creep through the opening, and glance toward the floor.

From what little Lucky has shared, coupled with his nervous hesitation, I expect to find an injured orphan boy, possibly bleeding from wounds caused by working too close to the trucks. As my eyes adjust, I indeed see a quivering child. However, the pleading, coffee-colored eyes staring back belong to a panicked girl. She is lying on the floor in the corner, as if she's afraid to move, yet her body trembles. Tears roll down both defined cheeks, and the puffiness in her features tells me that she's been sobbing for some time.

She is perhaps just a year or two older than Lucky, eleven or twelve at the most, and her appearance is striking. Her ebony hair flows out from beneath a faded denim sun hat that is pulled down around her ears. She wears a cotton shirt that was probably white once but is now decorated with a spattering of tan, brown, and grey stains.

And then I see the blood.

She wears dark cotton pants that are soaked nearly black around her pelvis and thighs. As fear lurches in my chest, I drop beside the child, praying that my concern is misguided.

"What's happened? Are you in pain?" I ask as I take her hand.

"My stomach hurts," she whispers.

"It's okay. Breathe deeply. What's your name?"

She continues to tremble and so I gently stroke her arm to calm her down, as I would do to assure my own child that everything will be okay.

After a moment, she softly answers. "Maly."

"Maly? That's a beautiful name," I reply. "It means *blossom*."

She nods, confirming a fact she already knows.

"Maly, has someone hurt you? Has someone touched you?"

I expect her to look away, but instead she shakes her head back and forth. "No one has touched me."

I turn to Lucky for confirmation. "Can you tell me what happened?"

"We were picking at the dump and all of a sudden she just started bleeding. She got really scared and began to cry—so I brought her here. We didn't know what to do."

As the true nature of the situation comes into focus, I am so very thankful.

"Maly, do you have a mother?" I ask, though I can already guess her answer.

"Mother is dead."

"And your father?"

She shakes her head again to let me know he is also either dead or out of the picture.

"I am sorry. Where do you live?"

Lucky interrupts. "She lives with her older brother. They haven't been here long."

I turn to the boy. "Can you get us some water? And do you have some clean rags?"

"I have two shirts."

"That will help."

Lucky gathers the shirts from a box in the corner that is surrounded by Buddhas, and then retrieves a bucket that he's filled with water from the jar outside. He sets it down and watches nervously.

"Lucky, would you mind waiting outside?" I ask. "I need time with Maly . . . alone. There are a few things I need to explain to her."

Lucky doesn't move, but instead fidgets with his fingers so he won't have to look me in the eyes. "Why? What things?" he asks.

"It's woman talk. I don't believe you'll want to hear it."

"But I need—"

"Just go. Please!"

Lucky leaves with a disgusted sigh, though I suspect he's listening just beyond the hut's thin walls. While I don't yet have a daughter of my own, I'm thankful that he's brought me here today, and I promise silently not to let this girl down. First, I try to calm her fears. With an equal mixture of clarity and concern, I do my best to explain to Maly the cause of her bleeding, what it means, and why there is no reason to be afraid. She listens quietly, nods often, and says little.

77

Next I help her to clean up. We rinse her pants as best we can, and then I wring them out and hang them up inside to dry. I let her bunch up one of the shirts to hold in place between her legs to capture any more bleeding. Then I rummage through Lucky's box and find a pair of shorts that fit well enough for her to use temporarily.

"You are experiencing what is called *rodow,* meaning *season,*" I add. "It's a moment to celebrate in a girl's life, not to fear."

"But not everyone is sent away when their season comes," she whispers in a voice so tender and timid I can barely hear.

"Sent away? Maly, what are you talking about? You won't have to go anywhere. Just explain to your brother what has happened—what we've talked about. He will understand."

At that moment Lucky screams from outside. "No, Sang Ly! He won't . . . she can't!"

He storms in through the door and plants his hands on his waist in a defiant stance that declares he's not leaving again.

"I was trying to tell you!" he says. "Her brother has joined a gang. Now that she's . . . well, a woman, they're going to take her to *Tuol Kork.*"

As the boy's words sink in, I comprehend the trembling, the fear, the child's tears. This stunningly innocent and beautiful girl of no more than twelve is going to be taken by her brother to the city's red-light district and be sold to a brothel as a child prostitute.

The notion is unthinkable to anyone civilized—but in Cambodia, it happens all the time. Usually the family is poor; sometimes the parents or relatives may even be unaware. At the suggestion of a distant cousin or an acquaintance, a man arrives and offers to pay the family a large sum of money, usually about $200, with the promise of a job for the child as a waitress in the city. But there is no restaurant, and by the time the frightened girl realizes what is happening, it's too late.

To the right customer, a week with a virgin will sell for more than the amount paid for the child. After that, she'll become one of hundreds of enslaved child prostitutes, forced to carry out unspeakable acts for as little as $2 a session. If she refuses, she'll be beaten. No matter how hard she works, her debts for room and board will always add up to more than the money she is able to bring in.

Unable to hold back any longer, Lucky's distress finally transforms into tears. He turns to hide his face, but as he does, his eyes pause on the girl—and for the first time I see her features brighten. His concern is instantly clear. When he turns back toward me, his plea is also unmistakable.

"Sang Ly, we can't let it happen. We've got to do something, and we've got to do it now!"

For as long as I can remember, there have been gangs at the dump. They prefer roaming Stung Meanchey over the streets of the city because the police typically refuse to patrol here on account of the horrific smell—and also because those who live at the dump are too poor to pay the policemen's bribes. The thugs are usually young, children in their early teens, often abandoned or without parents—at least any who care. Their crimes are mostly petty, but aggravating nonetheless. If they catch you alone, they will circle you and *ask* for money— theft by intimidation. If the buyer happens to be closed after a day of gathering and you forget to take your bag of recyclables inside, it's unlikely you'll find it waiting for you beside your house in the morning. At other times, the kids cause mischief just to be cruel—tipping over water jars, cutting slits in canvas recycle bags, dumping human waste in front of doors so that you step in it first thing in the morning (though considering we live at Stung Meanchey and encounter human waste all day long, I've never understood that).

Lately, however, the gangs have been getting more aggressive, more brazen, and nearly deadly. It is an interesting irony. It's because they are getting violent that Ki insists something must be done. For the very same reason—fear of violence—many of those living here refuse to get involved, and I can't blame them.

During the Khmer Rouge revolution in the mid to late 1970s, more than a million Cambodians were slaughtered by the vicious dictator Pol Pot and his government. Since that genocide, those who managed to survive have raised an entire generation of children who have been taught that to stay alive in the world, it's best to lie low, mind your own business, and let others do the fighting.

I walk to the plateau above the trucks to meet Ki so that I can tell him about Maly. However, he's been talking with some of the men at the dump about the gangs, and when he finally meets me he's too angry to listen.

"They are cowards," Ki hollers as we walk home, gesturing back at the men still sitting beneath the shelters.

"Try to understand," I say.

"I do," he insists. "I understand that the gangs almost killed me. I understand that if we don't do something soon, someone else will be next. I understand that if we just sit around—"

"Okay," I interrupt. "I get your point."

"They are thinking only of themselves!"

"And how about you?" I ask.

"What do you mean?"

"Are you protecting your family, or is it something more?"

"What are you asking?"

"I'm asking are you really wanting to protect others—or are you simply seeking revenge?"

He doesn't answer. I wait until we are far enough away that I'm certain no one else can hear.

"There's also a little matter that I need your help with—okay, a big matter."

I explain to him how I helped Maly, including her young age and her fear of what might happen if she returns home. When I tell him her brother is one of the gang members, I see Ki's muscles visibly tighten.

"What kind of animal would sell his own sister?" he asks in utter disgust.

"I don't know," I answer. "The real question is, how do we handle it?"

"We?"

"Yes. We have to help her!" Ki knows I'm right, though his hesitation raises a valid concern.

"How, exactly?" he asks. "We live in the same dump they do. I mean, we can try to hide her, but if her brother is in one of the gangs, he'll have them all looking for her. She'll never be safe if she stays here."

"We could try the police?" I suggest, already knowing his answer.

"For the right price," he confirms, "they will haul her to the brothel themselves—after they've had a turn with her."

"What do we do, then?"

"I don't know, but until we figure this out, tell Lucky to keep her inside. And be careful who you tell . . . people talk. If the wrong person finds out, one thing is certain."

"What's that?"

"It will be too late for the girl."

Sopeap arrives, but we do not discuss literature or learning. Instead, she spends her time once again listening to me read while she crouches in the corner and scribbles notes from her books.

Though I am worried about Maly, I try to act as if nothing is wrong. Still, I must sound ridiculously impatient as I read because when I pause, she answers a question I haven't verbalized—at least not in the last twenty minutes.

"Your reading is coming along well," she says, "but if we dive into the pool before it's full, we'll hit our heads."

"Is that a literature lesson?" I ask with a hint of sarcasm.

"No," she replies curtly. "That is a common-sense lesson."

For someone who insisted that we discuss literature *quickly,* she is taking her own sweet time. Sopeap also won't say why she is leaving the dump, just that she's been planning it for a while but has yet to finalize her timing. Whenever I press her further, she gets belligerent and calls me foolish for asking questions that are *none of my damn business.*

"Are you ready?" she asks out of the blue as she shuffles her notes.

"Yes," I answer, not sure to what I'm agreeing, but ready anyway.

"Fine. I've taught you how to read. Now let's teach you how to see."

She takes pages from her notebook and hands them to me.

"In time, we will learn from stories that come from all around the world," she announces. "Today, we will start with a few of the most basic stories ever written, timeless stories that come originally from Greece." Sopeap gestures to the papers now in my hand as she makes the introduction. "Sang Ly, meet Aesop, writer of countless children's fables."

I nod, as if Aesop and I are already best friends. She waves her hand at the words, seeming to demand that I begin. So I do.

The Dancing Monkeys

A prince had some monkeys trained to dance. Being naturally great mimics of men's actions, they showed themselves to be apt pupils. When arrayed in their rich clothes and masks, they danced as well as any of the courtiers. The spectacle was often repeated with great applause, until on one occasion a courtier, bent on mischief, took from his pocket a handful of nuts and threw them upon the stage. At the sight of the nuts, the monkeys forgot their dancing and became (as indeed they were) monkeys instead of actors. Pulling off their masks and tearing their robes, they fought with one another for the nuts. The dancing spectacle thus came to an end amidst the laughter and ridicule of the audience.

There are words I stumble through, words I don't understand. But I get the general idea—it's a funny story and I can't help but smile. Sopeap isn't as amused.

"One of the first lessons that I hope you grasp is that woven into meaningful literature, so tightly that it can't be separated, is a telling lesson, even in stories as short as this one."

"Always?" I ask.

"Always!" she confirms. *"Good stories teach!"*

"Perhaps it should speak a little louder," I reply, hoping to amuse. Instead she frowns.

"Sang Ly," she says, in a raised tone that instructs me to pay attention, "what do we learn from this story today?"

I want to say, "Don't throw nuts on a stage when monkeys are dancing," but I'm fairly certain that's not the answer Sopeap is looking for.

"Is the message always obvious?" I ask instead.

She lets out a frustrated grunt before explaining further. "Stories are often layered with meaning. If you don't learn from a story's message, if you gloss over or dismiss it—even if it's a message with which you don't agree—then you have wasted not only your time but the writer's time as well. So, I will ask you again, what lessons does this simple fable teach? What does it mean to you?"

I must get this right, but under pressure I get nervous, my blood pumps, my heart races, and my good thoughts run for cover, often not coming back until they are sure the coast is clear. She said that a good story will always have something to say, whether we agree with the message or not. What is she expecting? *Please, Grandfather, help me to know how to answer.*

And then a question pops into my head. It is sincere, and I don't mean to sound like I'm still stalling. However, as the words roll off my tongue, I fail miserably.

"What does this story mean to *you?*" I ask.

She replies with a breath, a sigh, an air of forced patience. It's only when her eyes drop, her shoulders slump, and the lines of her face wrinkle with such sadness that someone as dense as I can begin to realize that, like the stories she's describing, Sopeap is also layered. In silent tones her actions scream, *This is more than just another one of my ornery days!*

"Aesop reminds me," she almost whispers, "that during my life, there are times when I pretend to be something I'm not. He reminds me that when nuts are thrown on my own stage, I quit dancing, pull off my mask, and stupidly scramble to gather them. He reminds me that—"

She reaches out to touch the easel, not for balance but as if she's remembering. "I'm sorry, Sang Ly," she continues, "but I have not been a good teacher today. I am going about this all wrong. I still feel a bit tired from my last trip to the city. I'm going to go home now and get better prepared."

I want to know what she's thinking. I want to understand what goes on in her life and her head in between our times together. I long to understand the parts of her life that she keeps hidden—and perhaps, to share some of mine. Instead I ask, "Is there anything I can do?"

"Yes," she answers. "Please be here tomorrow."

I am about to go over to Lucky's to check on Maly when Ki arrives home unexpectedly.

"What are you doing here?" I ask.

He doesn't look happy. "There is something I thought you should hear."

"What is it?"

"I told you people at the dump will talk—well, there is a rumor going around that a young girl has been kidnapped. Now we've got more than just the gangs to worry about. Everyone will be keeping their eyes open for her."

My night has been miserable. Nisay is still hot and fussy with fever, and to offer even the slightest comfort to the child, I have to keep him constantly draped in wet rags. To make matters worse, Lucky arrived in the middle of the night with Maly. He thought he heard someone walking around his place in the dark, and so when the footsteps abated, he woke the girl up and they ran across the dump in the darkness to stay where they felt safe.

Ki Lim, who was awake most of the night with us, kissed me goodbye early to head out. There was little more he could do, and should we need to take Nisay to the doctor again, Ki thought it would be best if he got an early start to be sure we have enough money.

When Sopeap calls out, I'm the one who feels as though I've been up all night drinking. I swear it should be midnight, but the sun that fights its way into our home tells otherwise.

"Nisay has been sick," I say to Sopeap as I barely pull back the canvas. "I can't leave him today."

She twists at her watch, a gesture I have come to understand as a sign of impatience and frustration. For a woman so hesitant just a few short weeks ago about teaching me, her disappointment reads like tattooed words across her face. "We will try again tomorrow, then," she finally offers.

Nisay lets out a cry, and so I turn around to check him. When I turn back, Sopeap has taken a step closer. She doesn't look well herself. I am about to suggest she also go home and rest, but then I notice her eyes glancing inside to my floor where everyone is sleeping. A look of curiosity crosses her face. Without trying to be conspicuous, I lower the canvas to block her view of Maly.

"Do you really want to get out of the dump?" she finally asks, as if my haggard appearance doesn't aptly scream my answer. It is a ludicrous question. Does not everything about me shout that I want to be rid of this place?

"Absolutely," I say, short on sleep and patience, forcing myself to remain composed.

"People only go to the places they have visited first in their minds," she says, uttering the phrase as if secrets to the universe have just been shared. "Perhaps that is how learning can help you. However, first you must see it, feel it, and then believe it. When you do, where it takes you may surprise."

She clasps her hands and waits for my response, but by the time I realize she expects a confirmation, she has already lost patience and is waddling away through the trash.

I stand in the hot sun with bloodshot eyes that burn, a child that whimpers behind me in pain, and a brain that can't figure out the answer to the more important question:

What are we going to do to help the girl?

၅ ၅

CHAPTER
ELEVEN

It's been two days and Sopeap has not returned. My nerves are frayed. I don't want my teacher to know about Maly, and so each morning before it gets light, we sneak her back over to Lucky's. Then when evening comes, with Lucky nervous that someone will find her at his place, he brings her over after dark to sleep with us.

It's exhausting. To make matters worse, we still haven't figured out how to help—and I'm growing attached to the girl. When Sopeap doesn't show up on the third day, my emotions surrender and I do what I should have done the day we found Maly. I go to my mother.

"Sang Ly? Where's Nisay?"

"That's what I'm here to talk to you about. You know how I've always wanted a daughter?" She stops and turns, staring in disbelief.

"Are you pregnant?"

"Not that I'm aware of, no."

Her disbelief turns into puzzlement. "What, then?"

I gesture toward the floor and then sit at her side. I take a breath, grasp her hand, and explain as best I can why her own daughter is Stung Meanchey's most recent kidnapper. Of course, I've never been in this actual situation before, so when I finish and she says nothing, I don't know what it means.

I wait. She continues to think.

"Thank you," she finally answers.

"For what?"

"For helping a mother to feel like she has raised her child right. Now, as to your little problem, it will take me a day or two to work out, but I may have a solution."

Sopeap doesn't say where she has been for the last several days and I don't ask. However, the color has returned to her face, she is wearing a pair of *new* brown socks, and though she will always be demanding, she has never looked better nor been more amiable.

"Sang Ly," she begins, "I'm old and long past caring about what people think of me."

I had already figured out that part of the woman and so I bob my head in agreement.

Sopeap continues. "Two things happen when you get to be old. One, you gather experience and knowledge. You learn from your mistakes and thereby offer wisdom to others. The second thing that happens is that you grow forgetful, ornery, and senile, and when you offer advice, well, you sometimes just don't know what you're talking about. Often it's hard for everyone—including me—to know the difference. You see, I haven't taught for a while, and I stepped ahead of myself last time we met. I launched right into my lesson without giving you a most critical rule."

I ready my pencil.

"Literature should be loved."

I raise my head to question, but her lips are already answering. "When I was a child, my father visited a faraway country on business. When he returned, he presented me with a tin that contained a cake. He told me that it was special because it was the custom of that country to mix a small toy in with the batter and bake the toy into the cake. The toy was supposed to be a surprise, though perhaps he worried that I would bite into it and break a tooth or that I'd swallow it and choke. Either way, knowing the toy was there, I began to pull the cake apart, shoving pieces into my mouth, gulping it down, all the while looking for that silly prize."

"Did you find it?"

"I found it near the bottom. It had been baked into one of the corners, but by the time I discovered it, I'd eaten almost the entire cake."

"By yourself?"

"Yes, of course. But that's not the point. The point is that I ate my cake so quickly and with my heart so intent on finding the toy that, to this day, I can't tell you the flavor of the cake. I can't describe the texture. I can't say if it was delicious or bland. I can't even remember what country it came from. Do you know why?"

"Because . . . you . . . were focused . . . on looking for the toy."

Sopeap sighs again, but this time with relief rather than despair. I bite my tongue to remind my pride to stay seated.

"Yes!" she says. "Literature is a cake with many toys baked inside—and even if you find them all, if you don't enjoy the path that leads you to them, it will be a hollow accomplishment. There was a playwright named Heller, American, I believe, who summed it up this way. He said, '*They knew everything about literature except how to enjoy it.*'"

I scribble this quote also.

She continues, "Learning is an affair that takes a lifetime. Just be patient. As we delve into stories—which we will—you will soon understand. As Plautus said, *'Patience is the best remedy for every trouble.'*"

"How do you remember these quotes?" I ask.

"Unfortunately," she answers, "I have the curse of memory that only rice wine will erase. Macbeth had it right when he called memory *'the warder of the brain.'*"

"Do you realize," I point out, "that you just answered my question about a quote with another quote?"

Sopeap smiles—and we end for the day.

When Ki steps inside, next to where I am boiling our rice, I expect to see disappointment. He has been meeting again with a few men at the shelters, hoping to convince them to stand up against the gangs. Instead, as he pulls off his boots, I think I see him smile.

"You convinced them?" I ask, tempering my disbelief.

"Three of them," he says, "Okay, two and a half."

"It's a start, but three—er, rather, two and a half of you—can't take on the gangs by yourselves."

"Why not?"

We've had this discussion before and I already know how it ends. I plow ahead anyway. "Ki," I plead, "it's not worth getting hurt."

I wait for his rebuttal, but he instead throws me a question I don't anticipate. "You are *reading* to help our family; I'm protecting us with my knife. How is it any different?"

I don't care for his tone, the way he seems to mock me, but I stay silent—for all of ten seconds. "Perhaps they're not any different," I say to his astonishment as I let my supposed surrender marinate. "But at least my reading isn't going to get me killed, leaving my family behind and all alone."

If I were Ki, I'd get angry. He doesn't.

"There's a time and place for defending yourself," he says calmly, "whether it be with words—or with a knife. Keep reading; your stories will teach you that."

We've each said our piece and the ending is no surprise, though there is one thing he has said that causes me to wonder.

"I'm curious," I ask. "The half person you mentioned . . . are you talking about Lucky Fat?"

The corners of his mouth turn up ever so slightly, and that tells me that when he answers, I won't be certain if he's serious or teasing. Either way, I know from experience that I won't discover the truth for the rest of the day.

"No," he says with a straight and sincere face, "it's not Lucky. The person I was counting as a half, the gutsy person willing to also take a stand and fight with me—I was talking about Lena, *your mother.*"

The air is heavy and warm, enough so that I pull back my canvas and sit on the ground in the shade. I look to the distant hut of Teva Mao and listen for Nisay. My good friend has been anxious to watch my son of late, when Mother can't, and while I'm not certain, I suspect that Sopeap has made arrangements with Teva to forgive a portion of her rent.

I worry about Nisay, leaving him almost every morning for so long while I learn from Sopeap. Learning to read feels like the right thing to do, yet when my child cries as I pass him along to waiting hands, I want to throw away the books and pencils and just hold him close. But then, his constant whimpering throughout the day reminds me that if conditions don't change, he'll never improve. I wonder . . . is life so conflicted for everyone everywhere?

Sopeap notices my concern. "Don't worry about your son," she says. "He'll be fine."

"Will my learning help him?" I ask, needing to confirm that I'm making the right choice.

"Education is almost always good, especially when it brings us to an understanding of our place in the world."

"And literature will do that?"

"Sang Ly, we *are* literature—our lives, our hopes, our desires, our despairs, our passions, our strengths, our weaknesses. Stories express our longing not only to make a difference today but to see what is possible for tomorrow. Literature has been called *a handbook for the art of being human.* So, yes. It will do that."

"Will it help me to know how to get him better?"

She sets down her book. "I am a tired old woman who lives in a dump. I can't say if this is the right direction for you. That is a question only you will be able to answer. But I should warn you."

"Warn me? About what?"

"As you learn, as you read stories that speak to you and begin to understand how they relate to you and your family—you may find questions you weren't expecting."

"What kinds of questions?"

"The deepest questions of mankind: What is the meaning of my life? Why am I here at the dump? What's in store for me on this path? Do the ancestors listen and care about me? Why is life so hard? What is good and what is evil? What must I do about it? The list goes on and on."

"I don't understand. How does reading stories about others answer those questions for me?"

"That is what I'm hoping you will understand—every story we read, Sang Ly, is about us, in one way or another."

"But how . . . ?"

"Hold your questions, child. Let's not let the morning pass and find out that we haven't yet cracked open a book. We'll begin today with the story *Tum Teav* by Cambodian author Preah Botumthera Som."

She hands me a worn text. "I think you'll enjoy this story," she says. "It's about a beautiful adolescent girl named Teav. She is caught in a rather unusual predicament." Sopeap's eyes lock on mine, as if she can read my thoughts, and her words carry such wryness that I'm certain she must have found out about the girl. And if she knows, who else also knows?

I freeze, not budging, not breathing, until Sopeap finally points to the book and says, "Open to the first page and we'll get started."

CHAPTER
TWELVE

Mother is causing trouble again at the shelters, and I seem to be the only one to notice. By the time I arrive, she has convinced Sida Son and Jorani Kahn to build a large single shelter together rather than two smaller shelters of their own. "If you work together," she told them, "you'll create the best shelter ever seen at Stung Meanchey."

The problem is she knows full well that Sida and Jorani hate each other—and yet she persists. If my mother's motives were pure, if she were trying to get two friends to make up, I would applaud the woman. Instead she finesses the less-than-brilliant pair together, just so she can sit back and watch the show.

"Shame on you," I say as I take a seat beside her while the two women continue to argue about how far their cardboard should extend past their fabric roof. I would step in and break things up, but I know better.

"What would Father say if he were still alive?" I say to Mother.

"First of all, I don't know what you are talking about," she says. "And second, *you* should talk—you're the one who killed him."

Naturally I don't remember, and the story would change every time Mother or Grandfather would tell it. It was said that during my child-birth, Mother was in heavy labor, pushing and pushing, while I refused to come out. She was encouraged by the midwife while my father smoked homemade cigarettes as he paced nervously in the front yard.

Grandfather said I refused to leave the ancestors, who must have been gathered around telling jokes. I suspect, instead, that someone there must have warned me about my future at Stung Meanchey. Either way, my birth took hours. When I finally filled my lungs and announced to the village that I had arrived, the midwife ran out to deliver the good news and found my father stone-cold dead on the ground.

As a child, I liked to imagine that he gave up his life for me, that whoever was in charge that day had decided to allow a limited number of my relatives on the earth at one time. I convinced myself that I was the one destined to die, but then, at the very last moment, my father some-how pulled a *phlah bdo* (a secret switch) and volunteered himself instead.

It was just a child's silly story, but it helped ease the pain of one of my biggest regrets growing up: I never knew my father. To this day, I don't know what he looked like. Pictures were rare in the province, and the single photo Mother had of him was lost when I was still a baby.

"Do you want to stay for more?" Mother asks as Sida begins to curse and Jorani starts to throw trash.

I don't mean to laugh, but the two women are rather comical.

"It's no wonder we're both at Stung Meanchey," I tell her as we lean back and resist the temptation to clap. "It's no wonder at all."

Only when the fighting winds down does Mother lean over and casually mention, "You should also know . . . I have made arrange-ments for the girl."

I lurch forward. "Arrangements? For Maly? What does that mean?"

"It will be best if I keep the details to myself," she says, "for everyone's safety. Let's just say I've found a good situation, away from the city, where she will be safe."

"When?"

"I will leave with her tomorrow."

"So soon?"

"Yes, but there is one slight problem." I hate it when Mother mentions *problems.*

"What kind of problem?"

"To make this work, we're going to need the help of the Rent Collector."

I'm waiting outside my curtain when Sopeap arrives. I sent word that we needed to speak and, thankfully, she arrives on time.

"What is so important?" Sopeap asks, irritated.

"I'm sorry," I begin, unsure how to explain. "I just . . ." When I pause, she loses patience.

"Is this about the girl?"

I take a breath. "You know about her?"

"Since the day I saw her sleeping on your floor," she scoffs.

"I'm sorry. We wanted to keep her safe until—"

"Do you have a plan?" she interrupts.

"Yes, but . . ."

"Spit it out."

"We need your help. The girl—Maly is her name—will need money for the bus trip, and then for the family, to cover her expenses."

"Why are you telling me this?" Sopeap asks.

To me it seems obvious, but I continue. "The only extra we have is the money we're saving for next month's rent."

Sopeap's voice hardens. "Are you asking if I think helping this girl, a stranger to us both, is more important than you paying rent?"

I didn't expect her to be so belligerent, though I'm not sure why. Her question demands an answer, but I hesitate in my reply.

"Are you?" she repeats.

"Yes," I say. "I am."

There is no mistake in her tone. "I won't allow you to use your rent!"

"But Sopeap . . ."

Abruptly she reaches into her pocket and removes a tight roll of money, as if she expected this all along, and passes it to me. "This should be sufficient. However, offer it only to those you can trust—for the girl's sake. When does she leave?"

I am so taken aback, I say nothing.

"I asked, when does she leave?" Sopeap repeats, as if I'm hard of hearing.

"Tonight."

"So we won't be meeting today?"

"Not today."

"Then I'm going to have a drink—and tomorrow you can finally get your mind back on your studies." As she wobbles away, she calls out, "And don't be late with your rent!"

Life is a funny thing. One day I'm worried about our safety with Maly staying with us. Days later I'm scared to death to have her leave.

Even though the sun still beats down outside and we desperately need some air, we keep our canvas down until it gets dark.

Lucky is the first to say good-bye. He stands next to Maly, looking confused as to whether he should hug her or not. She helps him decide by wrapping her little arms around his neck. They whisper words we can't hear, and when the two separate, the boy quietly announces that he's going outside to look around and make sure it's safe. As he wipes his sleeve across his forehead and eyes, we all understand.

I step over to Maly next, and when she begins to tear up, I pull her close.

"I have something for you," I say as I present her a copy of *Reamker*, a book given to me by Sopeap.

"But I don't read," she answers.

"Not yet," I add, "but you will."

She touches the cover. "What is it about?"

"I have just finished reading it myself. It's a celebrated Cambodian epic that you are going to love. You'll fly away with Prince Rama and Queen Sita, fight giants, befriend monkeys, swim with mermaids, and rescue a forlorn princess. It's a wonderful world where good balances evil, friendships last forever, and magic keeps you safe—and every time you read it, you can think of us."

I hold her close a little longer until Lena reaches out her hand to indicate that it's time to go. Maly takes Lena's fingers and then hesitates.

I stoop beside the child. "Maly, be strong. You can do this."

"How will I live on my own?" she asks, gasping now as she weeps.

"You won't be—we'll all be here cheering for you."

She gathers her courage and nods, and then, as quickly as the child dropped into my life, she is taken away. Despite my head explaining to my heart that she is not my own daughter, that her leaving is for the better, my chest still aches.

១៣

CHAPTER
THIRTEEN

The stories that Sopeap brings are sometimes written by Cambodian authors. Most, however, are translated books by writers from distant parts of the world. Many are also in English, but with scribbled Khmer translations penned between the typed lines. I don't know where she gets them all.

I've learned that Sopeap not only taught years ago at the university in Phnom Penh but, prior to that, attended college in America, studying English. (She hasn't said, but her family must have been well-off to afford such blessings.)

The opening page of her book today shows a penned engraving of ocean waves and the splashing tail of a fish.

"We are reading a condensed version today," she says, "but even so, I suspect it will take us two days. The story was written by an American named Herman Melville and was translated by Khun Chhean."

Other than one or two Cambodian authors whose names have

sounded vaguely familiar, the author's names for the stories Sopeap brings are meaningless to me. She insists that will change.

Since I am new to learning and still trying to grasp the depth of the stories we read, on occasion Sopeap will explain what is going to happen beforehand, so that when I come to relevant passages, my brain will click and whir, my eyes will light up, and I will make her feel as though she is doing an adequate job.

"In this tale today," she begins, "some say Captain Ahab represents evil as he seeks revenge. The white whale, on the other hand, is said to represent good."

"Does everything always have to mean something else?" I ask before we get started. Who knew that literature was so tangled and complicated?

"That is a wonderful lesson, Sang Ly. Remember it."

"What was it again?" I ask, not certain to what she was referring.

She repeats it for me. "In literature, everything means something."

We open the pages and read.

Call me Ishmael. Some years ago—never mind how long precisely—having little or no money in my purse, and nothing particular to interest me on shore, I thought I would sail about a little and see the watery part of the world . . .

It takes four days instead of two to read the shortened version of the whale story, but these are four of the most exciting mornings I've spent at the dump—and they have helped take my mind off of Maly. The story ends in a valiant battle between the captain and the whale.

Captain Ahab is a consumed old man, bent purely on revenge for a deed his enemy committed long ago (if you must know, the whale bit off his leg). His words and actions are vicious, and even in his final moments, as he harpoons the animal from his sinking boat, Ahab cries, " . . . *to the last I grapple with thee; from hell's heart I stab at thee; for hate's sake I spit my last breath at thee.*" Yet in spite of his coarseness, Ahab is not completely repugnant. Wretched, certainly, but also consumed by a misguided desire for revenge.

Likewise, the white whale, which Sopeap reminds me represents good, isn't a pure creature either. Though he wins the battle—I presume signifying good prevailing over evil—he also kills the captain and his crew (except for the young man telling the story), an act far from benevolent.

Throughout the story, Sopeap's observation bounces back and forth in my head—*everything means something.* I can't help but consider Ki. He seems bent on revenge, perhaps to a small degree the same as Ahab. Yet Ki is a good man, a wonderful provider and husband. The question I keep asking is: *Is Ki Ahab or the whale?* It's uncomfortable because if Ki is not the whale, if he's more like Captain Ahab and his crew, I'm worried. Ahab and his crew all drown.

"Can you help me understand what this story says about dealing with evil?" I ask Sopeap with real intent.

"Can you be more specific?"

"How are we supposed to react to evil in our own lives? Should we battle, as Ahab and the whale? Or, is it better to steer clear and mind our own business, like people tend to do in the dump? What about Maly, for example? We helped her get away, but the gangs are still here—and they only get worse."

Perhaps because my teacher is educated and knows so much about literature, I expect a reasoned, deliberate answer. Instead, her glance darts back across her shoulder.

"If you are certain you are facing evil," she says, "and not ignorance, you must, if you can, destroy it before it destroys you!"

I have come to know Sopeap well, to read the emotion in her face, to understand her body movements and her quirks. When she twists her watch, she's impatient. When she throws her left foot to the floor harder than her right, she's angry. When she purses her lips and turns her head away, she's trying not to smile at something I've said that she finds funny. As she tells me now that I must destroy evil, a new emotion creeps across her face, an emotion that I have never seen in the woman in all the time I've known her. When she speaks about evil—true evil—the emotion that gathers in Sopeap's face is fear.

I don't mean to belabor the point, but I need to be sure I understand.

"I tell Ki that I'm learning about words and stories to help our family. He says he's protecting our family with his knife. Who is right? Which is best, protecting with words or with his knife?"

She is instant, certain, and solemn, and there is no misunderstanding her meaning.

"Fight ignorance with words. Fight evil with your knife. Tell your husband, Ki, that he is right."

၅

CHAPTER
FOURTEEN

While I wait for Ki near the shelters, on my own I find literature—at least I think so. The paper is stuck between two tattered magazines and I almost toss it aside. The title reads *Sy Mao's Advice for Growing Rice*. It's not the title that intrigues, but two handwritten words beneath. I read the page aloud so Mother, holding Nisay nearby, can listen.

Rice is the most important crop in the world. These tips will help you raise your rice properly.

Growing rice is challenging but not impossible. It takes patience, care, and a tremendous amount of work.

Even though rice adapts to many environments, it needs plenty of sunshine, water, and nutrients to thrive.

Rice comes in many varieties—brown, black, white, and red—including long-grain (slender), medium-grain (short and fat), short-grain (nearly round), sweet, sticky, and more. All varieties are good.

The secret to growing rice that thrives is to provide a proper environment. Clean out all noxious elements that may harm young plants. Use plenty of healthy organic matter.

Make certain your plants have plenty of room to grow. Stay close to remove sprouting weeds. Trying to care for too many plants at one time can be difficult and tiring.

While rice does best in certain environments, sometimes you have no control over natural conditions. Don't worry. Rice has an uncanny ability to tolerate both drought and flood.

Sometimes rice is planted in a nursery bed and then moved later to a garden. Other times, rice is sprouted right in the garden itself. Both methods work. The advantage of direct seeding is that you reduce transplant shock to the young and tender plants.

Above all, never take your rice plants for granted. Every plant is important. Care for them properly and they will grow to be mature, tender, and strong.

Good luck.

Sy Mao

At first glance the page appears to be nothing more than simple advice for gardening, and so, naturally, Mother is confused at my giggles.

I explain. "Though the page claims to be instruction for growing rice, beneath the title, someone has written the words '*and children.*' The title now reads, 'Sy Mao's Advice for Growing Rice *and Children.*'"

Mother is not following, so I try a different approach. "I'm going to read it again, but when I say *rice* or *plants,* in your mind think instead of *children.*"

As I read, I pause each time the word *rice* shows up, giving her time to grasp the new meaning. She is soon smiling as well.

Knowing that I've been in search of literature, she asks the same question I'm thinking. "Do two written words turn ordinary instructions into literature?"

I think through the question carefully, as Sopeap would expect, before I offer an answer.

"I don't know if it becomes literature," I say, suddenly feeling uncomfortably like the teacher. "I just know the two added words cause me to look at the ordinary sentences differently. And quite honestly, I find that to be magical!"

Sopeap must know that I'm excited because after I pass her a copy of *Sy Mao's Advice for Growing Rice,* I bounce around like a schoolgirl.

"This illustrates a lesson I'd planned on bringing up tomorrow," she says. "However, now is as good a time as any. Words, Sang Ly, are not only powerful, they are more valuable than gold."

I pause. Doubt must show in my features.

"You hesitate?" she asks.

"Well, yes," I say, "gold pays for food, clothing, rent—everything. What do words buy?"

"When you take your child to the doctor, how do you explain your son's illness so the doctor can offer help? Will all the gold in the world communicate what is wrong?"

"I guess not," I answer.

"How then does he know?"

"I tell him—"

"Precisely . . . with words. You use words. While gold may pay the doctor's bill, words have already helped save the child."

She doesn't quit there. "If you want to tell your husband how much he means to you, what do you do? Do you give him gold?"

"He would no doubt prefer that."

"If you gave him garbage trucks filled with gold, you would give only empty riches. To convey true love, Sang Ly, you whisper . . ."

She waits for me to fill in the answer. "Words."

"What words? What would you say to him?"

"I guess I would say, *I love you.*"

"Three words, Sang Ly, three simple words that communicate more, mean more, than worldly riches. Words provide a voice to our deepest feelings. I tell you, words have started and stopped wars. Words have built and lost fortunes. Words have saved and taken lives. Words have won and lost great kingdoms. Even Buddha said, '*Whatever words we utter should be chosen with care, for people will hear them and be influenced by them for good or ill.*' Do you understand?"

"I think so, except for one thing."

"Yes?"

"If words are so powerful, why do you—an educated woman who is able to speak and write many words—why do you live at Stung Meanchey?"

It is a long time before the teacher speaks. "Words are also like ropes," she finally says. "We use them to pull ourselves up, but if we are not careful, they can also bind us down—at times by our own doing."

"Are you saying you *choose* to live at Stung Meanchey?" I ask.

Often, when I raise an uncomfortable topic, Sopeap answers with a question. She says it's the sign of a good teacher, that it makes a student reflect. I think it's a sign of a teacher avoiding a difficult answer.

This time is no different. "Sang Ly," she replies, "don't we all choose to live in the dump in certain aspects of our lives?"

When I tell Ki Lim after dinner that Sopeap spoke about him, he throws back a glance of immediate disgust. "This ought to be good. What did my favorite teacher say?"

"She said that you were right."

"What?"

"You heard me—though I worry about how proud you are going to be now."

I have his attention. "Right about what?" he asks.

"That if we face evil in our lives, we should defend ourselves, stand up and fight, not tolerate it. She said there is no way to stop true evil but to destroy it."

"When she agreed with me, was she drunk?"

"I don't think she's drinking as much anymore, at least not before she comes to teach."

It takes Ki a minute to digest the notion: *Sopeap agrees with him on something.* While his shrug reads, *it's really no big deal,* the contentment radiating in his face screams, *I told you so.*

"Now that I've mentioned it, you have to make me one promise."

"What's that?"

"Don't be Captain Ahab."

"Who's Captain Ahab?"

"He's a guy who fights a big whale."

"What's wrong with that?"

"He dies in the end."

១៥

CHAPTER
FIFTEEN

Most of Sopeap's books contain no pictures. However, the first one she pulls out today has a hard cover with an illustration on the front that almost reminds me of Nisay's book.

"Are we reading another children's story?" I ask.

"Some may call it that."

"What would you call it?"

Sopeap considers my question. "I would call it . . . remarkable."

I think her pause was for dramatic effect, and it has worked, because I am reaching toward the book to get a better look. She moves it away and I surrender, letting my hands fall to my side.

"What is so remarkable about *this* story?" I ask.

"It was written in Cambodia many years ago. But more important, it comes from a rather distinguished family of stories—sisters, if you will, that deserve discussion."

I wonder if sometimes Sopeap tries to confuse me just for fun. I pretend to understand and move on. "What is the name of today's story?"

"It is called *Sarann*."

"Sarann? Who is Sarann?"

"Sarann is a Cambodian girl. Now, before you can ask any more questions, let's read it." She lets the cover fly open and begins. Her words are beautiful, and I am soon lost in the story as well.

Many centuries ago, when the Khmer Empire of Cambodia stretched from the farthest tip of Thailand to the costal shores of Vietnam and was regarded as the strongest kingdom in all of Southeast Asia, there lived, near the kingdom of Angkor, a wealthy rice farmer and his wife, with their only daughter, Sarann.

The family lived on the edge of the great river, Tonle Sap, in a beautiful home built on stilts to protect it from the seasonal rains that caused the water to rise. Since her father owned fields along the river and employed many servants to plant and harvest rice, Sarann had never lacked for any of life's comforts. Yet in spite of their wealth, she wasn't a spoiled child. Instead of thinking only of herself, as many children do, Sarann would help her mother carry food to her father's servants as they worked in the fields. At home, when her mother was tired, Sarann would sit by her side and brush her mother's silky hair; and if a family less fortunate in the village ever needed shelter, clothing, or food, Sarann would volunteer to help out, as best a young girl could.

While most days brought contentment, the moments

Sarann cherished most came each year when her parents took her to the Water Festival, an annual celebration that began when the waters from the great lake reversed their course to flow back down the river, the only place on earth where such a phenomenon in a river occurred. It was a celebration that also coincided with the full moon of the Buddhist calendar month of Kadeuk.

In addition to plentiful food, magnificent dancing, and sacred ceremonies, competing villages would race elaborately decorated dugout canoes, each carved with an ornate prow and stern that curved toward the sky. When a winner was declared, the king himself would present the prize, a ceremonial oar emblazed with the king's seal. Often the king would then take a ride in the winning canoe, bringing luck to the triumphant village.

It was at the Water Festival that Sarann's mother and father purchased her most prized gift, a silk *sampot* [a formal skirt], embroidered all over with beautiful threads of silver and gold. It was a special *sampot,* one that she would save until the day she married, and it came in an ornately carved box with a secure lid. It was presented to her at the festival and provided a moment she would never forget.

An afternoon rain had just passed as an eager sun poked out through the clouds to create a sash of rainbow color that draped across the sky. Sarann and her parents sat together by the river and unfolded the skirt. To Sarann, it meant that her parents realized she was growing up. It was a gift that also came with fatherly words of admonition: "My daughter, as you blossom and grow, always look for ways to serve others, and most important, never lose sight of your dreams."

But dreams, like rainbows, can be fleeting, for just after Sarann's fourteenth birthday, a fever swept through the village and both her father and mother were taken gravely ill. Within three days, her mother died, and her father would have followed had it not been for the hours Sarann spent by his side, replacing clean cloths that helped cool his head and whispering words of love and encouragement into his ear.

Even though he eventually recovered, the sickness had weakened his heart (and, some said, his mind). Fearing that the fever would return and take his life, thus leaving Sarann alone, he decided, in haste, to marry a widow who had recently moved to the village with her daughter. Even though she was regarded by many as the most beautiful woman in the village, others with perhaps more sensitive eyes regarded her as mischievous, cunning, and ruthless.

In spite of people's gossip, Sarann hoped the marriage would bring her father peace. Besides, she would finally get a sister—or at least a stepsister. Unfortunately, just a few short months after the wedding, her father's heart gave out and he died silently in his sleep. After his passing, the stepmother's true nature emerged. With her newfound wealth, she became obsessed with her own beauty and began to look down upon anyone who threatened her status—especially Sarann.

The vain woman spent fortunes seeking out astrologers, sorcerers, and magicians who would concoct spells and potions to preserve her beauty and help her remain looking young— but envy is hard to cover.

The stepmother greatly resented Sarann's natural beauty, and every day she would give the girl difficult and dirty chores—feeding pigs, shoveling sewage, digging for special mud in the jungle that was said to make one's skin radiant. But it didn't matter how filthy the job, because the radiance of virtue is equally hard to cover. And though Sarann's stepsister didn't condone the treatment that Sarann received at the hand of her mother, she did little to stop it.

As the years passed, life became more difficult for Sarann. Her skin became rough, her hair thin, and her cheeks hollow—yet she worked hard to remain cheerful. She would begin each day by opening her hand-carved box (which she hid in the wall of her room) to admire the golden threads of her *sampot* and remember the goodness and love of her parents. Silently she would repeat her father's admonition: "Always serve others and never lose sight of your dreams."

And then one day, a sorcerer came to the door to inform the stepmother of a rare flower with a yellow center and purple petals, with just a touch of white at each petal tip. It was a flower that grew only in the deepest, most dangerous part of the jungle. Men had tried to retrieve it, but none had. In fact, few had ever returned, most likely devoured by wild and ferocious beasts. It was said if the petals of the flower were rubbed against one's skin, they would draw such radiance and stunning beauty to the surface they would make the person irresistible.

With each passing day, the stepmother grew more delirious with envy and greed, wishing to have the flower for herself—so much so that she devised a wicked plan. She would send Sarann deep into the jungle to search for the flower. If she returned with the petals, it would be wonderful. If Sarann were instead eaten by ravenous beasts, it would be almost as wonderful. What plan could be more perfect?

Sarann was not so thrilled. She feared the jungle and understood its dangers, having been warned of them many times by her father. And so she refused to go. Her stepmother ranted, screamed, and threatened. She even hit Sarann several times across the face, but nothing would change the girl's mind. For there were no dirtier jobs she could be given than those she was already doing. She couldn't be made to work more hours, as there were only so many in a day. Quite simply, there was no punishment that she wasn't already receiving.

Then one morning, her stepsister (at the command of the stepmother) hid herself beneath a mammoth pile of clothing that was stacked in Sarann's room, waiting for mending. The stepsister watched Sarann remove her secret box from its hiding place in the wall, admire the embroidered skirt, and then whisper words of remembrance and love toward her parents. It was a scene so touching that the stepsister should have been moved to tears—but she wasn't. Instead, she dutifully reported to her mother what she had witnessed, then went about her own selfish business.

Later that day, when Sarann returned from slopping the pigs, she was horrified to find her stepmother calmly holding the open box above the noonday fire on which Sarann would cook their meal. "Please, have mercy!" Sarann screamed, but the stepmother knew no mercy.

"You will go into the jungle and return with the flower, or I will burn your precious *sampot* and the last memories of your pathetic parents forever."

Sarann left early the next morning, heading into the wild jungle in the general direction the sorcerer had pointed. She hiked until no more sounds of the village could be heard and no remnant of the initial trail remained. With every rustle ahead, she was certain she would meet her end and be devoured alive by wild beasts. But she wasn't, so deeper and deeper into the jungle she trekked.

When the night came, she found a tree and slept in its branches, though she was really only dozing off for a few moments here and there until the sun rose once again in the morning sky. Though she was incredibly hungry, thirsty, and tired, she continued on, getting farther and farther away from home with every step, constantly scanning the dense vegetation for a yellow-centered flower with purple petals that showed just a touch of white at each petal tip.

Soon her hands and feet, lacerated by the sticks, thorns, and sharp edges of the jungle's plants, became swollen, red, and bloody. Her neck and face, covered in bug bites, itched and burned.

By late in the afternoon, just when she doubted her ability to take another step, she looked toward a dark green thicket of spiny foliage. And there they were—the most vibrant and wonderful flowering vines she had ever seen, each displaying scores of yellow-centered blooms with deep purple petals tipped with brilliant white.

Even more peculiar, when she got close, she could see, perched on a vine next to one of the blooms, an Asian Fairybluebird, almost as vibrant and colorful as the flowers themselves. The bird was not alarmed by her presence, and it even looked as though it wanted to smile but couldn't because it only had a beak. Instead, it sounded a pleasant chirp and then flitted away, leaving her alone to admire the spectacular blooms.

Fearing she might be suffering the delusions of jungle fever, Sarann reached out to touch the flowers, just to see if they were real. They were, and she plucked a flower from its stem, which proved more difficult than she would have expected, and rubbed its velvety petals between her fingers.

She was still very hungry and thirsty, but the thrill of finding the flowers was so exhilarating that she forgot her pains and began to gather handfuls of the vines to take home. Then she realized that carrying them would be impossible because, at times, the vegetation in the jungle was so thick and matted that to pass through it took both her hands to bend back the leaves and branches. She would never be able to make her way back home carrying the flowers.

Then an idea blossomed. Though the blooms looked delicate, they were very hardy, and the vines were surprisingly wiry. She wove some together into a sturdy but lovely wreath. When she placed it on her head, it fit so perfectly that she felt just like a princess. Even better, the petals of the flowers were soft and soothing against her skin.

When she was ready she looked for the path out, but the jungle all around her appeared the same, making it impossible for her to remember the way she had come. Then she again saw and heard the bird that had been perched on the vine when she arrived. It seemed to be calling to her, bidding her to follow, and so she did.

Even though the trek out of the jungle was equally as tiring and treacherous as her hike into the jungle, she no longer seemed to notice or care. Just when she was certain that she must be nearing home, a handsome young man emerged from the brush. He looked as surprised to see Sarann as she was to see him.

With his eyes locked on hers, he tried to speak. "Hello. My name is—" But that's when he stopped, and it seemed peculiar to her that he'd forgotten his own name. It was several moments before he could continue. "Forgive my bad manners. What I'm trying to say is that my name is Kamol."

She was about to tell him her name when she realized, with embarrassment, how she must look and smell after hiking for so long in the jungle. She wanted to apologize for being filthy and scratched and red and swollen, but as she looked down, she realized she wasn't any of those things at all. The bites that had itched on her face and neck were gone. The cuts on her hands and feet that had throbbed as they left trails of blood had vanished. Her skin was instead smooth, soft, and radiant. And the terrible thirst and hunger that had plagued her—well, she hadn't been hungry since heading toward home. That's when she remembered the gentle and soothing flowers of the wreath that had been rubbing against her head. The sorcerer must have been right—the flowers had a powerful and magical effect.

Curious, she asked the handsome young man what he was doing alone in the jungle and learned he was gathering pyracantha berries that he would boil into dye with which to color his canoe for the upcoming race at the Water Festival. When she heard him mention the festival, her face brightened. They sat together on the fallen trunk of a tree and reminisced about the marvelous event and all the things they each loved to see and do. Before they knew it, the sun sat low in the sky and it would be getting dark soon. But when Sarann looked for the bird that had guided her home, it was nowhere to be found. It didn't matter. The young man knew the way, and, together, they walked out of the jungle.

Sarann could see her home in the distance, so she quickly thanked the charming boy before rushing away to recover her treasured *sampot*. As she approached her home, she saw her stepsister out front, watching rice that boiled in a pot over a fire. The stepsister looked surprised to see Sarann, as if she might be seeing a ghost, for the flowers had made Sarann so radiant and beautiful that she almost glowed—and quite frankly, neither the stepsister nor her mother honestly expected to see Sarann ever again.

Sarann was about to explain—to show her stepsister the flowers, and to tell her all about the bird and the boy, when she glanced down at the dancing flames of the fire and noticed the charcoaled remains of a box corner. Also littering the outer circle of ashes were glowing golden threads. As reality registered, Sarann couldn't help but scream.

"What have you done? What have you done?"

Hearing the commotion, the stepmother rushed from the house—but it was too late. Sarann ran as fast as her legs would carry her, with tears streaming down her face, back into the darkness of the wild jungle. When the vegetation became too thick for her to run, she dropped to her knees sobbing, praying that an animal would appear and eat her, for she could bear her misery no longer. And an animal did appear, but it wasn't a boar, snake, or crocodile. Instead, it was the Asian Fairy-bluebird that had led her previously from the jungle. It fluttered close, then landed beside her. Suddenly, before her eyes, it transformed into a beautiful woman wearing a flowing golden robe and holding the lovely green branch of a willow. She spoke to Sarann.

"What is the matter?"

"Who are you?" Sarann asked.

"I am the Goddess of Mercy. I have come to ease your burden."

"It's too late," the girl cried. "It is simply too late."

"It is never too late. You are barely just beginning."

"But they have burned my *sampot,* and I have nothing left to remember my parents."

"My dear," she answered gently, "you don't need a *sampot* to remember. Your heart is flowing with memories. Signs of their love and admiration are all around you, whether you choose to see them or not. All that your parents wish is that you have a happy and fulfilled life. I think it is time we get started."

The Goddess of Mercy then waved her willow, and, as she did, the lights in the heavens above began to swirl.

The sound of distant laughter caused Sarann to awaken from the spot at the edge of the jungle where she'd fallen asleep the night before. As she sat up and rubbed her eyes, she wondered if it had been a dream. However, when she looked down, she was dressed in a vivid red and gold *sampot* of the most striking hues. Her hair lay as a dark mantle draped gently across her shoulders, as if it had just been washed clean in the river and it now flowed radiantly from beneath the flowering wreath that still adorned her head.

When she heard voices, she stepped out from the jungle

growth and called toward the streaming throng of people, "Where is everyone going?"

"Why, to the Water Festival, of course. Have you been living in the jungle?"

They laughed but then invited the stunning stranger to join them as they walked to the river's edge. She hadn't eaten a good meal in days, and so upon arriving at the festival, she stopped first at the food sellers. She reached into an empty pocket, only to find that it wasn't empty at all but contained sufficient money for her needs. She bought a large bowl of cooked rice, pork, and vegetables, just like the one she and her parents used to share together. As she ate, she smiled, remembering how her father would make her eat the vegetables first, before she was allowed to fill up on too much of the sweet pork.

Next, she wandered through the sea of vendors offering drinks, fish, hats, sandals, toys, incense, clothing, and just about everything else one could imagine—even ceremonial *sampots*. She looked until she found one similar to hers, the one that had been burned, and she recalled the day it had been purchased.

"You are growing up, daughter," her father had said. "Your mother and I spoke and we agreed that even though you are still young, it is time for you to pick out your *Sampot Lbak*—the one most special that you will save until the day you marry."

As she listened again to the words that echoed distantly in her head, she whispered her reply, "Thank you, Father, for having so much trust in such a young and naive girl."

Sarann wandered to the river, where she and her father

would stand atop a stone wall built along the deepest edge of the river. (It was always too scary for her mother, so she would wait below.) Her father would climb up first and then take his precious daughter's hand to lift her gently up. It was the perfect spot from which to watch the races, as it raised them above an otherwise thronging crowd and allowed them to see the boats, even when they were still distant. Today, there was no one there to lift her up and hold her hand, so she climbed alone. While she was sad that her father wasn't with her, she was also grateful he had taught her how to climb by herself. Standing atop the wall, she felt an unusual peace.

Shouts from the crowd grew loud as the racing canoes appeared. It was just like old times, and, encouraged by those around her, Sarann also waved and cheered. Even from far away she could see that the canoe on the near side, closest to the wall, reflected a deep crimson red, almost the color of her *sampot,* and she guessed it must be Kamol's canoe.

The crowd roared as the crimson boat won, and as it shot past the finish line, Kamol, the head oarsman and navigator, turned his head for just a moment as if to acknowledge her. *He must be well loved in his village,* she thought. Not only would her newfound friend's victory gain him the respect of his village elders, but Kamol would also have the honor of meeting the king.

Sarann climbed down from the wall and pushed her way through the crowd to the place where the boats docked, to get a better look at the victorious oarsmen. To her surprise, the handsome boy noticed her peeking through the well-wishers and waved her to come forward.

"It's you!" he shouted as she approached. "You helped us win!"

"I don't understand. I just watched," she replied.

"To win the race," he said, "the navigator must pick out a distant landmark and then guide the boat hard and fast toward it. To deviate left or right will increase the distance traveled and slow the overall time. As we rowed toward the finish, I picked out a woman in a bright red gown, and I steered the boat toward her—never wavering. We were behind at first, but with concentration and focus on our goal, we soon pulled ahead. As we shot by the wall where the woman stood, I realized it was you, the girl from the jungle, and I don't even know your name."

"My name is Sarann."

The boy held out his hand to her as the crowd looked on, wondering about the beautiful girl in the red and gold *sampot*.

"Miss Sarann," he continued, "would you care to take a victory ride in the winning canoe?"

She was honored but also confused, for the king himself stood several yards away watching but had not yet stepped forward.

"The king is always the first," she replied.

"The king? Of course," said the boy, as he turned toward him. "Father, this is the girl I told you about. Is she not even more beautiful than I described? Shall I take her for a ride first?"

The king smiled, nodded to Sarann, and then waved his permission.

"You are Kamol, the prince of Angkor?" Sarann asked with disbelief.

Before he could answer, Sarann felt a terrible tug as the wreath was jerked off her head. She had not noticed her stepmother and stepsister, who had worked their way through the crowd, creeping up on her from behind.

"Finally, I have them. I have the flowers!" the stepmother shrieked as she tore a single blossom from the headpiece and furiously rubbed its petals against her face, arms, and hands. The stepdaughter followed her mother's example, tearing two flowers from the mangled vine instead of one.

Before the king could command his soldiers to step forward and arrest the two women, the flowers' magic began to take effect. But the petals' power was to bring beauty already deep within to the surface, to reveal one's true nature. Since the stepmother had long ago replaced any goodness with greed and vanity, there was no virtue left to surface. There, in front of Sarann, the king, the prince, and throngs of onlookers, she painfully twisted and withered into a common swamp leech, then dropped from where she stood into the river's muddy depths.

Moments later, the stepsister also began to change. However, instead of becoming a leech, she shrank into a small, lifeless rock—doing no evil, but doing no good—and she also rolled into the river with a plop and sank from view.

Seeing the danger the flowers posed to those in the crowd, the prince grabbed what was left of the magical wreath and, before others could touch it, flung it far out into the river, where it disappeared forever into the watery depths. Since the prince had also touched the flowers, all held their breaths to see what would happen to him. But, like Sarann, his true nature was already known and he could not be changed for the worse.

Instead, he stepped to Sarann's side, held out his hand, and helped her into his canoe for the victorious ride around the river. As they circled, those on the banks cheered for the girl who they understood would soon become the new princess of Angkor.

Sopeap turns the last page and waits for my reaction. "Did you enjoy it?" she asks.

"Oh, yes, it's a wonderful story," I answer before I fittingly add, "though I am very inexperienced in these things."

"Can you tell me why you enjoyed it?"

Speaking to a teacher, I feel duty bound to offer a reasoned and thoughtful reply, one that recognizes the story's qualities. The truth, however, is much simpler. "It makes me happy."

Sopeap tips her head as if to agree, but it's so slight I think I may have imagined it. "The story we have just read," she says, "can be found in hundreds of versions all over the world, in every country, continent, and culture."

"They all know the story of Sarann?"

"The girl's name is different and her circumstance will vary. However, the story's message is the same. She is *Ye Xian* in China, *Tattercoats* in England, *Aschenputtel* in Germany, *Critheanach* in Scotland, *Nyasha* in Africa, *Cinderella* in North America—which story is probably the most well-known—and the list goes on and on."

"Where did the story begin?"

"No one is absolutely certain. There are so many versions that researchers can't accurately count them. Some say there are hundreds, others cite thousands. Many once believed that the first Cinderella story was written in seventeenth-century France by a man named Perrault. Then they discovered a Chinese version told hundreds of years earlier. Still others say the first is *Rhodopis*, a story recorded in the first century B.C. by a Greek historian. It seems that every time old records are uncovered, another version pops up."

Sopeap speaks with genuine excitement.

"Do you understand, Sang Ly? People living on distant islands of the seas, isolated from all other civilizations, they also have their own Sarann stories as well."

"How? Why are there so many?"

"I think the answer lies in the story itself. Perhaps you touched on it when you said that it made you feel happy. It seems, quite simply, that as human beings, we are born to hope."

"To hope?" I ask, wrinkling up my brow. "But you told me that hope died at Stung Meanchey."

"And therein lies another lesson—*consider the source.*"

"I don't understand."

"Never rely on the advice of a disillusioned drunk."

"Then you do believe in hope?" I ask.

A longer pause, a deeper breath. "I believe the message of the story that we have just read anchors deeper than our doubts."

She can see by my face that my tired brain is working hard to process her comments and so she decides to make it easier for me. "Sang Ly, the desire to believe, to look forward to better days, to want them, to expect them—it seems to be ingrained in our being. Whether we like it or not, hope is written so deeply into our hearts that we just can't help ourselves, no matter how hard we try otherwise. We love the story because *we* are Sarann or Tattercoats or Cinderella. We all struggle with the same problems and doubts. We all long for the day when we'll get our own reward. We all harbor hope—and that's why it's such a problem."

"Problem?"

"Yes, an issue that bothered so many teachers at the university—myself included—a problem we could never explain away. Is our DNA to blame for this inherent desire to hope? Is it simply another survival mechanism? Is that why we love Sarann or Cinderella? Or is there more to it?"

"Such as?"

"I had colleagues who would dissect and quantify the stories, as though the paragraphs were laboratory frogs. They would split the sentences apart, dig through their insides, write up theories about the why and how and when—but in the end, when the letters all settled, their answers often pointed to something deeper. It would make them crazy. I'll admit that, at times, it still makes me crazy."

"When you say *deeper,* are you talking about the ancestors?"

"I am talking about the constant nature of *truth*. Look at Buddha's philosophy—it's about the path and our journey. That's what his teachings of the Noble Eightfold Path are all about. Do you see what I mean? Have you ever found a classical book of literature that isn't about a journey—whether actual or within?"

Other than the few I've read with Sopeap, I can't name any other stories. It doesn't matter. She answers her own question.

"There isn't one. It's not just Sarann and Cinderella. Look at all books, plays, movies—we keep writing the same plots, with the same characters, teaching the same lessons. Why do you suppose that is?"

"Nobody has an original idea?"

She eyes me intently. "Or is the *original idea* so intrinsic, inherent, and ingenious, so fundamental to our existence, that we can't help but be drawn back?"

I try to grasp what she means but can only shrug.

"I'm suggesting writers can't help themselves," she says. "Our trials, our troubles, our demons, our angels—we reenact them because these stories explain our lives. Literature's lessons repeat because they echo from deeper places. They touch a chord in our soul because they're notes we've already heard played. Plots repeat because, from the birth of man, they explore the reasons for our being. Stories teach us to not give up hope because there are times in our own journey when we mustn't give up hope. They teach endurance because in our lives we are meant to endure. They carry messages that are older than the words themselves, messages that reach beyond the page."

She takes a deep breath and waits.

"Your words today are all so beautiful. Why did you ever quit teaching? Why would you ever give up on literature?"

"Perhaps it gave up on me," she answers more faintly.

"Do you believe that our ancestors care about us, that they watch over us?" I ask Sopeap, still a bit unsure of the point she is trying to make.

She licks her plump lips, hesitates. "I'm inclined to, but . . ."

"But what?"

"We all want to be Sarann, to have hope for our future. While I also want to have my story end happily, there's a problem that keeps getting in my way—I wake up most days to find I'm just another ugly stepsister."

"Do you say this because not all our stories end happily?"

"That, Sang Ly, is the paradox," she continues, "the part that is perplexing. It seems that if we take these stories too literally, if we expect our personal lives to always end with a handsome prince, most of us will close our books with shattered dreams. Yet, on the other hand— and this is the part that frustrates—if we don't take the meaning of these stories literally, if we treat these tales as simply entertainment, we miss the deepest, most life-changing aspects of the stories. We miss the entire reason they even exist."

This time her pause is longer. Then her tone changes. "And if that happens, we grow cynical, teach literature at a university, and end up drinking rice wine at the dump."

Only when Sopeap forces a smile do I understand that her last comment is meant to be funny. "Besides," she adds, perhaps to relieve us both from an awkward moment, "if every story ended with a handsome prince, there wouldn't be anybody left in the kingdom to stand around and cheer."

๑๖

CHAPTER
SIXTEEN

On the far southeastern side of the dump, where the bulldozers have not yet piled mountains of trash, the ground turns to swamp and the water pools into small, irregular ponds, each a foot or two deep and a couple of hundred feet across. Reeds thrive around the edges, and, at certain times of the year, the snails that live in the water will grow big enough for us to gather.

Since I'm now seldom picking trash, and since Sopeap has only forgiven the single month's rent, I'm hesitant to spend too much of the money Ki Lim earns to buy pork at the market. Instead, when Ki arrives home early today, I grab one of the bags we use to gather recycled trash, ask him to watch Nisay, and tell him that I'll be back home shortly with dinner.

I once told a doctor, who asked what I fed Nisay, that on occasion we eat boiled snails. He jerked around excitedly, as if snails were a staple in everyone's diet, and then added that he'd eaten them at *Le Bouillon Chartier,* one of the finest restaurants in France. He was the same doctor who told me that the practice of scraping Nisay's skin was a waste of time, and I couldn't tell by his tone if he was mocking me about the snails or if he was being sincere. I presumed the latter, and so the next time I cooked snails, I explained to Ki that we were eating just like the rich do in France. I don't remember his exact reply, but I know it contained the word *chkuat* (crazy).

Teva Mao's oldest girls are playing out in front, and when they realize where I'm headed, they follow along for the adventure. As we approach the ponds, there are already others gathering, and in spite of the fact that we're talking about snails from the dump, I pick up my step anyway, worried I'll miss out. Though the water is muddy, a quick inspection confirms that the snails are still too small—until we wade out to where the water deepens. Not only are they larger, but they are plentiful. Then it starts to rain.

I work an area where the water reaches my knees but where there are still patches of reeds, and there I pluck snails the size of errant limes. As I gather them into my bag, the rain increases. It's a bit treacherous as I try not to slip, but I can't complain. The job is tolerable until I glance at my ankle while stepping through the water to see what looks like a black spot of mud.

In this life we all have our own phobias and fears. Lena hates snakes. Narin dreads stink beetles. Dara Neak can't stand the thought of spiders. I, in turn, am terrified of leeches—just like the one now attached to my ankle.

I'm not stupid enough to leave my bag behind, but I clutch it tightly and high step out of the water as if I'm about to be eaten by a swamp creature—which I am. Once I reach the safety of higher ground, I toss my sack aside and reach down to pull the miserable creature off of my skin, but I can't. Either my fingers are too slippery from the snails I've gathered or my hands are too shaky from my panic.

No matter how hard I try to grab hold of the monster still sucking blood from my body, I can't get a grip. I try an alternative tactic, which entails repeatedly stomping my foot against the ground, as though my pants have caught fire at the dump, hoping to shake the leech loose; but the stubborn little animal doesn't budge.

"Girls! Come quick!" I scream, as if the swamp water has also caught fire and if they don't come this instant, we'll all be consumed. They continue splashing at each other and giggling.

I scream louder.

When they finally reach me, Vanna, Teva's oldest, rolls her eyes.

"Pull it off, quick!" I say, and she reaches down to give it a try. It stretches out, long and plump, sliding through her slender fingers, and I'm certain it's getting longer and plumper every second.

"This one's hard to get off," she says as she tries again and fails miserably.

Teva's youngest pipes up next. "Usually they let go once they've had their fill of blood."

It's an interesting tidbit of advice that I have no intention of testing out!

"Quick, give me your sandal," I say to Vanna.

She slips it off and hands it to me. Using a flat end, I finally scrape the wretched leech from my leg. After I do, blood continues to ooze out from the spot on my skin where it has been attached.

"I'm going home. I'm through gathering snails," I declare with a pout as I pick up my bag and stomp away, looking carefully where I step. I feel like a tantrum-throwing child who refuses to play when she doesn't get her way, but I don't care. Teva's girls don't care either. They shrug, wave, and then, after I'm distant, laugh at me.

By the time I arrive home, I've calmed down. I give Ki the snails I successfully gathered before the cruel leech attack, watching as he dumps them into our Styrofoam box. He swirls them around with water to clean them off, then mixes in a little salt to draw them out of their shells. As he works, I rehearse the vicious assault in more vivid detail. He tries not to smile but does a poor job hiding his amusement.

"Where exactly did it bite you?" he asks, and I can't tell if he's concerned or just teasing. I think I've already shown him, but to eke out as much sympathy as possible, I twist around and pull up my pant leg so he can see for himself.

"It was right here—" I point to my wound, but when I look down, there's nothing there. I must have mixed up which leg got bitten. I twist to the other side and pull up that pant leg instead. "I mean it was—" It's not on that ankle either, which is confusing, and suddenly, I can't remember exactly where it bit me.

No matter; Ki can hardly contain himself. I want to join his laughter, as the situation really is hysterically funny. Instead, I shake my disgusted head, bend down, and transfer our dinner into a cooking pot, promising myself not to speak another word to the man until well into the evening.

"I have been thinking about something you said last time we met," I say to Sopeap after we finish talking about the story we have just read.

"Then you *do* listen."

I ignore her sarcasm. "You said we all want to be the story's hero."

"Yes."

"Well, I asked Sida Son what she thought about heroes."

"What did she say?"

"She chuckled and told me to look around at where I lived. She said to let her know when I saw a hero walking past, but that I'd grow old waiting—and then she left."

"Perhaps she's looking for the wrong kind of hero."

"I don't understand."

"Heroes come in many varieties—some are reluctant, others are willing; sometimes heroes act alone, other times they represent a group. Seldom are heroes perfect."

"Then what makes them heroes?"

"Most teachers will agree that the true mark of a hero, what sets him apart from everyone else, is sacrifice. A hero gives something up, sometimes even his own life, for the good of others."

"Does giving up *time* for another count, like you teaching me how to read?"

Our discussion so far today has been friendly. Instantly Sopeap flashes anger. "Don't pander to me! I won't tolerate it."

I don't understand how she can turn so mean so quickly. "I'm not . . . or I don't think I am. I don't even know what *pander* means."

She isn't finished. "Understand, child, I'm nobody's hero."

As always, I should shut my mouth. But when she gets angry for no reason, it makes me . . . well . . . *angry*. Rather than show it, I decide to play dumb.

"But you *are* teaching me—isn't that a sacrifice?"

It works. She steps so close I have a hard time focusing on her eyes. Her tone reaches out with invisible fingers and grabs my neck. "Don't you *ever* assume that I'm doing this for you. I am *not* a hero—not to you, not to anyone! Do you understand me?"

I'm not certain exactly what point I've proven, but it feels as though there must be one in there somewhere. "Yes," I answer. "I'm sorry."

Sometimes when I get Sopeap angry, we finish early for the day. I think if I had to put up with me, I'd drink also. But today, she gathers her composure and keeps going.

"There are other vital characters beside the hero. Stories are littered with characters you will recognize from our everyday lives. We should talk about them as well."

"Like who?"

"Have you ever known someone who pretended to be something they were not? A friend, perhaps, who later crossed you?"

"Yes, of course."

"Then you have met a shape-shifter—and yet it's not always a person. Fate is the most maddening shape-shifter you will ever encounter."

Perhaps it's because my face is all scrunched up that she thinks I don't follow. I do. It is just that she is talking so fast I have to concentrate to not miss something. "Tell me about others."

"Do you have friends or acquaintances who are always mischievous and making jokes?"

"Everyone does."

"Not only do these people provide relief with their wit, but their often impish actions point out the absurd, things that need to change."

"Just like Lucky Fat," I say.

"Explain what you mean."

"The other day Lucky joked about how ridiculous it is that the buyer pays less to women and children when they bring in scrap than to a man—and he did it right in front of the buyer's face. I thought it was funny, but the buyer seemed annoyed. Yet, when he paid me that day, it was as much as if Ki had gone."

"Then you are already acquainted with the benefits of a trickster." Sopeap raises her arm to cover the lower part of her face, then crouches at her waist. She glances wildly about the room, and when she speaks, her voice almost sounds sinister. She is actually acting; it's a side of the woman I have never seen. "And then there's the mask of the shadow," she says, "a cunning character indeed."

"The shadow character must be the evil person, like the gangs," I say.

"It could be," she agrees, standing back up straight. "Sometimes, the shadow is the villain, but a shadow may also be someone who simply disagrees with the hero and tries to pull him or her in a different direction. And sometimes the shadow isn't a character at all."

"Why not?"

"At times the shadows can be within us—all of our dark secrets that try to tear us apart, secrets that we can't or don't admit, even to ourselves."

"There is something you've said that confuses me," I say.

"Some of the things I say confuse me also. What is it?"

"If the shadow isn't always evil, if it can also be someone who disagrees, does that mean Ki is a shadow when he tells me I'm wrong?"

"Good question. Remember, from the shadow's point of view, *we* are the shadow and he is the hero. And here is something else just as confusing: sometimes these characters are all mixed together. We may find that any character in the story can temporarily wear the mask of any or all of these, even the hero."

"Then how do I keep them straight?"

"Often we don't. That is why literature—and life—are so exciting. These characters can be right in front of our faces and yet we don't see them."

Sopeap hesitates.

"What is it?" I ask.

"Also think about this, and then we will finish for the day. All of these characters we have discussed, and many more that we

135

haven't—their struggles aren't always evident. In almost every story, the fiercest battles often take place within."

Sopeap places her books in her bag, a sign that tells me we are finished for the day. Perhaps it's the confusion still pinned to my face, or that I'm finally silent and not asking incessant questions, but either way, just before heading out the door, she leaves a thought that I sense will percolate in my head for the rest of the afternoon.

"Just when we think we have our own stories figured out," she says, "heroes arise in the most unexpected places."

The *Momordica charantia* is a tropical plant grown in Cambodia that is widely known for its edible fruit. The fruit is a grassy green color and comes in a variety of shapes and sizes, though typically oblong with bluntly tapering ends. In short, it looks like a skinny cucumber with a horrific case of warts. It is also called *bitter melon,* and rightly so. Of all the fruits in Cambodia, there is none more bitter or acrid to the taste.

Teva Mao says the leaves of the bitter melon plant stimulate digestion, reduce fever, and just may help my son. When she returns from a trip into the city, she brings back some leaves that she purchased at the market, and I am most thankful. Nisay is not as excited. I don't care. He's been getting worse and I'll try anything. I boil the plant until the bubbling water has leached color from the leaves, turning the liquid a pale emerald green. It actually looks quite delicious, until I take a sip. My lips tighten and purse and my tongue involuntarily blocks access to my throat. It makes me wonder: If I can hardly stand its taste, how am I going to get Nisay to try it?

Ki thinks it's funny, so I give him the job of feeding it to the child.

He starts with a spoonful, and while Nisay is eager on the first try, he's not stupid. I question how much of the liquid the boy actually swallows as green splashes trickle down his bare chest. On Ki's second try, Nisay cries, spits, and jerks his head sideways, and it's plain to everyone—okay, at least to me—that this is not going to work. Ki, however, can be as stubborn as Nisay. He tells us that he'll be back, and he soon returns with a small container of juice from a fruit called *Tieb,* also known as *custard apple.* (I have no idea where he got it, and he refuses to tell me.) While the bitter melon is known for being sour, the custard apple is known for being sweet. On the third attempt—Nisay twists away at first—Ki finally forces a spoonful of the sugary liquid against the child's lips. The fussing stops, Nisay turns to Ki with interest, and his tongue pokes out of his mouth, as if to say, "Hey, something is different here!"

The transformation is so swift we can't keep from laughing, and Nisay now looks like a baby bird waiting for breakfast. I almost feel sorry for the child, as I can see what's coming. He gulps; he realizes; he coughs; he cries. Ki then presses another spoonful of the sweet liquid to his lips and the process starts all over again. It is parenting by deception at its finest, and my husband is quite proud of himself—in spite of the fact that our son will have obvious issues with trust well into adulthood.

Still, it's a happy day and I have hope that the medicine will help. But by the next morning, there is more diarrhea, this time a pasty green color, and my son cries for most of the morning before I hand him to someone else, someone who is not his mother, someone who doesn't care about him as much as I do, and I trudge back home to learn about literature because it's supposed to somehow, in my warped mind, help my child.

When Sopeap finally arrives, she asks, "Are you okay, child? You look as though you've been crying."

១៧

CHAPTER
SEVENTEEN

Dreams are curious.

Most dreams are nonsensical scenes that cause us to giggle when we recall them in the morning. Others are frightening nightmares during which we are attacked by gangs, chased by garbage trucks, or endlessly falling in menacing darkness. A few rare dreams are so real, so detailed and profound, that they alter the course of our lives. Last night I had such a dream.

It was not of my childhood. I didn't speak with my grandfather or try to decipher his often puzzling advice. In fact, I didn't utter a word. Instead, when I awoke in the morning—or thought I had—I opened the flap on the front of our little home at Stung Meanchey to find the entire dump covered in a blanket of white ash. I assumed that the fires must have been especially terrible to create so much ash, but then, as I looked over the horizon, I could see Jorani Kahn. She was waving me to follow, and it was then that I understood Stung Meanchey wasn't covered in ash at all—it was covered in snow.

I have never seen snow in person, never felt its touch against my skin. I only know about snow through occasional pictures of faraway countries that we find in discarded travel magazines—and from Jorani Kahn's stories. She once visited a place called *Co-lo-ra-do* in America with her father when she was a child. She told me about molding snow into balls like cotton, but heavy like mud, and throwing them at other people for fun. She said that the piles of snow in the mountains were so tall that they would almost reach the height of the trash at Stung Meanchey.

I didn't have time to play in the snow. Nisay had been sick again and we had no money for the doctor. I had to work, but when I looked again for Jorani Kahn to tell her, she was gone. Instead, I saw only stillness—no rumbling trucks, no clanking bulldozers, no scavenging workers, no grunting pigs, no clucking chickens, no boisterous children, no buzzing flies. It was completely and utterly silent.

In spite of the unusual scene, I snatched my picker and an empty canvas sack, as if it were just another normal day of work. Yet the fact that it was just an ordinary day is partly what made it so extraordinary. I stepped out into the snow, but as I began to dig down through the sheet of white, I realized the putrid trash was no longer there beneath. Everything dirty at Stung Meanchey was gone—no germs, no stench, no toxic water, no smoke, no fires, no bustle, no gangs, no rotting food. The filthiest place on earth had been made clean.

As I turned about, marveling at what had happened, in the distance I could see my home province of Prey Veng. I understood that this was impossible, since Prey Veng and Stung Meanchey lie far apart, a distance that requires a long trek by bus, much hiking, and lastly a ride by boat—but I could see the province anyway. And in my village home, a man stood waiting with his hands stretched out in my direction, as if he wanted me to hand him something, or perhaps he was beckoning me home. At first I assumed him to be my grandfather, for he often visits me in my dreams. However, this man stood too tall, too straight, too broad to be my grandfather, even in his younger years.

And then he spoke.

"You should have come sooner. Why didn't you come sooner?"

He repeated the question three times before I responded. But just when I was about to ask his name and what his question meant, I awoke with his voice still ringing in my ears:

"Sang Ly, you should have come sooner."

"Do you dream?" I ask Sopeap before we end for the day.

"As in goals, such as '*reach for your dreams*'? Or do you mean waking up relieved that I wasn't actually working naked in the dump?"

Until I came to know Sopeap, I didn't realize how funny she could be.

"I mean seeing people and places in your dreams that are familiar, but then not understanding what they mean—if they mean anything at all."

"You're talking about serious dreams?"

"Yes."

"The only real dreams I have anymore are usually not pleasant."

"Nightmares?"

She nods. "Perhaps a symptom of old age."

"I'm sorry," I say. "How do you keep them away?"

"Rice wine. Why all the questions?"

"I had a dream that feels important, but I don't know for sure."

"I guess that would depend on whom you believe."

"How so?"

"William Shakespeare called dreams the 'children of an idle brain, begot of nothing but vain fantasy.'"

"What's my other choice?"

"Dreams have also been called a sign of ambition. I think the quote was: 'Dreams, indeed, are ambition; for the very substance of the ambitious is merely the shadow of a dream.'"

"And who said that?"

"That was also William Shakespeare."

"He couldn't make up his mind?"

She shrugs. "I would say if it feels important it probably is. Our subconscious can be downright persistent in prodding us along our path, even if it's a road we'd rather not travel."

"Then dreams matter?"

"Absolutely. Some of the world's most important stories, works of literature that have changed lives, have come through dreams."

"Seriously?"

"Let's see. Many sacred writings of Buddha depict specific dream images. Then there is Lewis Carroll's *Alice in Wonderland,* a perfect example of a story inspired by dreams. There's *Kubla Khan,* a poem by Coleridge that's considered one of his greatest works. It celebrates creativity and our connection to the universe—and it was composed one night after a dream. Robert Louis Stevenson, a Scottish novelist, was a vivid dreamer, as was Bunyan, who wholly attributes his *Pilgrim's Progress* to dreams. Cambodian writer Nhean Uy composed several of his dreams into stories. Give me time and I can probably list dozens, perhaps even hundreds more. And let's not forget Carl Jung, the Swiss psychiatrist. He was the grandfather of dream psychology. He believed that literature and dreams weave together in astonishing ways. He documented a connection between the dreams of his patients and figures in mythology—even with people who had never read mythology."

"How is that possible?"

"His conclusion was that both came from a deeper source."

"But how can I know what *my* dreams mean?"

"If you listen to Jung, he said that to learn from our dreams we should ponder them. I believe he said, 'Consciousness succumbs too easily to unconscious influences, as these are often truer and wiser than our conscious thinking.'"

"I don't understand what he means."

"It's his way of saying that dreams are more important than we can ever imagine—we just need to listen."

Nisay is filthy, so we step around to the side of the house where I pour water over the child with a tin cup to try to get my little puppy clean before his father comes home. Too late. Ki arrives early and rushes around the house to find us. Before he even opens his mouth to say a word, his face tells me something is wrong.

"What has happened?" I ask.

"Don't worry. Everything is okay. It's Lucky Fat."

"Tell me! What's happened?"

"When he wasn't at the dump today, your mother dropped by to see if he was okay . . ."

"And?" My eyes lock on his, willing him to continue.

"Apparently, some in the gang are still looking for the girl."

"They went to Lucky's? How did they know? What did they do to him?" I'm raising my voice to the one person in the dump I shouldn't.

"When he wouldn't tell them anything," he replies, "they decided to teach him a lesson."

My heart picks up a beat and I wish Ki would just spit it out. "Please tell me if he's okay."

"They roughed him up and smashed most of his Buddhas. In the process he was hit in the eye by one of them. It's swollen shut, but Lena is with him now and it looks like he's going to be fine."

"He's a child. How could they hurt a child?" It's a stupid question, as I'm talking about those willing to sell an innocent girl into a life of prostitution. Though I've always been the pacifist, I instantly want to bash in their faces with a stone Buddha myself.

"What are we going to do?" I ask, ready to take Ki's knife and go after them this instant.

"I've just been meeting with more of the men. It seems that Lucky is well liked. This, coupled with Sopeap's words, which I shared, suggesting that we fight against evil . . . well, it looks like I'm finally making some progress."

"What are you saying?"

"I'm saying the number of men finally willing to stand up and fight—it's now closer to thirty."

១៨

CHAPTER
EIGHTEEN

Sopeap decides to sit today because she's feeling a bit tired, so we share space, side by side, on the floor where both of us can see. She opens the volume to a marked page. "I think it's time for a tragedy," she says.

"Really? I'm not sure I'm ready for more tragedy."

"We never are, Sang Ly."

She hands the book over and then explains, "This is the story that many believe inspired Shakespeare to write *Romeo and Juliet*."

I nod agreeably, as if it's common knowledge, as if I've heard of the story of which she speaks.

"In the original story," she continues, "they were called Pyramus and Thisbe."

"Why did he change their names?"

"He didn't. The two are different stories about different people. It's believed that the Pyramus and Thisbe story was the first . . . well, let's begin and then you'll understand."

This time she asks me to read, and I begin slowly.

Late in the afternoon, when I reach the shelters, I witness a sight at Stung Meanchey more miraculous than snow. Four trucks are lined up in a row, each methodically purging its load, and no one—I mean *no one*—stands near to sort trash. I stare at the peculiar scene, certain it's not a dream, but not sure what to make of it, while my mind attempts to process an unfamiliar sound. Mixed in with the beeping of the backing trucks and the humming of the swarming flies, I hear what could be the cheers from a children's soccer game. Yet, as I glance around, I see only emptiness.

It is then that a woman runs past from behind. I recognize her, but I can't recall her name. She often waits at the shelters in the afternoons while her husband, who is new to the dump, works the trucks. "Hurry, they're just over the hill," she says, panting and pointing to a direction that I now identify as the source of the sound. "They've caught one of them," she adds, with utter excitement resonating in her voice. "They've caught one of the thieves who beat the boy."

By the time I approach the horde, the yelling and jeering has all but ceased. I push through the circle, past strangers, neighbors, and friends, making my way to the middle of the melee. As I break through to the very center, I stumble and fall to my knees, not prepared for the scene that waits. They have given the culprit some room now, because he isn't going to go anywhere. He's no more than a boy. His eyes are open, but they gaze directly into the sun. His arms are pushed underneath him, as if he could jump up and run, except he is lying on his back and his limbs twist in ways they were never meant to bend. Fresh blood oozes from his mouth and ear, and his shirt has been torn from his body to reveal puncture wounds, certainly caused by the sharp metal hooks from the picking sticks that we use to separate the trash.

The boy—now just inches away from my face—is dead.

Then I notice something familiar in the shape of his defined cheeks. I blink, and the scene begins to tip and spin. My head feels light and I realize that I'm hyperventilating. I cover my mouth, not only to control my breathing but also to subdue the contents of my stomach that are trying to push their way out.

"He's the one who beat Lucky," a man calls out. "A thief," another adds. "We caught him stealing red-handed," someone else exclaims. Their asserting voices mix and muddle together in swirls of lawless justification toward the boy who can't respond.

"What did he take?" I ask, to no one in particular.

A woman across the circle answers. "There were four of them who tried to steal a bag of cans from Menn Chim. Lucky was resting two shelters over, still fresh from his beating, and he recognized at least three of them."

I look for Lucky, but I don't see him anywhere.

"What is the boy's name?" I call out. "Please, does anyone know this boy's name?" I am hoping that I'm wrong, that it is not Maly's brother lying dead before me, but then a voice answers. "I don't know his name, but he's the boy who has been looking for the runaway."

Before I can properly process the answer in my head, I heave and vomit into the garbage on the ground.

It was just days ago I wanted to kill the criminals myself. But my desire was for revenge on crooks, thugs—dark images of evil that gathered in my head when I pictured the men who beat my husband and Lucky Fat—not boys, especially this boy.

And then I feel Ki's trembling touch on my back. He pulls me up from the ground, away from the broken body, through the crowd that begins to thin, as many retreat toward the trucks. Ki is breathing heavily, clutching his knife with his other hand.

"What happened?" I ask as we find a place to sit in a swirl of garbage, not certain I am ready for his answer. He takes a minute to catch his breath before speaking. His words are halting and his hands shake. As I look at my own, I see they tremble as well.

"I was working with the men . . . near the trucks . . . when someone up at the shelters began to point and shout. A few men began chasing them, then others followed. Soon it was everyone."

He looks at his hand and realizes he still holds his knife, then glances around as if there should be someone to take it, some easy place to put it. There isn't.

"When one of the boys tripped," he continues, "they caught him. The crowd was screaming *thief* and *robber* and hitting him with their pickers as I ran past."

"Who?"

"I don't know exactly—everyone, I guess. They had surrounded him, so I chased after the other three with Chey and Pran Teo. We were close to catching them, though I remember thinking I wasn't sure I wanted to."

Ki pulls up the leg of his pant, his hand still quivering, and slips the knife into its sheath. He wipes his fingers against his shirt.

"They made it to the streets," he says, "near the factory on Choam Chao, and we lost them . . . and I was glad. Then, by the time we got back . . . well, that's when I found you kneeling beside . . . ." Ki doesn't know the victim's name, doesn't yet realize his identity, and doesn't want to call him *the boy,* so he pauses for a second before he continues. "I could see he was dead, and then I . . . didn't want you to have to look at him."

"It wasn't right they beat him. It wasn't right that he die," I manage to mumble, as tears that have been waiting in my eyes run down both cheeks.

147

"I know, Sang Ly," Ki answers, with fear still trailing in his voice. "I just wanted to stop them . . . I didn't mean for this to happen . . . "

And then neither of us has anything further to say. We just sit together in the garbage of Stung Meanchey and weep for the killing of a thief, a crook, a thug, a brother—a boy—whom we didn't even know. And amidst my quiet tears, a vision of a white whale and an angry captain rows into my head. It was so exciting at the time to read the story with Sopeap—the captain bent on revenge, harpooning the whale from the sinking ship, then being dragged to his death with a rope tangled around his neck.

Sopeap insisted that I understand the underlying theme—*good vs. evil*. But I wondered at the time, why, if that is the critical message, wasn't it better defined? Was the author an amateur writer, not up to the task? In the story, Captain Ahab wasn't always despicable and the whale wasn't always pure. Instantly I realize that the man who wrote the words understood the world completely—and I can't help but wonder if he ever lived in a dump like Stung Meanchey.

When our breathing softens and our eyes dry and our stomachs finally settle, Ki lifts me up from the trash and we clasp hands and walk together to pick up our son. Just before we arrive at Mother's, Ki stops. "I am sick knowing that a boy has been killed," he says. "But there is something I need to make clear."

I take his hands. "Yes?"

"I want you to know that if he or any other gang members like him—boy or not—ever tries to harm you or our son, I will not hesitate to defend you."

We pick up Nisay and finish our walk home in silence because, in spite of the power that so many words carry, as so eloquently explained by Sopeap, neither of us can find adequate meaning to the guilt, sorrow, anger, relief, worry, and overwhelming anguish that mix in our hearts.

In the morning, with the dead boy's image still burned into my head, I leave a note for Sopeap, telling her I'll be back soon. Then, with Nisay in one arm and a small white sack in the other, I swing by for Lucky Fat. He agrees that my idea is fitting, and we head out together.

In Cambodia, when someone has perished it is common to make an offering, a gift to appease the person's soul. As we approach the spot where the boy was killed, a woman who lives close also arrives with an offering. She tells us that the police never showed up, that when she went to bed late last night, the body was still there, torn and broken, but staring peacefully toward heaven. By morning, the body was gone, and she could see fresh bulldozer tracks where the garbage had been pushed around during the night.

"May your next life be more peaceful," Lucky pronounces, and then we lay out the gifts we've brought—a banana, a can of rice, salt, incense, and a small Buddha statue that Lucky found still intact.

Lucky's eye is looking better, and on the walk home, he is talkative and happy once again.

"How do you think she's doing?" Lucky asks.

I don't need to ask who. "I'm sure Maly is doing well."

And then Lucky speaks words that confirm he is more mature than his young years let on. "I think her brother will now be in a place where he can finally watch over her."

"Yes," I admit, "I think you're right."

I had considered telling Sopeap on my return, if she were still there waiting, that the last twenty-four hours had been too emotional for me to continue our study of books today. Yet, as I contemplate life and death, justice and mercy, Captain Ahab and a thief at Stung Meanchey, I wonder if it isn't a perfect time after all.

ด៩

CHAPTER
NINETEEN

To wash clothes at Stung Meanchey, I stoop down over a large blue bucket that I keep behind our house and I scrub and scour our clothes against each other until they are clean—well, as clean as they will ever be at Stung Meanchey. While some women at the dump use a washboard, a few rub their clothes against a flat rock. They say it reminds them of home, doing laundry by the river in the province.

Our clothes are typical Western styles—sweats, T-shirts, shorts—many with popular name-brand logos. We don't wear American clothes to be stylish; we wear them because they are cheap. All of the major companies have factories in Cambodia, and we can buy blemished seconds for just pennies.

Ki comes around the house to where I work to bring me Nisay's towel. It suddenly needs washing. Before he can say anything, I ask him a question that's been rattling in my head.

"Sopeap said that in books, stories foretell other meanings—she called them metaphors."

"Metaphors? What do you mean?"

"According to Sopeap, it's using a word or phrase to explain a different meaning. It would be like when I tell you Stung Meanchey is a prison. It's not really a prison, and there aren't any guards, but it feels like there could be."

Ki glances down at the dirty towel he still holds in his hand, and I can tell he's thinking it was a mistake to come out back at this particular moment. He can't help but voice the obvious.

"So?"

"Well, I have been back here doing laundry by myself for nearly an hour—washing mostly yours and Nisay's clothes—and I've finally figured out its true meaning."

"A metaphor for laundry?"

"Yes."

"The fancy words you've been reading are mixing up your brain. You do laundry because *our clothes are dirty.*"

"See," I explain, "I think it means that since we both wear clothes, you should help me do the wash—I think that's the metaphor that was speaking to me."

"Fine," Ki says. "Then I think it means I should take off your clothes right now to wash them."

He steps behind me and tugs at my shirt—only he hasn't washed up yet from his day of work and the stench of garbage lingers.

I protest. "I think it means that you smell too bad for that right now. And besides, it's still light and Nisay is up."

"Okay, then," he says. "That means that I'd better take a bath so I'll be clean *later* when Nisay is not up."

I'm trying to remember exactly when I lost control of this conversation. "Well, that means if you're going to bathe now, this early, then you'd better give your dirty son a bath along with you."

151

"That means—you have a deal!"

Ki leaves with a grin, and I hear him tell Nisay that it's time to step outside for a good scrubbing because Mommy and Daddy have something to do later. Then I reflect a little longer on who is really getting the better end of the bargain.

Metaphors in literature can be a very confusing thing.

Grandfather had a saying: *If you know a lot, know enough to make people respect you. If you are stupid, be stupid enough so they can pity you.*

I wait for the right moment, put on my pity face, and then make a request of my teacher. "I would like you to bring a certain book to read next time."

She is pleased that I've taken some initiative—that is, until she hears which book. "I'd like you to bring Nisay's book, the one that you—"

"I remember the book," she interrupts. She isn't angry but rather faceless, like a book with its cover torn off. "Why that book?" she asks.

"Last time I held it, I couldn't read the words. Now that I can, I'm curious. It seemed like a beautiful story."

"It's a children's book," she answers.

"Yes, I understand."

"It's not a typical children's book."

"Are you trying to say you'd rather I not read it?"

"I'm saying that if you're going to read it properly, the way that particular book was meant to be read, I insist that you read it with your son sitting in your lap."

Her passion intrigues me. "I can do that—but I have a condition as well."

"You're giving *me* conditions now?"

"Yes, this time I am."

"And your condition is . . . ?"

"I want you to be there when I read it."

I have either left her speechless or she has a lot to think about. "Why?" she finally asks.

"You are the teacher. We may need to discuss it afterwards."

There's a heartbeat of uncomfortable silence, followed by contemplation, surrender, and a nod of agreement. "I will bring it tonight."

As Grandfather said: . . . *stupid enough so they can pity you.*

The thought was charming—my young child, Nisay, would sit patiently on his mother's lap, waiting for each page to turn, listening intently as the story unfolded. Like so many classics, my plot is pure fiction. Instead, Nisay wants to maul the book and then eat it—if he can just get his hands on it. We decide the only way he won't destroy the thing is for him to sit in Ki's lap beside me so his father can physically restrain him, if needed, and otherwise force him to listen. It also lets me concentrate on reading.

I wonder when the Model Parent Award will arrive?

With the soul of a teacher, Sopeap stands behind us, observing but saying nothing, and for a split second, I think I catch the corner of her mouth turning upward.

The book's cover is more alluring than I'd remembered, and as I flip through a few of the pages, just to get a grasp of the task at hand, I recall the striking illustrations of mountains, trees, and oceans.

"Are you going to begin?" Ki asks impatiently.

"Certainly."

I read the title, *Love Forever*, and then I turn to the first page.

> If I were the trees . . .
> I would turn my leaves to gold and scatter them toward the sky so they would circle about your head and fall in piles at your feet . . .
> so you might know wonder.
>
> If I were the mountains . . .
> I would crumble down and lift you up so you could see all of my secret places, where the rivers flow and the animals run wild . . .
> so you might know freedom.

I'm using inflections in my voice to keep Nisay's attention. However it's Ki whom I've roped in. He sits wide-eyed as a curious little boy at story time.

> If I were the ocean . . .
> I would raise you onto my gentle waves and carry you across the seas to swim with the whales and the dolphins in the moonlit waters,
> so you might know peace.
>
> If I were the stars . . .
> I would sparkle like never before and fall from the sky as gentle rain,
> so that you would always look towards heaven and know that you can reach the stars.

If I were the moon . . .

I would scoop you up and sail you through the sky and show you the Earth below in all its wonder and beauty,

so you might know that all the Earth is at your command.

If I were the sun . . .

I would warm and glow like never before and light the sky with orange and pink,

so you would gaze upward and always know the glory of heaven.

But I am me . . .

and since I am the one who loves you, I will wrap you in my arms and kiss you and love you with all of my heart,

and this I will do until . . .

the mountains crumble down . . .

and the oceans dry up . . .

and the stars fall from the sky . . .

and the sun and moon burn out . . .

And that is forever.

It's a treasure. I turn to thank Sopeap for allowing me to read it, but she is no longer standing by the door watching.

Sopeap is gone.

It's early when Sopeap calls out. She has stopped by to ask if we can put off meeting for today. She has a touch of the flu and needs to rest. Before she leaves, however, I grab Nisay's book.

"I don't think my son listened to a word, but Ki enjoyed it," I say.

"Nisay will. Just give him time."

When I try to hand her the book, she waves me away. "Actually," she says, "I would like your son to have it as a gift."

I want to tell her *no*, that it's too important, it means too much to give away so easily—then I remind myself, giving it away probably isn't easy at all.

"We will treasure it. But may I ask why it means so much to you?"

"Yes. I have also come to share its story."

We sit on the ground and, once she is comfortable, she begins.

"This book was written by a dear friend. We taught together at the university. We had both studied in the United States years before and had discussed the many children's stories that are published there every year. We wondered why few such books were written for Cambodian children. My friend was tenacious and passionate and created a book, first crafting the words, then hiring an artist to paint the illustrations. After everything was perfect, I helped her find a small, local publisher."

"Did it sell?" I ask.

She hesitates, stepping cautiously among banished thoughts.

"We didn't get a chance," she says haltingly. "Just weeks after the publisher delivered the first copies, the Khmer Rouge soldiers pushed into the city. The schools and universities were ransacked. Books were stacked in great piles and burned. Those who had written them were tortured, shot, and burned as well. Can you imagine dying for having written something so beautiful?"

"She was murdered?"

"Yes. And the illustrator—and thousands like them. There were so few copies printed in the first place that I presumed all had been lost—until the day I saw it on your floor. I wasn't sure if life was offering me a second chance or slapping me in the face. Sometimes the two can be confusing."

"I am so sorry to hear about your friend."

"Though it's been many years, I still miss her. However, she was not the reason I was so overcome the day I visited your home."

"No?"

"Sang Ly, my friend had no children." A pause, a sigh, a hesitation. "The story was written about me—and my son."

The tap on the wooden post outside our front door is timid, and when I come out from around back with a pan filled with water to cook rice for dinner, I find my cousin Narin waiting.

"Sang Ly, I am sorry to disturb you."

I can tell by her trembling tone, the panic in her face, that this isn't a social call. My own heart quickens. "What is it? Is Ki all right?"

She shakes her head. "It's not Ki."

"Who, then?"

She leans up against the house, and so I do likewise. "Do you know Makara Hong?" she asks.

"No."

"She sells fruit in the city, near the French clinic."

"Yes. I mean, no. I don't know her, but I know the fruit stand. Why?"

"We've become friends. Makara's older sister lives in the Dangkor district of Phnom Penh."

As Narin pauses, I must ask: "Please, what does Makara or her sister have to do with me?"

Narin quickens her pace. "Her sister works as a nurse at the hospital. I went with Makara to meet her, to pick up some money." Narin shifts her weight uneasily. "We talked, and when she found out that I live at Stung Meanchey, the sister said they were treating a patient there from the dump."

"Who?"

"She said it was a woman named Sopeap—Sopeap Sin."

"Treating? For what? What are you saying?"

"Sang Ly, she has something wrong in her chest. Cousin, I'm here to tell you that Sopeap is very ill, perhaps dying."

I hear her words, but I don't believe them. "What does that mean? It's not true. This woman at the hospital is mistaken. Sopeap was here. She just left and she said nothing about . . ." My own words trail as my mind darts back—the vomit, the blood, the stumbling, the bad days—how could I have not seen it?

Narin continues. "She said it's a tumor in her chest; it's pushing against her heart."

"Cancer?"

"I guess."

"Did she say anything else?"

"Yes, she . . ." Narin hesitates.

"What is it? Please tell me!"

"The time that Sopeap has left is very short."

២0

CHAPTER
TWENTY

Sopeap hobbles in and drops her bag on the floor. I say nothing as she leans down and removes a small yellow paperback book. She opens it to a marked page and then holds it out away from her face so that she can focus.

"We're going to read parts of a story today from a Japanese author, Yasunari Kawabata," she announces. "This is a story I would often read to my students."

I can hold my tongue no longer. "Why didn't you tell me?" I demand.

She stops, looks me over, but I don't give her the time to decide *if* and *what* I know.

"You're dying," I scream, "and you said nothing to me!"

She closes the book. "I told you I was going away." She answers with such composure, it's confusing. "I just failed to mention how far."

I want to jump up, to cry, to yell, to hit her in the chest myself until she understands that I feel the same pain in mine. "Why didn't you tell me?"

"I had planned to—just not yet."

"I deserved to know."

"I was waiting for the right moment. It was your fascination with learning, your childlike desire to drink in the stories. It was so— refreshing. I just didn't want to spoil it, for either of us."

"Spoil what?"

"Your innocence, your hope for the future, your trust in the words and messages that stories carry. I didn't know how to make you understand."

"Understand what—that all stories aren't happy? That life can be miserable?" I should settle down, but I can't help myself. "You think I'm too stupid to realize that? Did you forget that I have a sick child, that I live in a disgusting dump?"

While I'm the one behaving hysterically, Sopeap remains calm. She takes a long and steady breath, as if drawing on a pipe. "You may have a point," she says. "There's a possibility that I may have been thinking about myself—trying to rewrite things that should be left alone."

I don't pretend to understand what she's talking about, but her tone hints of remorse. I should tell her that it's okay, that I understand—but I don't. I am still too angry.

"What did they say is wrong with you?" I ask instead.

"It's a long list, but if you're referring to my medical condition, I'm told it's a growth contracting the artery that feeds my heart. Apparently, arteries don't like to be contracted."

"Can they operate? Can they cut it out?"

"They could if . . ."

"If?"

"*If* I were younger, *if* I had gone in sooner, *if* I had more money,

160

if I were living in America or Europe or any other country in the free world that has modern facilities. Life is full of so many ifs."

"How long have you known?"

"A while."

"Please, how long?"

"The doctor broke the news to me the day I threatened to kick you out—not one of my better days. It was a bit emotional and confusing."

"You should be home resting."

For the first time, Sopeap bristles; her voice hardens. "I'll do no such thing! We're here to learn about literature. I've taken the time to translate much of the book myself and, by damn, you're going to listen! And just so you know," she says, waving her crooked, pointing finger directly between my eyes to be crystal clear, "there will be no negotiation on this point. I'm going to show up here every day until I think you are ready, or until I . . . well, until you are ready."

She opens the book and lets her finger find the sentence.

"Besides," she adds, "I can't die yet. I'm just starting to like you."

Our lessons become a blur. I listen; I make notes; I try not to ask contentious questions. Now that I know about Sopeap's condition, there are little things I notice: long breaths from the teacher that I once thought were meant for drama's sake in telling the story but that I now realize are to ease the pain in her chest; her choosing to sit beside me, not so I can see the page but because she's too tired to continue standing; her finding excuses to end early so I don't have to watch her stumble outside, fall to her knees, and vomit.

There are times my eyes water—I simply can't help myself—though Sopeap's eyes never do, and I admit to feeling a bit hurt. It causes me to recall a conversation I had with Ki the day I found out that Sopeap was sick.

"How could she sit there reading stories so casually, knowing the entire time that she was sick—and then never tell me?" I asked with complaint.

"She wasn't angry?" Ki inquired, a bit surprised.

"No, she hasn't been angry for a while."

"Then don't you be angry," he said.

Since my husband obviously wasn't understanding, I would need to better explain. "It's just not right. She needs more time."

He paused, letting me settle down, and then he asked a question that still lingers. "Does she need more time—or do you?"

How ironic that Sopeap is the one dying and yet I'm the one feeling sorry for myself because she doesn't mind that she'll be leaving!

I let my thoughts wander again and only snap awake when I realize my teacher is speaking to me.

"I'm going to bring one of my favorite books tomorrow," she says.

"What's it called?"

"It's a story that is . . . well, it's my favorite," she says.

"What is it about?"

"It's a metaphor, but then, what in literature isn't? It's an old story that seems tragic at first, but in the end . . . well, I don't want to ruin it for you. No, this is a story best understood if you don't know the ending."

"Then you won't tell me?"

"Tomorrow. We will read it tomorrow."

"Sang Ly! Sang Ly!"

Even from far away, the terror-filled echo of my mother's cry yanks me from the floor to my feet. I bolt to the front yard. She is out of breath, chest heaving, eyes wide with horror, and Nisay is collapsed lifeless in her arms.

She mutters so fast I can barely understand her. "He was playing . . . on the floor . . . not crying at all . . . he slumped over . . . I can't wake him up . . . I've tried and I can't wake him!"

"Nisay? Nisay!" I pull open his eyelid, but his pupils are rolled back. I press my face close to his, strain to feel any signs of life. I think he's breathing; I hope he's breathing; I look heavenward. "Please, Grandfather, help him to keep breathing."

I take him from my mother's arms and, out of instinct, turn toward the house for Ki. *Wait, he's not home.* It's late. The sun is setting. He should be here—but he's not. He is still picking at the dump. Who else can help? Teva Mao. I speak first to Mother. "Run to the trucks. Find Ki. Tell him what's happened. I'll take Nisay to Teva."

I don't know how, but Teva knows about such things. Surely she can help. She is just a few houses away, over the slight rise of garbage that separates the view of our two homes. With Nisay cradled in my arms, I do the only thing I can think of—I run.

My left sandal flips off, but I don't turn to retrieve it. I fly across the garbage with a single bare foot toward Teva's, oblivious to anything sharp or dangerous that may cut my feet. As I reach Teva's home I scream, "Teva! Help!" There is no answer, no sound, no bustle inside to see who may be calling. "Teva, please!" Teva Mao is not home.

I check Nisay again and he looks terrible. I want to scream, to cry, to curse, to plead to the ancestors, but none of that will help my child.

The clinic! I will take him to the French clinic.

I retrace my steps back toward home. My lost sandal sits patiently in the trail and, miraculously, it's facing the right way. I slip it on almost without slowing down. I pass our home, heading down the slope on the opposite side, until the ground levels out to the trail that leads to the city streets.

On a good day, I will walk with Nisay to the clinic. Today is anything but good. I am panting by the time I reach the street where the motos cross. I wave frantically but the first two don't stop. Perhaps they realize I have left what little money we have at home. The third to approach jerks his *tuk tuk* to the curb beside me. He is an older driver.

"Please," I beg, with all the motherly compassion I can muster. "I need help. I must get my boy to the clinic on Khemarak Boulevard, near the Russian hospital. He's sick!"

He hesitates, as if he also knows I have no money to pay, but then he glances at my son. "Get in!" he says.

We climb into the two-wheeled cart hitched behind the motorcycle, and before I'm even settled, he lurches out into traffic. Any other day, I would be furious. Today, I am only grateful. As we weave in and out of the busy city traffic, I whisper encouragement to Nisay. "We're almost there, son. They are good doctors. They will help and you'll be fine."

Except for the sway of the moto as it darts back and forth, Nisay is motionless. And then the moto brakes to a stop and I jump out. I pay little attention to the pained looked on the driver's face. I ignore his grimace as he stares past me to the clinic entrance. Only when I turn do I understand—the windows and doors are all covered with grates. The clinic is closed.

"No," I scream. "Open, please open!" I command the doors, as if I expect the chains to obey and part. They don't.

And then time blurs. I am in such a frantic frame of mind, wishing, hoping, pleading for someone to help, that I can't be certain what is really happening and in what order. I am riding again in the moto, but I am crying hysterically because I don't know where the driver is taking us. It's my worst nightmare. Instead of endlessly falling into blackness, I am riding though the nighttime streets of Phnom Penh with my dying son lying limp in my arms, unable to wake up or get out of the racing moto.

But I can't be dreaming because surely in a dream, such pain and panic would have caused me to wake up screaming—and Ki would console me and tell me that everything is fine.

Instead I am alone and my dreams are not only real—they get worse.

We arrive at a tall glass building. When I realize the driver wants to put me out on the street, I refuse to get down. He pulls at my arm while I scream at him. "How could you! How could you!"

He physically yanks me out as I grasp my son, but I continue to stand in the street shrieking in anger and pleading for help. Then someone else touches my shoulder. She's an older Cambodian woman, dressed in a white uniform of the sort that medical workers wear. I am standing in front of the National Children's Hospital off of Kampuchea Krom Boulevard.

The woman escorts me to the entrance with my son. Just before passing through the doors, I turn to thank the driver, to apologize for my conduct, but I can no longer see him. He is gone.

My child is taken from me and I think I tell the nurse what is wrong with him, but later, as I try to remember, I can't be sure. I'm asked to wait in a room, but when I enter there is no place to sit. The seats are full of other desperate people living nightmares of their own.

I find space against a wall, relieved to feel that it's solid, and slide exhausted to the floor. I grab my knees as the adrenaline that has filled my body retreats. I may throw up, but I'm too tired to find a bathroom. I am uncertain whether I doze off or just stare blindly at the distant, whitewashed wall, but sometime during the night, the woman who escorted me into the hospital touches my shoulder to get my attention. She needs information. I give her my name and tell her where we live, and when she hears *Stung Meanchey* she doesn't bother asking if we can pay. Before she hurries away, she says that my son is fine, that a doctor will find me soon to tell me more. To those watching, it must look as though she has delivered awful news, because as she walks away, I am so relieved that I cover my face and sob.

There is a clock on the wall and at 2:10 A.M., I remember my own clock at home. I worry about Ki and the panic that he must feel, not knowing what's happened to his wife and child. Then, an hour later, he runs into the waiting room. He is sweating and breathing heavily. When he sees me, still leaning against the distant wall, the relief that spreads across his face is so palpable that I feel it from across the room. It washes over his body, and by the time he reaches me, he slumps beside me on the floor. He puts his arm around me and he asks, "How is Nisay?"

I hug back as best I can while sitting. "They are taking care of him. He's going to be okay."

We say nothing more for several minutes, content to simply be together in spite of the circumstance.

"How did you find us?" I finally ask.

"I've been checking all of the hospitals. I'm so glad you didn't go to the one on the north side of Phnom Penh." And that's when I realize he ran to each one.

In Cambodia, it's unfortunately common for husbands both to drink and to beat their wives. Other families are abandoned, left to fend for themselves. Instead, my husband runs through the city for the better part of the night to make sure that his wife and son are safe.

We sit together on the floor for hours, taking turns resting as we wait for the promised doctor. Late in the morning, a haggard-looking man in a white coat appears. He is rushed and I expect we won't talk long.

"I am Doctor Chan. Your son will be fine. He was severely dehydrated and we've given him fluids throughout the night. We'll be discharging him now, so you're free to take him home."

I can't express enough joy that Nisay is okay, but I also understand that he's going home because we have no money to pay for his stay.

"How can he be better so quickly?" I ask.

The doctor doesn't answer but instead offers instructions. "It's critical that you give him plenty of liquids and—"

"I try to," I blurt. "But he has diarrhea so bad, and then he won't eat or drink anything."

"I've got some pills that should help."

"When the pills run out, he always gets sick again."

"Just remember, plenty of water. Now, I've got several other patients waiting, so if you have any questions, the nurse should be able to help you."

And as quickly as the doctor appeared, he is gone. I don't blame him, and I am not bitter. I sit in an overflowing hospital waiting room, brimming with desperate mothers, including many who lost their loved ones. How can I be anything but indebted to this man?

Nisay is sleeping when the nurse hands him to me, but I can see that his color is back. They don't ask for payment and we can't offer, but instead we use what money Ki has with him to take a moto home. I hope to see the driver who brought me, to pay him and to thank him. When the moto stops, I look, but it is not him.

It's nearly noon by the time we arrive home, and our energy is spent. In spite of the heat, we close the tarp on our home to block the light and we lie down. I let my eyes close and invite the smells and sounds of the dump to swirl in my head and join me in slumber. They oblige, drifting across me like a nonexistent breeze that will soon make everything right in the world.

"I love you, Ki. Thank you for finding us," I whisper—or think I do. Then, as I drift to sleep, I open my mouth wide toward the heavens because all around me something wonderful is happening. For the second time in a month, snow falls from the sky to cover up Stung Meanchey.

As the man calls to me again in my dreams, his face remains obscure. However, the distance in his tone, the inflection of his voice, his guarded manner, all remind me of someone, a forgotten acquaintance from years past. He is like the person you bump into at the market and recall as a friend, but no matter how hard you try, you can't remember his name. Then, after a few days pass—or a week, or even a month—the name jumps into your head, as if it's been hiding behind a curtain in your mind, planning for just the right moment to step onstage.

When I awake, Ki is no longer beside me. His boots are not in the corner, and I presume that he's gone to the dump to pick. I can tell from the color of the light peeking in through the cracks that it's already late afternoon, and I am starving. I hope that he can make enough in this short day to buy more than rice.

Nisay lies beside me, breathing heavily. I'm not surprised. It's always the same after our visits to the Western doctors and the modern hospitals. They give him medicine—sometimes vitamins, other times antibiotics, always names I can't pronounce—and almost immediately, he feels better. He's content, his diarrhea goes away, his appetite comes back. But then the pills run out, and in spite of the doctor's insistence that my son is fine, his fever always returns.

Nisay will soon awake, and I'm counting on the fact that he'll be hungry. I roll away slowly so as to not disturb the child. He doesn't move, though I'm sure his slumber will be short-lived. I'm also thrilled there's no mess around him to clean up.

We still have a kilo or two of rice but nothing more, so I quietly stack several small pieces of kindling into the lower opening of my clay cooking stove, which sits obediently in the corner. I click and touch the handheld lighter to the wood beneath until the flames burn on their own. It doesn't take long to retrieve water from outside, pour it over the rice, and then place the pan on top where the heat is already converging. It will soon boil and, with any luck at all, Ki will arrive in time with something more—vegetables, pork, beef, anything. I'd even settle for more snails, if it weren't for those nasty leeches.

As the steam dances away with the smoke, I'm taken back to my childhood, realizing that mothers have been cooking rice in Cambodia this same way for hundreds, perhaps thousands of—

And then, in the middle of my thought, I remember!

The admonition in my dreams is from a man in the province, a man I haven't seen in years. Even then, as a child, I kept my distance and he kept his. It's not that he was cruel to me or any of the other children, or hurtful in any way. It's that childhood rumors, even those borne of young imagination, can leave impressions that linger. The man lived up the river from our home, perhaps ten minutes by boat, three times that following the river's path by foot. Since leaving the province, I've seldom given him any thought. But now he's shown up in my dreams, and I can't help but wonder if it's coincidence or if my overwhelming desire for Nisay to get better is creeping into my subconscious.

I forget the name of the Swiss psychiatrist whom Sopeap quoted, but he believed that dreams are important, that we should ponder them for meaning and answers to our life's problems. This entire notion now makes me nervous. The man calling to me from my dreams, insisting that I *should have come sooner,* is Bunna Heng. While some Western doctors and other medical professionals might call him a witch doctor, he is better known in the village of my childhood as *the Healer.*

I'm not bothered by what modern doctors think, for their remedies haven't proven overwhelming. Instead, his words are what make me anxious.

"You should have come sooner."

If my dream is about Nisay, and if I *should have come sooner,* does that mean I am already too late?

If the Swiss dream doctor was right, if the stories and images of our dreams do matter, if they truly offer insight, understanding, and even warning, then I had better listen carefully.

As my rice boils, I instinctively understand what I must do. I need to travel with my son to the Prey Veng province of my childhood and visit the Healer—and I must leave as soon as possible.

Most of our clothes fit into two worn suitcases—gifts from the dump. Everything else of value—my cookware, clay stove, utensils, sleeping mats, and even my broken clock—I hide underneath our raised floor, which I access from the rear of the house. Still, nothing is secure. Everything we own could be taken at night, or anytime, for that matter, and nobody would notice. But we have no choice.

I have not seen Sopeap since arriving home from the hospital, and my stomach tightens every time I think about her. It's a distress overshadowed only by worry for my son. I presumed Sopeap would drop by to schedule our next lesson, and I could say good-bye then, but she hasn't. I've been to her home twice, wanting to explain the reason for my departure, but there has been no answer.

"Should we stay one more day?" I ask Ki for the hundredth time. "She may be back soon." He ignores me, knowing another minute later I'll tell him to hurry, that we need to leave now. In truth, I can't honestly say if my urgency to get Nisay to the Healer is a prompting or paranoia. At times it's so hard to tell the difference.

We have counted our money and have just enough for the trip there. How we'll afford to get back is still unanswered. I've convinced Ki that we should leave the dump the long way, out the western pathway, the one that leads past Sopeap's home, to check for her one last time. We step from the house, ready to leave, when I see Lucky Fat running toward us.

"She's coming!" he says, tired and breathless. And it's true. Sopeap trudges down the distant path, a slow but unmistakable silhouette against a backdrop of towering garbage.

"I'll take Nisay and the two suitcases and wait for you on the corner of Boeung and Keng, by the chicken farmer," Ki says.

"You can't carry everything. Leave me a suitcase, and I'll catch up soon."

But he somehow takes both suitcases anyway, along with the child, and then motions for Lucky to follow. The boy looks disappointed that he can't stay and listen but he obeys. I study Sopeap as she approaches, once again finding myself at a loss for the right words to convey the mix of aching and gratitude that tangle in my heart.

"How are you feeling?" I ask as Sopeap shuffles beside me and then rests against the floor where it steps up into the house. She looks exhausted.

"My artery feels a bit constricted," she says, reaching for her chest. Then I catch the slightest glimpse of a grin. "It's my new favorite reply," she adds.

I return a smile. "Seriously, are you doing okay?"

"I'm still here. Besides, it's nothing a sip of rice wine won't help."

"You shouldn't drink, knowing you're going to die."

Apparently I'm the only one who follows my logic. "Why *wouldn't* I drink, knowing I'm going to die?" she asks.

I change the subject. "I came by several times, but you weren't home."

"Yes, I had some additional business in the city—rent collection duties. It took longer than I expected. I was happy to find out that Nisay is feeling better."

"Who told you?"

"I hear these things. I *am* still the Rent Collector, you know."

But then her gaze drops, her demeanor darkens. "I do wish we could have finished. There was so much more I was hoping to talk about."

"We will," I say.

"Did we ever read the phoenix story?" she asks, ignoring my reply.

"No. I don't believe so."

"That's too bad. It's one of my favorites. I think that's why I was saving it."

"We'll read it together later," I tell her, "just as soon as I return."

She is silent as she studies the garbage at our feet. "Of course," she finally answers, but the words ring with hollow conviction. And then she adds, "No matter how much we cling to hope, our stories seldom end as we expect."

"Is that a quote?" I ask, uncertain whether she is referring to herself or to me.

"No, that's a fact," she replies. Then she reaches into her bag, a gesture I'm going to miss. "I brought you something to read—for the road."

"You did?" My voice brightens.

She takes out a bound leather volume and hands it to me. "It's so that you can read to your son."

"Thank you." I take it from her aged, experienced hands. I fidget with it, saying nothing more. In the same way I read her body language, she reads mine.

"What is it, child? Spit out your question."

"I just . . . well . . . I've been thinking about you being sick . . . wondering about what happens . . . you know . . . when you leave Stung Meanchey?"

"When I die?"

"Yes. How do you think it works? Are the ancestors really waiting? I don't know a lot about these things—and I wonder."

"These are questions pondered, argued, and discussed by some of the most intelligent men in the universe."

"What did they decide?"

"I believe they are still in committee."

"That's a joke, right?"

"If you must ask, it wasn't a very good one."

"Do you ever talk to your ancestors?" I ask.

"Mostly we wrestle."

"Wrestle?"

"Yes, and I don't recommend it. You will always lose."

"I am looking for a serious answer."

And then she sighs. "I'm sorry. I shouldn't joke with such bad arteries, should I? The problem is you need a sincere answer, and I don't think I'm the person who can best offer it."

"Why not? You're the teacher."

"Because I distance myself from heaven and then complain that heaven is distant. Look, as you continue to study and learn, you will find many opinions. You can believe writer Darany Ma, who suggests we face a cold and silent universe, or you can listen to Phirun Vann, who sees a power that guides our steps—"

"That's my point," I say, interrupting. "How do I know? I love what you've taught me, I've loved reading our stories, but at times, it can be so . . ."

" . . . damned confusing?" she asks.

I smile, and then, in true Sopeap fashion, she answers with another quote. "The poet Hunt said, 'There are two worlds: the world that we can measure with line and rule, and the world that we feel with our hearts and imagination.' I think if you follow his advice, you'll do okay."

"I will miss your quotes—I don't always understand them, but I will miss them."

We then sit quietly, neither of us speaking, yet there is no awkwardness in the moment. Sadness? *Perhaps.* Regret? *A little,* but it mixes with the right amount of contentment.

"Good-bye, Sang Ly," she finally says.

"Good-bye, Teacher."

២១

CHAPTER
TWENTY-ONE

The streets of Phnom Penh are a constant buzz of commotion as thousands of scooters, bikes, cars, buses, trucks, and especially motos weave, bump, sway, honk, hum, and rattle together in a maniacal sea of mechanical chaos—a tumult that we always manage to survive. We wait in front of the terminal near the new market downtown, where the lines of buses are parked so uniformly together they feel like mismatched dominoes that could topple one another at any moment. Finding the correct bus was once a dreadful task of stress and worry that entailed asking several people the same repeated question, hoping for enough consistent answers to be fairly certain we were lining up in the right place. Now I simply read the destinations posted in each front window.

As I do, an elderly woman watches and then approaches. "Can you tell me which bus leaves for Seim Reap?" she asks.

I scan the window signs until I find her bus, then point assuredly, letting her know that I am certain. She bows graciously and disappears into the crowd.

Our bus doesn't load for forty more minutes, so we park ourselves near the terminal and eat some of the rice that we have packed for the trip. We decide to delay buying pork and vegetables until after we get off the bus. Food will be less expensive near the river, and the more of our money we conserve, the sooner we'll be able to return.

As we eat, a man walking past catches my attention—he is carrying a stack of brightly colored books, though it's not just his books that give me pause. He sets them down near an adjacent garbage can with the spines toward me, and then he proceeds to clean out his pockets, throwing scattered items away. Naturally I long to read the titles, to learn what the books are about, to thumb through their pages and attempt to read them myself. However, as these thoughts roil through my head, I also have the odd desire to tear open the bag of garbage and see if he's throwing anything worthwhile away.

It's such a striking display of the emotion that now clashes in my heart and head that I'm certain it's more than a coincidence—and I know who is to blame. I speak heavenward. *"Funny, Grandfather—very funny, indeed."*

Our bus is a rickety old thing that bears the scars of boisterous children who long ago grew to adulthood. The still visible names carved into the seat backs are foreign. Before its happy retirement to Cambodia, it appears our bus served time in Thailand. It coughs grey smoke that wafts up on both sides rather than in back where a working exhaust would be located. The fumes dissipate as we pull out of the station and creep north through the traffic away from the city. The passengers seated around us are also hot, impatient, and grateful to finally be moving. In the seat to my right, a younger woman cuddles a sleeping baby—a little girl, I think. It would be quite a touching scene, except Nisay has just begun to cry and the mother keeps throwing glances toward us, as if wondering why I can't keep my baby content like hers.

Two rows forward and across the aisle, a businessman sits alone with an array of papers spread out on his seat that dare anyone to try to sit beside him. Since the bus is not full—and perhaps even if it were—he looks capable of defending his territory. He is ranting to the man seated in front, complaining about the bus having no air conditioning. It makes me consider our home at Stung Meanchey, not only without air conditioning but without electricity and with only a tarp for a door. I am just grateful for the wind now blowing through the windows as we clear the city and pick up speed.

Seated directly in front are two old women with similar features, perhaps sisters, who take turns pointing out scenes on the street as if it's their first time in the city and they've booked a low-budget tour.

As I study the travelers who surround me, I wonder about their stories. Sopeap taught me that stories are all around us, that we are swimming in literature, even at Stung Meanchey. If literature is about *us*—our hopes and dreams, our trials and struggles—could she have been talking about people: friends, neighbors, strangers, enemies? At first I dismiss the thought, since most people's stories feel so mundane compared to the exciting tales of dragons and maidens, old men and boats, young love, and valiant war. I suppose that outwardly that may be true, but she also taught that life's most difficult battles are those fought within—and that would include everyone.

The longer we drive, the harder Nisay wriggles and the louder he cries. I had hoped that the bus's vibrations would soothe his fussing and settle him down, but they're doing just the opposite. I rock him back and forth and begin to hum. I want to think that my actions are to ease his discomfort, but I fear I'm just trying to deflect the piercing glares from my fellow riders. Their expressions speak louder than words: *Terrific. No air conditioning, uncomfortable seats, stifling heat, and now a screaming child!*

Ki offers to take Nisay, but instead I stand up in the aisle and hold him over my shoulder, bouncing him softly and pleading with him to close his eyes and sleep. Even I am losing patience with the child, though I shouldn't, because my heart also aches for him to feel better. Like most on the bus, I am sweaty, tired, and irritated. What nobody else can understand is that, in addition to worries about my son, anxiety over Sopeap also rakes me with concern.

Then Ki motions me over and offers a second time. "Sang Ly, let me hold Nisay and you read him a story. See if that will settle him down." At first I shake my head, thinking that it will disturb our fellow riders even more—and then I glance around. At this point, *nothing* is going to make matters worse.

I pass Nisay to Ki and pull the book that Sopeap has sent from my bag. I can see from the cover that it's a volume of short stories from India and Southeast Asia. Too bad; long stories would have been much better, as we have a lengthy trip ahead of us. Nonetheless, I thumb through and stop at a chapter with a picture of a tiger on its opening page. Surely Nisay will enjoy a story about tigers. Below the picture is a paragraph about the author. His name is Rajam Banerjee. It says he was born near Sawai Madhopur, in Northern India, and that he wrote this story over a hundred years ago, a fact I find stunning. While almost everything that surrounds us in life gets old and wears out, stories, like our very souls, don't age. It was translated into Khmer in 1963. I also read that Mr. Banerjee wrote adventure stories and—

Ki touches my shoulder to encourage me—no, to *beg* me—to quit reading silently and begin.

"Tiger Road," I announce, as I let my finger underline the words as I read, "by Rajam Banerjee."

I find that it's a story about a man traveling across India in search of riches. He describes the conflicting beauty and sometimes harshness of the country with such vivid words that pictures of the place come rolling into my mind as I read.

The man works his way deep into the heart of the country in search of ivory, near an area called Ranthambore. He narrowly escapes with his life after a large tiger kills his only horse while the man watches helpless nearby.

The description of the tiger killing the animal is so gruesome that I quit reading and glance over at Ki.

"Should I keep going?" I ask. "Do we really want to read our son a story about killing?"

Nisay is still crying, not paying attention. Ki looks down at the fussing child, rolls his eyes, and then slings a glance of disbelief toward me, as if to ask, "*Seriously?*"

I keep reading.

Without a horse to pull his small wagon, the man appears to be stranded deep in the Aravali Range. Rather than try to walk out and save his life, he becomes so angry at the tiger that he grabs his gun and sets out in the moonlight to track the animal down and kill it himself—unless it kills him first.

After several more chapters, Nisay is still whimpering and I find myself reading loudly to get him to pay attention. When I realize that I must be making those around me absolutely crazy, I prepare to deliver my sincerest apologies. Except the sight that greets me is most unexpected. The woman across the way, who was sitting against the window, has shifted toward the aisle to be closer. The businessman, who not long after we began the journey buried his face into his work, has put down his papers and is watching me. Most surprising are the two old women in front. One has turned sideways, with her legs in the aisle, so that she can point her ear in a better direction to hear. To my disbelief, her companion has pulled her legs up into squatting position on the bench and twisted herself completely around in the seat to face me directly. It looks most uncomfortable, but her tip of the head lets me know that she is just fine—and then she speaks. "Please, dear, keep going."

The mother across the way chimes in to agree, and so I point my finger back to the spot where I left off and I continue.

With anger filling the man's heart, he tracks the tiger throughout the night, finally realizing the animal has taken refuge in a tract of dry reeds. Knowing it would be suicide to enter the reeds alone, where the tiger could see him but he couldn't see the tiger, he waits until morning's first light. Then, with a strike of a match, he sets the reeds ablaze.

After reading in such a loud voice for such a long period of time, my mouth is getting dry—and then it hits me. Not only is Nisay no longer crying, but other than the vibrations of the bus as it travels across the uneven road, it is quiet. Everyone surrounding us is silent and attentive. The bus is only about half full, but I can see that several of those who were sitting in the front of the bus have moved back to take open seats closer to where I sit. Though I'm not a fast reader, nobody seems to mind. When the businessman sees that I'm licking at my lips, he passes a bottle of water to the old woman on the aisle and gestures to her to pass it along to me. I nod my thanks to both. For a trip that started out so uncomfortably, I instantly feel as though I'm surrounded by friends. I open the bottle and take a long drink. Then, with all ears still focused in my direction, I pass the bottle to Ki and continue our Indian adventure.

The fire burning toward the tiger is so hot that it sends spouts of fire twenty feet into the air, filling the sky with smoke and ash. Still the man waits patiently with his rifle poised, ready to shoot the moment the animal emerges.

When the tiger finally bolts, he's followed by a smaller female and two adolescent cubs. The man takes careful aim, but just as he's about to squeeze the trigger, a bit of burning ash drifts into his right eye. He dances in pain and rubs his eye vigorously, clearing it out just in time to see the tail of the last tiger disappear into the surrounding brush.

If ever there was an angry man, it was he. He should have given up at that moment and turned around toward home to escape with his life—but he doesn't.

I am about to start the next chapter when Ki leans over and whispers, "How much is left? We're not that far away from where we get off."

When the old woman in front hears his question, a look of panic fills her eyes. "Please," she pleads, "read faster. You must finish."

Ki continues, "I'll walk up and show the driver where to pull over. You keep reading. You can finish it for me later."

He scoots past me to the aisle with Nisay and heads to the front of the bus. I press on.

I continue to read pages that describe the man chasing the tigers through a ravine.

Then, when the brush thins, he catches a glimpse of brown stripes, raises his gun, and shoots the first of the four beasts—one of the young cubs.

However, when he opens his gun to insert another cartridge, it jams, leaving him helpless as a tigress creeps toward him on her belly. He steps back cautiously, all the while banging at the jammed cartridge with his hand until his palm begins to bleed. He is certain that death is imminent, but then realizes the tigress is approaching because he's backing right toward the other cub.

After finally dislodging the stuck cartridge with his knife and taking up a new position, he raises his site, squeezes the trigger, and drops the second cub. Instead of fleeing, the tigress turns directly toward him. In a matter of moments either he will kill the tigress or she will kill him. The animal stops to growl with such an expression of diabolical fury that he hesitates. Then, finally, he fires, killing the creature barely in time.

With a single tiger left, he should count his revenge sufficient. Instead, he follows the final ferocious beast to a rise of boulders where the animal waits, lashing its tail. Before the man can raise his gun, the tiger springs from the cliff in one mighty bound.

As I turn the page, I realize the bus has slowed, and with a tiger hurtling through the air—I stop. I don't know what to do because we are at our destination. "I'm sorry," I say, "we get off here."

"No, you can't," the old woman nearest the window insists. "You must finish."

"How much is left?" the businessman hollers.

I flip the page over and see that there are not quite two pages.

"Just a page or two," I say. "But I'm reading as fast as I can."

And then the businessman, a stranger to everyone on the bus,

offers an act of kindness and sacrifice that I find admirable and moving. "I'm going to go and have a talk with the driver. I'll stall him while
she finishes." And then he pats his wallet. "Trust me, I'm persuasive."

He turns to the old women. "You two listen very carefully and
then tell me how it ends." Then, without hesitation, he strides away
toward the front of the bus.

Sopeap said that literature has the power to change lives, minds,
and hearts. Until this moment, reading to others on this rickety old
bus about tigers in India, I had not fully understood what she meant.

"Don't worry," I announce to everyone. "I will finish."

High into the air the massive creature flies, leaping in one great
arch. Just as he reaches the highest point of his spring, the man pulls
the gun to his shoulder and fires. The bullet hits its mark, but it is too
late. The tiger falls upon the man and sinks his great white teeth into
the man's thigh. The man screams in agony as the tiger's teeth grate
against his bone. He counts himself as dead—but then the tiger's grip
loosens.

The animal stands and roars with a sound that shakes the very
rocks before swaying to and fro and then falling over dead. The man
ties a handkerchief around his wound to stop the flow of blood. Then,
with the aid of local villagers, he makes it out of India alive—though
he remains a cripple for the rest of his natural life.

I close the story's last page and glance about at pensive faces and
pondering thoughts, mingled with splashes of satisfaction. Old woman
number two, as I have named her in my head, is the first to speak. "He
was crippled," she says, nodding her belief that the ending was just.
Then she adds, "But he shouldn't have shot the tigers."

The woman across the aisle leans my direction. "You are a very
good storyteller. We enjoyed it very much."

Others agree, and I'm not sure what to say until satisfaction trumps embarrassment. "Thank you," I finally mutter as I step toward the front of the bus.

The businessman, standing beside the driver, watches me approach. Ki Lim steps down off the bus first with Nisay, but before I can follow, the businessman stops me. Everything about the man is meticulous, including the quality of his clothes, and I can't help but wonder why someone of stature would even ride this bus.

"Thank you," he says as he reaches out and clasps my hand. When he does, I feel him pass along money.

"No, please, I can't accept this," I say. "I was just trying to calm down my son."

"I insist you take it. I had decided, even before the journey began, that it was going to be a miserable trip—and, well, you proved me wrong. Trust me when I tell you, you were better than book-on-tape."

He is obviously used to getting his way, and I realize any protest will be in vain. I push his gift into my pocket and bow. Besides, I am flattered. An important businessman has just politely thanked *me*—Sang Ly, a scavenger from Stung Meanchey. I bow again as graciously as I can, all the while suppressing a spontaneous grin. I step off the bus.

Ki Lim, Nisay, and I all stand together at the side of the road as the bus drives away and complete strangers wave their good-byes.

"What did he say?" Ki finally asks.

I pull out the folded money and look at the amount. It's enough to cover all of our fares and then some. "He said I'm better than *buk-on-tape,*" I tell him.

Ki wrinkles up his nose. "Who is *buk-on-tape?*"

"I have absolutely no idea."

CHAPTER
TWENTY-TWO

It takes a little more than an hour to hike from the road to the bank of the river where the boats stop. We are tired, hot, and hungry, so a ride on the water will be welcome. With some of the businessman's money, we buy a dinner of rice, pork, and dragon fruit. We should eat it more slowly, but we don't. After we finish, I rest with Nisay in the shade while Ki arranges with one of the boats to take us down the river to the village.

Back at the bus station, we borrowed a phone and called my Uncle Keo to let him know we would be coming. It apparently paid off, as we are greeted by waves and shouts from the path along the river as we near our village. It is two distant nephews who have been assigned as a welcoming party. After the boat drops us off on the bank, the boys volunteer to each carry a suitcase. We don't complain.

The villages along the Mekong River (or almost any river in Cambodia) are all laid out the same. Homes are built to hug the river-bank and can dot the water's edge for miles. Behind the homes, where the flooding river deposits its annual mud and silt, lie the partitioned fields of rice that have provided sustenance, livelihood, and hope to countless generations. Beyond the fields of groomed rice lies the jungle.

Uncle Keo's home is a short walk. For three years, Uncle has worked for the provincial government, though I'm not certain in what capacity. Every time we ask, we get a different answer. Even Auntie can't say for sure. Either his job is very shady or it's very uncertain, as he keeps changing responsibilities. Regardless, the position comes with benefits. Two and a half years ago, he received a load of wood to build a new home across from his old one. A little more than a year later, he became one of the first in the village to get a phone.

As we arrive, Aunt and Uncle greet us warmly. "It's so nice to have you back. How is my little monkey?" Auntie asks. She's looking at me, but she must be talking about Nisay, as I haven't been called *little monkey* in twenty-five years.

"He's not doing well," I say. "That's why we came: to see the Healer."

Her quizzical look answers my monkey question and we both laugh. She waves us to follow her up the ladder and inside.

Auntie prepares some fruit while Uncle catches up. "How is your mother?" he asks.

"Stubborn," I say, not trying to be funny but getting a chuckle in response.

We chitchat—rather, gossip—about the province, the dump, and the difficult life living in either place. He tells us that Munny Sap, a dozen houses up the road, was bitten by a pit viper in the middle of the night and died three days later. I tell him that Prak Sim was run over by a garbage truck and died instantly. I am about to explain that my friend Sopeap Sin, an ornery and wonderful woman who has taught me to read, has something constricting her arteries, and I plead to heaven that she'll still be alive when I get back—but I stop myself.

During the conversation, Uncle mentions that after our call, he tried to contact the Healer to let him know we'd be coming, but learned he'll be up river for at least another two days. My heart sighs. He must sense we are tired, so, as the conversation wanes, he tells us we will be staying in his old home to the west but that his mother-in-law has moved in recently so it's a space we'll need to share. When I assure him that it won't be a problem, he restrains a grin. I'm not clear if it's a warning to us or payback toward his mother-in-law.

The old home's stilts are not quite as high as his new home's, portending to the heavier flooding as of late, and I offer gratitude that it's not the rainy season. Once the river's waters rise, the only way to get to any of the homes along it will be by boat. When we enter behind Uncle, an old, pearl-haired woman grunts; it's apparent that she's none too pleased to welcome invaders. I don't remember her from my childhood, and I'm sure I should, but then Uncle explains she's been living in Stung Treng with a sister-in-law. However, *circumstance* (a term on which he doesn't expound) has made it necessary for her to relocate to the province. The way he now emphasizes the word *relocate* makes the woman sound as though she were a convict, and I soon understand why.

Her things are spread out, almost too neatly, across both rooms, though notably concentrated in the smaller area where we'll stay.

"Nana," Uncle says, taking a scolding tone, "I told you, we're having company for a few days."

She doesn't reply.

"I call it *magic hearing*," he says, talking to us as if she weren't there. "It works on the oddest occasions, such as when it's time for dinner. Then, when work needs to be done, it fades away . . . *magically.*"

I think I see the old woman scowl.

As Uncle gathers her things and tosses them into the adjoining room to make space, I attempt to make peace. "I'm sorry. We won't be here long. We're just here to take my son to the Healer."

If she understands, she doesn't let it show.

"Make yourself at home," Uncle says with enough cunning in his voice I can't help but think he's hiding something. He's halfway down the ladder when I hear him call out, "Goodnight, Nana." Then I hear him laugh.

Ki, who has hardly said a word, glances at the woman now fussing with the pile Uncle has created on the floor. He decides to retreat as well. "I'm taking Nisay down to the river for a quick bath. You get things situated here."

I'm not sure why *he's* leaving. He's the one with a knife. Then again, Ki bathing Nisay is an offer that's hard to turn down.

I'm alone with the woman, who still hasn't uttered a decipherable word—and then I take out Sopeap's book. Her eyes brighten; the corners of her mouth reverse position; her new grunting echoes glee rather than disdain. *That's it,* I decide. *Who doesn't like a story?* Tomorrow I'll read the tiger story again so that Ki can hear the ending. The old woman can listen and it will be just like our ride in on the bus.

I will read her literature, she will understand that we mean her no harm, and all can be right with the world once again.

The air is magnificent and the sun eager as the countryside welcomes us home as old friends. Uncle has arranged with a village farmer to let Ki Lim help plant rice. While he won't make as much per day as recycling trash at home, at least it's something.

I cart Nisay down to the river to let him watch the local villagers rise out from the murky flow atop their massive water buffalos as they cross from the opposite bank. If he were feeling well, Nisay would laugh, giggle, and clap. Today he barely opens his eyes. His fever and diarrhea were especially acute last night, and our roommate was none too happy about it. Still no words from the woman, but I listened to enough of her groans and mutters to make me decide that we'll spend the day outside.

When the water-buffalo parade is over, I wander with my son along the river path, tracing many ancient steps that intertwine into my childhood. I wish Nisay could have known his grandfather, but then again, I could fill a bushel basket with my wishes, and for what? We rest beside the twisted roots of a banyan tree for shade, to eat some of the food Auntie prepared, but we don't stay long.

"We need to go," I say. "You know what Grandfather said. *'We can't claim heaven as our own if we are just going to sit under it.'*"

Then I remind myself, he's also the grandfather who said, *"If you are going to do wrong, at least make sure you don't get fat from it."*

When I realize we've wandered close to the Healer's home, I decide to drop in and set a formal appointment. I understand that it is not necessary for him, but it is for me. The Healer's wife greets us, and at first I don't recognize her—too many years have passed between already distant neighbors. When I explain the reason for my visit, she agrees politely. "Yes, come back in two days. He will see you then," she says.

I bow my thanks and we leave. "Two more days, Nisay," I tell my child on our walk home. "Two more days and then you can finally get better."

As we reach home, smoke wafts from the open windows, though I'm fairly certain—no, I'm positive—it's not Ki cooking us dinner. Then I see him standing several yards away speaking with Uncle. Nisay sees Ki as well and gurgles something I consider close enough to *Ba* (Daddy) that I pass the child off. Then I climb the stairs to our room.

When I see the source of the smoke, I let out a horrific scream. "NO! STOP!" The crazy old woman is boiling rice on her ceramic stove. Adjacent, and providing the fuel for the stove, is my book of short stories with most of the pages torn out and in flames!

From my shriek of death, the woman must think I'm about to kill her, which I will commence to do shortly, but first I try to pull the burning pages from beneath her stove. It's too late. I instead snatch what remains of the book from beside her as I contain another battle of my own—fury versus tears. Before a winner is declared, Uncle and Ki rush in, responding to my lament. I want to ask Ki for his knife, but before I can, tears throw a knockout punch. Clutching what's left of my book to my chest, I slump helplessly to the bamboo floor, whimpering like a distressed child. It is several minutes before the men's consolation registers.

"She's just getting so old and ornery," Uncle says. "She doesn't think clearly all of the time. She didn't realize anyone here reads. All she's ever used old books for is to start fires."

I don't buy her innocence, but my only evidence of her malice is the satisfaction that glows from her face. I wipe at my cheeks, draw back my shoulders, and attempt to regain my composure. "The book was for reading to Nisay," I manage to mutter.

"Perhaps we can find you another?" says Uncle, missing the point of the old woman's vengeance.

"She should replace it," I demand.

Uncle glances at the cover, still in my hand, then says, "That may be difficult, unless you can wait until the next time I head to the city. Other than a handful of basic readers used by the teacher at the school, I don't know of any books in the village."

I know this to be true—or at least it was when I was growing up in the province. Yet the words still stun. Even at the dump, the filthiest place in Cambodia—perhaps on the entire planet—I can always find something to read.

Even by morning I keep a suspicious and wary eye on the old woman. Auntie must presume I'm planning wicked revenge because she invites me to carry Nisay down to the river with her while she scrubs clothes. Mostly it appears she just wants to talk.

"Your mother mentioned you and Ki are happy, in spite of your financial challenges with Nisay," she adds.

"Mother? When did you speak to Mother?"

"We talk on occasion."

"You do?"

Auntie chuckles. "The province is remote, but dear, we do live in the twenty-first century."

The way she calls me *dear* almost reminds me of Sopeap, and I find it comforting. Auntie continues, "Since we got our phone, she's been borrowing a few cell minutes every month or two. I'm not sure from whom, but it's enough that we've managed to stay caught up. She's so proud that you're learning to read—though a little nervous."

"Nervous?"

Auntie hesitates. "Don't say anything."

"Of course not, but why would she be nervous?"

"That may not be the right word. She's proud of you and wants to always live close so she can watch her grandchildren grow up."

"Grandchild," I clarify. "Singular, not plural—and why would my reading interfere with that?"

"I think now that you're reading, she worries you'll find a job and move away from Stung Meanchey. She says you hate the place."

"She's right. I *do* hate the place. It smells. It's filthy. The air is smoky all the time. Nisay never gets better. Here in the province life is so . . . peaceful. I miss being here."

"Yes . . ." Auntie says pensively, "memory can be such a pernicious monkey." And then she smiles.

"I'm not sure what you're getting at."

"I'm saying that the province is no different from the dump. It's just as hard and unforgiving—in many ways, harder. Have you already forgotten the reasons you left?"

"But you do okay."

"Since your uncle started his new job, things are better. But they haven't always been—and who knows what the future will bring? Most of the families here struggle. You know that."

What she says is true but I'm not willing to concede so easily. "Yes, but—"

"Sang Ly, do you love durian fruit?" she asks, changing the subject so abruptly, I sense an ambush coming.

"Yes . . ." I say cautiously. "I guess so." And it's true. I do like the taste, though it does have a bad reputation. While it's considered one of the tastiest fruits in all of Cambodia, it's also the worst smelling—so bad, in fact, it's actually banned at many hotels.

"I think, Sang Ly," she says, "that the dump is a lot like the durian fruit."

"You're right. They both *stink*."

192

"Correct, they do. But that's not what matters. What's important is what you find beneath. That is what makes the durian so popular."

"Seeds?" I say, being obstinate.

It doesn't slow her down. "It not only tastes good," she says, "but it's one of the country's most nutritious fruits."

And then she goes in for the kill. "The dump is like the durian. Though it's smelly, it provides a way for families to stay together—families such as yours. Even though it's putrid, it provides nourishment."

I presume the lesson is over. It's not.

"On the other hand, Sang Ly, the province is like the dragon fruit. Its bright colors are pleasing and attractive, and it smells delicious—and it is. However, if one were to eat only dragon fruit, he would starve. It doesn't provide enough nourishment on its own."

I lean over and clasp her hands, as if to offer thanks for her lesson. Only now, she stops scrubbing and turns to make eye contact. It's obvious she is not yet finished.

I reply with a gracious bow as she continues.

"Coming home from time to time is a good thing—and you are always welcome. Returning to one's roots is healthy and admirable. However, if it's at the expense of following your own path in the world, or of losing sight of what matters most, then I think you'd be making a mistake."

If she wants to get serious, so can I. "Auntie, what if fate tries to keep me in the dump? It's so ugly there. That can't be right."

"If it does, then so be it. But remember, the province, though beautiful, has its own pockets of ugliness. While the dump is ugly, it also has pockets of beauty. I think finding beauty in either place simply depends on where you decide to stand."

And then Auntie points to her scrubbed clothes. "Now, Nisay's not that heavy. You have a free arm. Help me carry this wash back home, will you?"

២៣

CHAPTER
TWENTY-THREE

As I hold Nisay in my arms while we travel up the river, there is a thought I can't shake from my mind. If people are placed in our path, if events happen for a reason, if everything has meaning and the characters in stories and myths mimic those of our own lives and dreams, why did the Healer—a man who was always cold, uncaring, and distant—show up in mine? Is he an unlikely hero in my story, the man who finally helps my son? Or will he turn out to be just another shape-shifter and once again dash my hope into disappointment?

Ki decided it was best for him to keep working the fields, to ensure we'd have sufficient money to get back home. Auntie agreed to come in his place to help me. Now, as we step out of the small boat onto the riverbank, I must appear to be nervous because Auntie puts her hand on my shoulder and delivers words that encourage. "Everything is going to be fine. Don't worry."

The Healer waits nearby the path and greets us.

"Hello. It's good to see you," he says as he bows graciously.

He's a wiry man of medium frame, wearing plain black shorts, sandals, and a dark T-shirt with white English lettering. I haven't seen him in years, so I'm not sure exactly what I am expecting, but he's not nearly as intimidating as I had remembered. In fact, if I passed this man on the street, I probably wouldn't even notice he was there.

"How have you been?" he asks, and though I can't imagine he actually remembers who I am, I'm impressed that he pretends.

"Fine," I tell him, before I remember that I'm not fine at all. "Except that my son has been sick. That is why we've come."

"What is wrong?" he asks, sounding surprised, though I don't know why he would be, since he knew we were coming to see him, and he *is* the Healer.

As we walk, I tell him about Nisay's diarrhea, his lack of appetite, his constant crying, and my despair. I tell him about the hospitals, the Western doctors, my treatments of *Koah Kchol* and *Choob khyol,* and the modern medicines that work only for a short while. He disparages none of it but simply says, "I'm sorry to hear. You should have come sooner."

"We would have, it's just that we live in the city now and—" His reply was so typical, so expected, that I'm halfway through my response before my ears tell my brain to hold up a minute and pay attention to the words he just spoke—*you should have come sooner!*

In my dream his admonition was definitive and certain. Today his manner is casual and quiet. As I try to decide if there is actually a connection or if my imagination is now having a terribly good laugh, the Healer reaches out and touches Nisay's cheek. At first it appears to be a friendly touch, something a grandfather might do, but when he leans forward to smell the child's breath, I understand he has already started his work.

"Don't worry," he says, looking into my eyes, "I can help him."

195

We reach the steps to his treatment room, a separate hut also on stilts that is apart from his home. He leads the way up and Auntie follows. I take a breath, tell myself it will all be okay, praying that this time it actually will, and then I follow with my son. I sit down cross-legged on the bamboo floor opposite the Healer, with Nisay in my lap. Auntie stands distant to stay out of the way.

We all watch attentively as the man unwraps a plastic bag tied with rubber bands and then separates several used syringe needles, a sharp silver knife, a spoon, and a small plastic jar that contains two irregular-shaped black rocks. Though I watch in silence, Nisay doesn't. Just as with his treatments of *Koah Kchol* and *Choob khyol*—or at any recent doctor visits, for that matter—my boy begins to protest the moment we sit. The longer the Healer prepares, the more I realize Nisay may have a point.

After the man lights incense, he uses his knife to break off a mea-sured portion of the coal-like medicine. He places it in the underside indentation of a broken, overturned teacup and grinds it with the cor-ner of a wooden block into what soon becomes a sticky, pasty mixture that he continually sniffs, as if the odor will tell him when it's ready. His splotchy fingers and the dark lingering residue caked beneath his nails tell me that this gummy tar—whatever it may be—is his medi-cine of choice.

An array of needles waits patiently in a tin, and he selects one that must work well because it looks as though it's been used often. He coats the sharp end in the pitchy mixture. "We are ready," he announces.

He instructs me to hold out Nisay's arms, a task that proves dif-ficult. Nisay too recognizes that the show is about to begin and resists mightily. The more I try to straighten his arm, the harder he pulls it inward, wailing his fear.

"Be calm. This will help you," I whisper—words that I hope will console, but that I fear may instead confirm that this boy's mother is nothing but a *neak kohak* (big, fat liar).

The Healer pokes Nisay first in the center of his left wrist—he wails louder—then again slightly to the left, and yet again on the other side to the right. The black tar must seal the wounds quickly because, though the needle pierces my son's skin, there is no blood.

There is a Cambodian proverb Grandfather loved that says, *For news of the heart, watch the face.* At this moment, I think it would be more apt to say, *For news of a mother's heart, watch her child's face.* Nisay is terrified and my heart weeps.

The poking and screaming, the tense muscles and tears, all continue on the opposite wrist, and then the Healer moves to the boy's feet. The man must sense that I reach a point where I can't bear to watch my son's fear and pain any longer because he sets the needle down. I expect him to say he is finished. Instead, he passes me the teacup that holds the rest of the menacing concoction and says, "Put some on your finger and place it in the boy's mouth."

My son is sobbing so hard in my arms that when I reach my finger into his mouth, he gags. I try again but only manage to spread more of the inky goo on the outside of his lips than inside. I look to the Healer for guidance, letting my despair-filled expression plead for mercy.

"Just a little more on his tongue."

I scoop the last of it on my finger, push it deep inside his mouth, and let it coat his throat and tongue the best I can. The Healer then speaks words that cause my eyes to tear. "It is over."

Auntie steps beside me and takes Nisay, while I take money from my pocket. "Let me take him outside," Auntie says. "We will wait for you down by the river."

My legs have gone to sleep, and it takes a moment to properly stand. There is a small table that holds the burning incense where the offering of money is placed. It is customary to leave payment, but there is no set price that the Healer charges. It is up to the patient to decide. Yet as I unfold our money and count, the Healer waves it away.

"No payment is needed today."

He waits until my gaze meets his, as though he wants to be sure I share his conviction, his words that address the real concern still weighing down my heart. He speaks in a tone so matter-of-fact, I almost *do* believe him. "He will now get well," the man assures.

I don't mean to be a skeptic, to lack hope, or to harbor fear. However, experience has been my diligent teacher. Still, I hate it. I don't want to raise a child of doubt. I want my son to believe, to hope, to dream that the future holds brighter days.

Grandfather, where is the balance between humbly accepting our life's trials and pleading toward heaven for help, begging for a better tomorrow?

And then Sopeap's lesson drops out of hiding and into my head. "Whether we like it or not, hope is written so deeply into our hearts that we just can't help ourselves, no matter how hard we try otherwise. We love the story because we are Sarann or Tattercoats or Cinderella."

And it must be true; some hope must remain in my heart, for I am standing in the hut of the Healer. If all hope had died at Stung Meanchey, I would not be here.

I am so caught up in my own internal brooding that it takes a minute for the Healer's next words to register. "The way you stand there so perplexed, you look a lot like your father," he says.

"You remember my father?" I ask with such surprise it causes a man who had yet to smile to offer what some might call a grin.

"Assuredly. We were good friends. We grew up together, not terribly far from here."

"I didn't know. Mother never mentioned that."

"That is my fault," he replies with reluctance. Though I wait for an explanation, he offers none.

"I wish I could remember him," I say, speaking of my father. "Unfortunately, I don't. He died the night I was born."

"Yes, I know," the Healer says, with a still solemn tone. "I was with him."

"No . . . but . . . you couldn't. You were with him? I was told he died alone, in front of our home, while Mother gave birth inside."

"Half of your story is correct," he says.

"Which half?"

His pause is evidence of his reluctance, but I don't turn away. When it is apparent that I'm not leaving until I know more, he motions for me to sit once again. "Your mother was in labor. I waited with your father in front of his home. He was so pleased to finally have a child."

"He was pleased?"

"Beside himself. I mean, he was also worried, as all new fathers are; but he couldn't wait to teach you about life."

"What happened?"

"As we talked, he lost sensation in his left arm, hand, and fingers; then he began having difficulty breathing. I was just learning the art of healing from my father, but I wasn't married yet, and I was still trying to decide if my father's path should also be my own. Sang Ly, what I'm trying to say is that when your father collapsed, I didn't know how to help."

"What did you do?"

"I ran to find my own father, hoping he would know what to do— but I made the wrong choice. By the time I came back, others had discovered your father on the ground, and I was too late."

The man leans toward me with eyes that plea for absolution.

"You couldn't have known," I tell him.

"That may be true," he says. "I couldn't have stopped death from coming, but I should have been with your father when it led him away. Nobody should have to pass away from this world alone."

It's a reminder that stabs at my heart with thoughts of Sopeap. I reach out and touch the Healer's hand, but he is not yet finished. "I have one more regret," he says. "I wish I had been closer to your family. I convinced myself that staying away would make it easier to forget. It turns out, it only deepened remorse—though I suppose there was one bright side."

"What is that?"

"Had your father not passed away as he did, it is unlikely that I would have become a Healer. After his death, I promised myself I would learn all that my father could teach about the ancient ways of healing—so that the next time, I would know what to do."

The Healer's eyebrows rise when I ask my next question. "What did he look like?"

"Your father? He was a handsome man—looked just like your grandfather. Yes, imagine your grandfather, but take many years off." Then he pauses. "You have never seen a picture of him?"

I lower my head. "I know of no photograph. Mother said the one taken at their marriage was lost when the river flooded."

The Healer's previous sadness skips to excitement. "Please, wait here."

He climbs down the stairs and hurries next door to his home. When he returns, he passes me a small black-and-white photograph of two handsome young men standing in front of a rice field. The man on the right indeed bears a striking resemblance to Grandfather. It is a peek into heaven, and I am left without words.

"Please, take it with you," the Healer says.

The photo is old. It is stained and it is grainy—and it is, without a doubt, the most wonderful gift I have ever been given in my young life.

"He would have been proud of you," the Healer says as I prepare to depart.

Perhaps he didn't listen earlier. "We live in the dump," I remind him.

He nods warmly. "It doesn't matter where you live, Sang Ly, it is *how* you live."

It sounds as though he's been talking to Auntie. I don't know proper protocol with Healers—what is acceptable and what is not—but I reach out and clasp his hands in mine, pull them close, then offer a sincere bow of gratitude. He returns my bow.

With thanks complete, I place Father in my pocket. By the time I reach Auntie and Nisay, they are sitting at the river's edge watching a man fish. Nisay's crying has ceased.

As the sound of the boat's motor mixes with the splashing river, I glance at the picture once more and then slide it into my bag, where it will stay safe and not get wet. I gaze heavenward toward a man I can finally picture.

Thank you, Father, for helping your friend decide to become a Healer so that he could be here today to help Nisay. Thank you for not caring where I live. Thank you for being proud of me. Oh, and when you get a moment, tell Grandfather that if he has something to say, he will have to wait in line. You and I have a lot to catch up on.

As we say our final good-byes, Auntie is somber.

"Give this to your mother," she says, passing along some folded bills. "Tell her it's to help cover the phone calls, since she's always the one to call me."

I take the money, bow to her and Uncle, and thank them for their kindness. Ki says his good-byes the way most men do, with a quiet tip of the head and few words.

I carry Nisay. Ki has a suitcase in each hand. We are a few steps away when I notice the old woman, our book-burning roommate, clinging to the distant stairs. Perhaps she wants to be certain we are actually leaving.

"Ki, wait," I say. "There's one more thing I need to do."

He glances at the woman, then at me. His expression reads, *Don't do anything stupid.* I answer by trading him Nisay for a suitcase. I then open the lid and remove my torn-up book. I have already inventoried the damage. She ripped out sections randomly, and no complete stories remain.

When Ki understands what I'm doing, he smiles—as do Uncle and Auntie. The old woman eyes me warily until I step to where she lingers and present my parting gift—the rest of my book.

Once the woman realizes I'm bestowing a peace offering, the suspicion in her eyes melts into wonderment. Her wrinkles turn upward and her old hands shake with glee. She snatches the book's remains from my fingers, says not a word, but immediately shuffles around to gather matches, a pot, and her old stove. Shortly the *crazy girl who wanted to murder her* will be but a distant memory, while she happily cooks rice and vegetables for her dinner.

២៤

CHAPTER
TWENTY-FOUR

Ki's head rests against the closed window of a bus that thankfully has both air conditioning and plush seats. When catching a bus ride home from the province, you wait by the side of the road and take whatever comes along. Today the ancestors were smiling.

Thank you, Father.

Nisay is draped across Ki's chest and both are sleeping like content babies. The scene is so picturesque I wish I owned a camera. The black spots on Nisay's wrists and feet remain, since I forgot to ask the Healer when to wash them off. At this point, I'm not taking any chances.

I try to sleep myself, but my occupied mind is holding my tired body hostage. The bus slows to a stop near a crossroads on the highway to let an elderly couple disembark. As I wait, I can't help but glance across my husband and our sleeping son to the faces of the villagers who mix and mingle along the road. I'm certain that each of them has an interesting life story to tell.

And then I see her.

I lean forward as my heart quickens. Just to be certain my eyes aren't playing tricks on me, I slip out of my seat and into the empty row in front, where I can scoot right up against the window.

Yes, there is no mistaking that girl. It is Maly, walking beside a well-dressed woman who is perhaps older than I am, but not by much. The two carry half a dozen rolls of brightly colored fabric, as if they are returning from the market. As they pass parallel to the bus, they chat contentedly together.

I want to pound on the window to get the girl's attention, to chase her down and wrap my arms around her and tell her that I've been thinking about her, that we've all missed her. But as I reach for the latch to slide open the window, my hand freezes.

Does Maly know about the death of her brother? Does she know that Lucky Fat wonders daily about how she's doing? Are the memories she holds of Stung Meanchey ones she hopes to forget?

As my questions swirl, I remember the story I read with Sopeap about Pyramus and Thisbe. It was about two children in love whose homes were separated by a thick wall—and yet they found a crack through which they could sometimes speak. I touch my fingers to the glass as Maly turns down a dirt road that leads to a distant village. I notice her giggle and laugh as she converses with the woman. She doesn't even realize that I am there.

I imagine this is how it must be with our ancestors. They watch us closely, full of love and concern, sometimes whispering encouragement through a crack, but mostly just satisfied to know that we are happy.

When I scoot back to my seat beside Ki, he lifts his head and glances up. "What's the matter? Sang Ly, why are you crying?"

"It's nothing," I tell him as I reach down to grasp his hand. "I was just allowed to peek through a crack in the wall. Let's go home."

It's late when we finally arrive at Stung Meanchey, but there is enough moonlight shining over the dump that we can see our way. When we reach our shack on the mound, my feet become anchors and I jar to a stop. My mouth opens, but no words escape. I carry one suitcase while Ki holds the other and our son, and my suitcase hits the trash with a thud.

While I can't seem to verbalize my disbelief, Ki fills in for me. "It appears we've been robbed."

We have been more than robbed—we've been plundered, pillaged, and raped. Our home is completely empty. Except for its three bare walls and a roof, which surprisingly remain intact, there is nothing left.

I dash around back but don't have a light. Ki brings his lighter, and, with one flick of a finger, my fears are confirmed. They've even taken our possessions that were stored beneath—my washtub, my pans, my stove, our quarter sack of rice. They've taken my books and magazines, our sleeping mats and pillows, Ki's long rubber boots, our empty plastic jugs, and our old Styrofoam cooler still filled with empty snail shells.

The ground that once held our ceramic water jar, the same one we've used since moving to Stung Meanchey, is bare and empty. Ki's picking tools are also missing, as well as our supply of empty sacks that we fill with recycled trash.

We stumble back around front and confirm that our canvas—the one that served as our fourth wall, our front door, our protection from the elements—isn't just folded up onto the roof. It's nowhere to be found. They have even taken my broken clock.

Every last thing we own—except what we have carried home from the province—is gone.

I hear the sound of a distant, gurgling brook as an animal pulls at my face in the darkness. I am dreaming—only it is not a dream at all. When I open my eyes, it's no longer dark. Nisay is beside me, and he is wide-awake and grabbing at my hair. I sit up in the unfamiliar surroundings and then remember we are at Mother's. Late last night, when we discovered that all our earthly possessions were gone, we decided to sleep here for protection in case it rained.

My husband is still asleep behind me, as is Mother across the room. I lie back down, pull my naked baby close, and realize there is no mess, no diarrhea to clean up—and he is trying to talk to me. I don't know what he is saying, but his voice is loud enough that Mother wakes up next. She takes a quick glance and then comes over for a better look. She can hardly believe what she sees.

"Nisay looks very good," she says, not wanting to sound too hopeful too soon. She throws open the door to let in more light, just to be certain.

"He has been much better," I tell her. "He slept all the way home on the bus. He's had no diarrhea and he does seem more alert."

Mother couldn't believe her eyes and now she doesn't believe her ears. "No diarrhea?" she asks, shaking her head.

"Not yet."

She reaches down and picks up the child, who is more than happy to oblige. I want to laugh with her as she plays with the boy, but I remind myself that hope was dashed too soon before, when his sickness returned. Yet that happened when his medicine ran out. Currently, he is taking no medicine.

"You look as though you are starving. Is my grandson starving?"

Mother says, speaking now in baby-talk to Nisay. "We must cook you a big breakfast to celebrate."

Ki, now awake, sits up. He is less cheery. "I should go to work," he says, "but I have no boots, no picker, nothing."

Of course, he is right, we have nothing. And yet, if Nisay is truly better, *we have everything.*

It is a simple notion—accepting that Nisay is going to be fine—but it's a hope that I've kept caged in my heart for too long. When I finally crack open the door to the possibility, gratitude rushes past so quickly to reach the sunshine, there is nothing I can do to stop it. My lips begin to quiver as tears roll down across my cheeks and past my nose. I can't help myself, and the first reaction I see from Ki is concern. "It's okay," he says, instantly apologetic. "I can get another picker."

I try to explain that it's not about the picker, but my words mix with sobs to create sounds only a mother can decipher.

"She'll be fine," Lena confirms. "Just give her a few minutes." And then Mother turns to address us both. "And don't worry about the things you lost. We are making arrangements."

"Arrangements?" we both mumble.

"Two days ago, Teva Mao noticed your home had been robbed. We have been gathering things for you since. She has an extra stove. Narin has a pan you can use for cooking rice. I have extra pickers. Oh, and Pran Teo thinks he can get a large piece of canvas from his nephew in the city. He will know for sure today. We are all just glad to have you home."

Home. I let the word ring in my head. Stung Meanchey—a dirty, smelly, despicable place where our only possessions can be carried in two hands.

"Yes," I confirm, "we are *home.*"

Ki has gone with Pran to pick up our new front canvas—new to us, anyhow. Before the men left, Pran mentioned casually that it's bright yellow with orange lettering and a picture of a chicken—though he said he had no clue what the words say. I wasn't sure if he was teasing, but I told him I could hardly wait.

Mother, Nisay, Teva Mao, and I are organizing our home, and, before my eyes, friendship is soothing the sting of injury. Teva is carrying water to fill up our new jar while her daughter, Vanna, keeps an eye on Nisay, who is becoming a handful. Other neighbors are dropping off extra food, sleeping mats, pillows, and cooking items. Love abounds, even at Stung Meanchey.

The one person I long to see is Sopeap Sin. I excused myself this morning and hurried to her house, but there was no answer. I will try once again this afternoon after everyone leaves. But when Lucky Fat shows up, my plans change. He carries a bag that I immediately recognize as Sopeap's.

"Sopeap asked that I give this to you," he says.

"What is it?"

"I don't know. I can't read."

Inside I see only a notebook. "When? When did she give it to you?" I ask, my whole manner pleading for more information.

"She came by three days ago to see if you were back. She didn't look real good—she even looked thin and that's something I never thought I would say about Sopeap."

"Is she home now? Did she say anything more? Have you seen her since?" I don't mean to bombard the child with questions. I just have to know. Lucky Fat looks confused, as if he's not sure which to answer first. His single reply covers them all.

"I think she was leaving."

I would ask where, but what would be the point? I rummage through the bag to make sure there's nothing else inside, and then I lean against our step and thumb the notebook's pages. There is a letter in front.

Dear Sang Ly,

I am sorry we could not see each other again. As I've said, endings sometimes disappoint. Still, I want to finish what we started. I have put together a few more lessons—I trust they will answer your countless questions.

Thank you, Sang Ly, for listening to this miserable old woman whose bones don't deserve your friendship. You are not a foolish girl after all.

Be well,

Sopeap Sin

P.S.: I have left a few books for you at home. My key is behind the water jar.

With rising anxiety soon to trump neighborly friendship, I consider leaving the gathering and running to Sopeap's myself to confirm what I already know to be true—she is no longer there. Then Ki and Pran approach carrying a bundle of canvas. Though it's clear that Pran was kidding about the chicken, the material is indeed bright yellow. At the moment, I couldn't care less. Worry must be parading across my face because Ki immediately asks what is wrong.

"Sopeap is gone," I say, holding up the papers for him to see.

"What are those?"

"They appear to be more lessons, but Lucky Fat says that she has already left."

"To go where?"

"He doesn't know. The note doesn't say either. She would never tell me where she was going."

"When?" he asks. "Do you know when she left?"

"According to Lucky Fat, about three days ago."

Ki glances at the canvas and then at Pran. "Three days," he repeats. "Well, I guess we could see if she's returned. Let me get this canvas put up before Pran has to leave and then I'll go with you to check her house."

While Ki works, Mother takes over duties watching Nisay, and I sit on a piece of cardboard, out of their way, to leaf through Sopeap's lessons.

As I turn the pages, I realize these are different. There are no printed stories, no translations from English, no pamphlets or books. Instead, every page is written on notepaper in Sopeap's hand.

The title on the cover of the bound bundle reads, *The Essays of Sopeap Sin*. The volume is thick with many lessons, and if I read them all, I'll be here for days on end. Every one looks interesting, at least at first glance. I see a story about her college life in America, another reminiscing about her first love, and several that apparently come from the time she taught at the university. It's the title of the last story, however, that grabs me and won't let go. It is called simply *The Epilogue*.

It catches my attention because I had asked Sopeap about the word *epilogue* and its meaning when I came across it in several of the stories we read together. She explained that an epilogue is often used by an author to step out of the story, to speak directly to the reader once the story is over, to bring the narration to its close. She said the epilogue is the moment when the author gets to explain what happened to the story's main character after the story ended. She also called it *the final chapter*.

I'm hesitant to read it now, not only because of what I may discover but because of another lesson Sopeap constantly drilled into my head: *Never read the ending first.*

What my teacher despised were readers who flipped to the last chapter, read the ending, then turned back to begin their stories with smug and wicked smiles dripping from their faces. I can still hear her admonition—actually, it was more of an order.

Child, unless you are opening a dictionary, you start at the book's opening page and you read the story through. If it's terribly dreadful, then just put it down and move on. What I will not tolerate is reading ahead. It's not fair to the reader or to the author. If they meant to have their books read backwards, they would surely have written them that way!

Ki watches my hesitation, but I don't have the time or patience to explain. Nor do I have the emotional energy to read her final words aloud. I tell everyone that I would like to read silently. They all seem to understand.

Then, with Sopeap's threats sounding in my head, I bite my lip, plead in silence for forgiveness, and begin. As I do, a voice echoes.

You're a foolish girl after all!

២៥

CHAPTER
TWENTY-FIVE

The Epilogue
by Sopeap Sin

There is an old Cambodian folktale in which Sovann Som, a hunter, is lured into the jungle by a temptress, but instead of finding his desired riches, he is silently strangled to death by a snake.

It's a story to which I, and the rest of Cambodia, should have paid more attention.

By early 1975, factional fighting and civil unrest had lasted for so long in the provinces around Phnom Penh that on April 17 of that same year, when Khmer Rouge soldiers claimed victory and marched through the streets, even soldiers in the opposing army cheered. We were just so glad to finally have the war over, nobody seemed to care who had won. We didn't understand that peace at any price is a fool's bargain. We welcomed apathy with open arms, invited it over for dinner, offered it keys to the spare bedroom, then silently slept while it sneaked up behind and cut our throats.

We wanted change. Could the new leaders be any worse than those who had just been overthrown? I would find out that very day.

Reports blaring over the radio instructed everyone to stay inside—most obeyed. However, I wasn't worried. History had taught me that Cambodia had always adapted to change in government. This time would be no different.

My husband, Samnang, wasn't so sure. Though he wasn't an elected official, he worked directly with the Minister of Education. In addition, he came from a respected family with numerous political ties. Defeat of the Republic, with a new regime in power, would probably mean he'd lose his job. But his connections had always served him well, and I had no doubt they would come through again.

Because of the recent rocket attacks aimed directly at the city, we hadn't left the house for three days and I was stir-crazy. With the shooting over, and to simulate a sense of normalcy, I grabbed a basket from the cupboard and announced that I was going to make a quick visit to see how Samnang's sister, Channary, was faring. Samnang was hesitant to let me go alone, but at the same time, he didn't want to miss any news that might come across the radio. Since our infant son was asleep in the back bedroom, he motioned for the housekeeper to accompany me.

"Be cautious," he instructed.

"We'll be fine." I assured.

My trek was not as adventuresome as it might sound. We

lived in a modern, three-story home in the central part of the city with a beautiful garden roof where I grew rumdul and lotus. At the back of the home, a narrow bricked path, concealed from the front entrance, connected a dozen similar-sized homes with what amounted to a disguised entrance. Since most of the homes were owned by family and friends, it offered not only convenience but a safe and easy method of escape should the unlikely need ever arise.

Channary's home was the farthest away, but still only a short distance. I let the housekeeper carry the basket and I led the way, all the while wondering about eggs.

Recent fighting in the outlying provinces had driven many to the capital to seek refuge. The influx of people had caused shortages at the market, and prices had skyrocketed. Twice I'd been to the market to find eggs and twice I'd come back empty-handed.

Like my husband, his sister seemed to know everybody. She had mentioned that a family nearby had purchased several hundred chickens and were now selling eggs to acquaintances. She felt confident she could get me two or three dozen without a problem.

It appeared she was right. As we approached the back of the house, I could see a basket brimming with eggs sitting on their table near the kitchen. However, as we entered, my sister-in-law was nowhere to be found. I called out. "Channary? Channary?"

No answer.

The housekeeper was nervous. "I think we should go back."

"Nonsense. There is nothing to worry about."

Not knowing exactly how many of the eggs were mine, I carefully transferred three dozen into my basket, leaving what looked to be an equal number behind. I scribbled a note, letting Channary know I'd dropped in, and we then headed home.

Once again, the housekeeper carried the basket while I walked a step ahead. As we passed though the yard gate and out onto the path, in her haste she tipped the basket, spilling and breaking several of the eggs. I was furious and snatched the basket from her.

"Foolish girl! Be careful. Those are expensive."

Perhaps I should have been more understanding. After all, they were just eggs. At the time, however, I felt she needed to be taught a lesson. She had been with us for almost a year but hadn't made much progress in her effort to learn how to serve others. She had come from the province, and as a favor to a mutual friend, I had agreed to let her learn at our expense. What the girl didn't know was that two weeks earlier, in spite of the time we'd already spent training her, I'd decided to let her go. However, with the confusion of the war and the fact that I had yet to find a suitable replacement, I simply hadn't found the right time to break the news. Perhaps she sensed change coming. A week earlier, when I lectured that she needed to be more disciplined and take responsibility for her actions, she bowed her head and apologized, "I'm sorry. I will do better. I will try harder."

Words—hollow words. I was growing weary.

As we reached our yard, the housekeeper opened the gate and stepped through first. I followed, careful not to spill any more eggs.

Once we were in the yard, four waiting Khmer Rouge

soldiers pointed their rifles at us and ordered us to move inside. My grip on the basket tightened. It was a moment when time slowed, when heightened senses seemed to observe and record every sight and sound.

As we entered the house, two more soldiers leveled their gun barrels at our heads. Across the room, my husband stiffened in his chair. The soldier behind him was but a boy, dressed in a man's uniform. Yet even though he was just a child, hatred smoldered in his eyes.

My hands began to tremble, causing the shaking eggs to click nervously against one another, till I was certain all of them would break. I glanced at Samnang. Ignoring the warm steel barrel ready to end his existence at any moment, his gaze shifted rapidly about the room, and I could tell he wasn't just weighing the gravity of the situation but also processing possibilities for escape. My breathing quickened. Did he really have a way out?

I'd often taught my students, many no older than the boyish soldiers who held us captive, that words are powerful. "Life-changing!" I would say as I'd lecture to the class. "Words demand justice, encourage freedom, change minds, and soften hearts—and words save."

What I didn't understand was that in spite of their power, word meanings are sometimes hidden or disguised. I also didn't anticipate the words my husband would speak next.

"Soriyan, it's okay. Come here. If we are to die, let it be together."

With the threat of death looming, Samnang called out across the room toward me. Only he wasn't looking at me. Rather, he was staring intently at our young peasant housekeeper, Sopeap Sin. She may have been a clumsy girl, but she

wasn't stupid. In an instant, her puzzlement jelled into understanding. She grasped what he was asking, what he was hoping.

She looked toward me for just a moment, as if to seek my
approval. As our eyes connected, I expected to see a reflection
of my fear. Instead, her face shone with confidence. Normally,
when we spoke, she looked toward the ground. Not today—
and our gaze shared words, silent words: "I am just a clumsy
peasant girl, a housekeeper, who has often let you down. But
today, I will finally make things right. I will make my family
proud, and I will make you proud. No matter what happens, I
will not spill the eggs again today."

And then she made her decision without me.

When Samnang called my name a second time, Sopeap
was quick with her reply.

"I'm coming."

With calmness and assurance, as if she were a princess in
the king's palace, she strode toward him.

The soldier behind Samnang furrowed his brow in confusion and then cast a glance at another, perhaps his superior.
Sopeap didn't offer either man time for mental debate. The
girl I'd berated moments before carried herself like a woman of
culture, a wife, a mother, a queen.

In turn, I, her teacher, stood frozen, desperately clutching
my half-basket of eggs.

If Sopeap expected the guns that tracked her to fire, she
never let it show. The guns remained silent. My heart wanted
to leap from my chest and protest, but instead, my will cow-
ered in silent fear.

When she reached my husband, he calmly ignored the
threat of a gun against his head, stood, and pulled Sopeap

close. As he did, the soldier's focus shifted away from me and toward them. My husband's plan—one that my mind was finally comprehending—was working. And when Samnang was certain, in his grasp of Sopeap, that the soldiers couldn't read his expression, he stole a glance in my direction.

His eyes assured that this was the best choice, the only choice—and his soft gaze offered a silent good-bye.

Words are powerful. I could have used them to call out, "No, this is not right. I am Soriyan. I am his wife. I am only holding this basket of eggs because the housekeeper was too clumsy." But in my cowardice, I said nothing.

She could have called out. "Don't harm me. I am Sopeap Sin. I am just a villager. They are the educated ones. They are the ones you seek."

But in her bravery, she said nothing.

Boom!

The bullet from the young soldier's gun sent Samnang reeling backward; blood spattered across our furniture; soldiers laughed.

"No!" I screamed, opening my mouth for the first time and letting my basket of eggs scatter across the floor.

Boom! Boom!

Sopeap twisted sideways, first from a shot to her chest, and then from another that entered her head just above her ear. Her limp body slumped over Samnang's.

And then our baby, asleep in the back bedroom, began to cry.

All six soldiers turned, startled at the unforeseen interruption. I tried to step forward but was grabbed around the neck as others readied their weapons to fire.

"Don't kill the child," I pleaded. "I will take him."

The soldier nearest the bedroom headed toward the cry first.

Boom!—and the cries of my child ceased.

The deafening sound of the gunfire in the bedroom served as the impetus for my body to begin heaving deep, convulsive breaths. The walls and ceiling began to constrict, bend, and sway. The soldiers yelled commands, but I couldn't understand their words as their voices distorted into strange and meaningless clamor. Though I tried to remain standing, my legs buckled beneath me and I collapsed onto the hard tile floor.

"End it now. Please, end my life now," I sobbed to no one listening.

If they understood my pleas, they didn't obey. Their aim wasn't to kill the peasants or farmers, but rather the educated. And as far as they were concerned, the only person left alive in my home that day was a clumsy, illiterate housekeeper. To them, I was just Sopeap Sin—and so that is who I became.

Two days later, I was marched out of the city with hundreds of thousands of refugees. Only in farming could we serve the good of the new society. I was relocated to the district of Khum Speu where I was assigned to a group growing rice. The Khmer Rouge would lead Cambodia back to a better time, a time before Western culture had corrupted society, a time when farming flourished and the worker ruled—and they would do it by force.

I had read essays describing the horrors of genocide committed during the Chinese Cultural Revolution. I had lectured on Jewish literature detailing the atrocities carried out by Hitler. I had read the words in my head but never comprehended their depth in my heart—until I lived them. Only later would I realize that there are no words harsh enough, no paragraphs wide enough, no books deep enough to convey the weight of true human sorrow.

Every day I expected to die. "Traitors of the society" were identified, trucked away, and massacred. After all, in the new Cambodia, in the perfect Khmer Rouge society, there would be no need for the educated—no doctors, no lawyers, no mechanics, no engineers, no drivers, no merchants, no students, and certainly no teachers. I watched children starving, old people being beaten to death with sticks, entire families being branded as traitors and murdered because a distant relative had once visited America.

It was utter insanity.

By the time the Vietnamese army overthrew the regime four years later, well over a million innocent people had been brutally exterminated. Those of us still alive had been bruised in more sinister ways.

I eventually made my way back to the city—but life was different. Just as my home in Phnom Penh had been destroyed, I was also damaged beyond recognition. I mostly lived on the streets, sometimes hoping to heal, but mostly drinking to forget.

Then, in 1995, I found my way to the river Stung Meanchey and I let it swallow me. It felt tolerable, perhaps even comfortable, as a place for old, discarded, and spoiled things to finish out their existence—even if that thing was me. Still I remained Sopeap Sin, it being less painful to never look back. I swore silence and waited for my story to fade away with the stories of others, a heartbreak too full of shame to ever share. But then another illiterate, backward girl from the province reminded me that even tragedies offer lessons worth repeating.

Pay attention to my final lesson, Sang Ly.

I could have saved the life of Sopeap Sin, my housekeeper, but I stayed silent. I have been paying the price ever since. Be careful in your choices. Consequences, good or bad, will always follow.

I offer my final good-bye, Sang Ly.

From your teacher,

Sopeap Sin

"No!" I scream as I finish reading Sopeap's last words. "You are wrong! That is not the lesson. That is *not* the lesson!"

I dry my cheeks on my shirt. My fingers tremble. Ki rushes from the back of the house to my side, though all he can do is wait for my explanation.

"Her name is not Sopeap Sin," I cry, shaking my head in disbelief. I speak the words a second time, as if repeating them will add more understanding to all who now listen. "Her name is Soriyan, not Sopeap Sin."

Teva Mao tilts her head as she tries to make sense of my ranting.

"Sopeap Sin was her housekeeper," I say.

"Her housekeeper? What does that mean?" Ki asks.

My resolve has never been greater. "It means we must find her before it's too late. She's the teacher and she doesn't even understand her own lesson. We must find her! Will you help me?"

CHAPTER
TWENTY-SIX

Though I know that my teacher's real name is Soriyan, I continue to call her Sopeap Sin. Not only does it seem fitting, but it's too difficult to explain the situation to others who won't understand.

Mother volunteers to trek across the dump to visit Sopeap's home again. She returns to announce that nobody answered and the neighbors confirmed that they had watched her leave. No surprise. I continue to read through the essays, though my eyes grow tired and, once the sun sets, I'm not certain I'll be able to continue by lamplight. The stories are entertaining and enlightening, though not all are happy. Some make me laugh, others border on the tragic, all teach important lessons—perfect literature. A number of the lessons are evident; most are hidden deep beneath the layers—so typical of Sopeap.

There is a story about the first year of her marriage and it makes me smile. Each morning she wrestles with her husband so as to not be the last one up, as they have an agreement that the last person out of the bed has to make it—and it teaches me about endearing love.

There is a story about a roommate with whom she lives in college while attending a university in Boston. The girl makes an elaborate quilt with her sisters for their ninety-five-year-old grandmother, but when they present the quilt, the old woman is so surprised, she has a heart attack and dies—and it teaches me about irony.

There is a story about two desperate parents who trade a child they can't afford to feed for a bicycle, so that the father can ride to work. However, both the bicycle and the child end up at the dump. She calls the child *Lucky*—and I can't help but wonder.

There is a lesson on poetry with an untitled work from Sopeap that teaches me about anguish and how simple verse provides a glimpse into our souls.

I scream in the dark at my weakness, with disdain not heard.

I seethe at my failure in the daylight, hidden by an impenetrable wall never seen.

I shed tears of shame in quiet moments that race to my lips, and only I taste.

I breathe in the smoke of despair, sickened by my selfish, filthy smell.

I plead heavenward, begging for solace, send a miracle to heal my fallen heart.

No heavenly hand carries my pain.

No light disperses my sorrow.

No voice offers answers.

Only a peasant girl interrupts and asks that I teach her how to read.

The ancestors have a very funny sense of humor.

Though the stories are tragic, moving, and enlightening, none appears to tell me the whereabouts of my teacher. Then my cousin Narin drops by just as the sun sets. She has heard at the shelters that friends have gathered to help us get settled and she wants to see how she can help. When I see her, my tired mind makes the connection.

"Of course!" I say aloud, remembering her friend Makara, whose sister works at the hospital treating Sopeap. "If Sopeap is sick, surely that's where she would be."

If we leave now, there will still be time. Ki nods his blessing, then counts out enough money to pay for a moto. I leave with Narin, hoping that we'll find Sopeap alive and ornery, complaining about the nurses.

It is not the hospital where I took Nisay, but the place is just as crowded and hurried. The waiting room is filled with different faces, but the worry, pain, and frustration are the same. The woman at the desk pages Makara's sister, and within a few minutes, she rushes through the door. Though she appears happy to see Narin, it's also clear that she can't talk long. After polite introductions, I get right to my question. "Have you seen Sopeap Sin, the woman you were treating from the dump?"

"Sopeap? I haven't seen her for several weeks."

"Wasn't she coming here for her treatments?"

"She was, yes, but she quit—it was quite a while ago."

"Quit?" I am confused. "Why would she quit?"

"She said the drugs made her too weak, caused her to be ornery, clouded her thinking. She said they interrupted *things* that she needed to do. We can't force someone to go through treatment."

"No, I understand," I say, as my brain tries to assemble pieces that don't fit. "One last question," I plead, though its answer is for me and not in hopes of finding Sopeap. "Had she continued, would the treatments have made a difference?"

The woman pauses to think, then offers her best medical opinion. "In Cambodia—no. Had she decided to go to Thailand, then perhaps yes."

"Thailand?" I ask.

"Yes, didn't she tell you? There is a foreign hospital there offering study treatments that are experimental but promising. She turned them down—for the very same reasons."

The eastern sky is just beginning to glow across the horizon, waiting for a sun that is building enough courage to peek out and start another day at Stung Meanchey. Halfway to Sopeap's home, I jerk to a stop. "Wait, I forgot my bag," I say, "to carry back the books."

"What books?"

"In her note—didn't I tell you? She left some books for me."

Ki shrugs a no. "If there are too many to carry, we can come back later."

As we arrive, Ki assures me that she is definitely not inside.

"How do you know?"

"Look at her lock. It's been secured from the outside."

I tap on the door anyway and listen. There is no response.

Technically, Sopeap doesn't live in Stung Meanchey, at least not in the homes that dot its perimeter. Hers is located on a skinny western street that skirts out of Stung Meanchey at a diagonal. I don't recall how I learned which home was hers, since she's never actually invited me over. From the outside, however, it appears to be two rooms, solid walls, and a pitched roof. The openings are shuttered tight. What I most envy, however, is her front door that locks. Still, in a world where everything means something, I'm also reminded that, like her home, Sopeap allowed very few people inside.

I bang harder, loud enough that a neighbor comes out from next door, looking irritated. "She's not home," he says, stating the obvious.

"Do you know where she went or if she'll be back?" I ask.

"No." And with a turn of his head, he disappears.

I hurry around to the side and kneel to reach behind her water jar. My fingers clutch a rusty metal ring that holds a single key. I turn to see the neighbor peek out from behind a window opening and then turn away. I pay him no mind but hurry to the front and shove the key into the lock. It clicks open.

"Are you ready?" I ask Ki. He deflects my question with a shrug.

I push open the front door and let the light that is now bathing the dump wash inside and illuminate the room.

"Sopeap?" I call out, knowing I will hear no answer.

As I glance around, my mouth drops open and my heart races. I reach out to confirm with my touch what my eyes try to register. Every wall in the room is stacked with books—hundreds of books.

There is a single sleeping mat against one wall. On the other side of the room is a cooking stove, black and dull, yet the modern kind with a chimney that bends on top to vent to the outside. Beside it is a tattered cabinet with a door swung half open. Inside, I see rice, a plate with aging vegetables, a container of cooking oil, and assorted cooking utensils. Opposite, on the other side of the stove, sits a small desk with a chair pushed beneath.

No matter where I stand in the room, I am close enough to reach books. I lean over to scan the closest titles. Though some are in English, most are translations into Khmer. I pull one at random from the stack and open its pages. It is *Vorvong and Saurivong,* a popular Cambodian legend. This version was written by Auguste Pavie.

I move to the next. It's written in English, but between each line, Sopeap has penned in Khmer words. I let the cover flip closed, but the title is so worn, I can't read it.

"What's it about?" Ki asks.

"I have no idea."

I pick up yet another. This one is printed in Khmer, with the name of the translator in type larger than the name of the author—an American named Steinbeck.

I keep reading titles and find there are Cambodian stories, Russian stories, Chinese stories, African stories, and stories from countries that I've never heard of.

"It doesn't look as though you gave up on literature at all," I declare.

"If these are the books she's giving to you," Ki says, "you'll not only need a bigger bag, we're going to need a bigger house."

I shift my attention from the books to anything else in the room that may offer a clue as to where Sopeap has gone. I take a step closer to the small desk that holds an open ream of paper, a cup filled with pens and pencils, and a scribbled list with the names of twelve families—and it includes ours.

"What does it say?" Ki asks.

"It's a list of those from whom she collected rent. Our name is at the bottom."

That's when it dawns on Ki for the first time. "If she's gone, who is going to collect our rent?"

"Who, indeed?"

We scour the place a bit longer before Ki gives up and asks, "Now what?"

"Let's start with the neighbors," I say, "and then everyone on Sopeap's list." I realize the man I've already encountered next door won't be much help, so I try the neighbor on the opposite side. After I call out, a middle-aged woman comes out to greet us.

"Good morning," she says, as if we were good friends.

"Good morning," I reply. "I am looking for Sopeap Sin, from next door. Have you seen her?"

She shakes her head sadly. "She is sick. She has not felt well. I think she left to get help."

"When? When did she leave?"

"A few days ago."

"Do you know where she was going?"

"No . . . no, she didn't talk much." Then the woman's eyes brighten, as though she has just solved the secret to the universe. "Lately she has been friendlier," she adds.

Though I appreciate her enthusiasm, I was hoping for something more. We try other nearby homes and fail on all fronts. With no visible clues as to where Sopeap may be or even if she is still alive, we decide to head back home so I can read through more of her essays. We are halfway there when Ki asks a curious question.

"If she goes away and we never see her again—"

"Ki, don't say that!"

"No, hear me out. If she goes away, won't the landowners send a new person to collect the rent?"

His question perturbs me, and I ask, "Do we have to worry about that now?"

"You're not understanding," he adds. "One way to find Sopeap might be to track down the landowners."

I don't mean to squeal, sounding like the pigs that neighbors raise at the dump, but I do. "You may be right. Where would we find them?" And then before he can respond, I answer my own question. "Teva will know. Hurry, let's go."

២៧

CHAPTER
TWENTY-SEVEN

The Ministry of Land and Records is located on Norodom Boulevard, near the Singapore Embassy, exactly where Teva described. It's a modern, three-story structure with a red tile roof and a contrasting whitewashed exterior. Trees partially mask the building from the street, but as we come near, I can see it's quite inviting—except for one problem. There is a gate and a uniformed guard through which everyone who wishes to enter must pass.

I tell Ki to announce our business, hoping it will sound more official.

"Can I help you?" the guard asks.

"We are here to research the ownership of several pieces of property," Ki says with such authority that I want to run over and give him a hug—but I don't. We must have passed the test because the guard waves us toward the building entrance.

The interior marbled floors are clean and swept. As I look down at our dirty and worn clothes, the contrast ensures I am instantly self-conscious. A second sentinel waits, this time behind an information desk, to further screen would-be intruders.

"May I help you?"

"We are looking for the Department of Records," Ki says, but as he pronounces the title, I realize he's said it incorrectly. It should be the Department of *Land and* Records. Either way, the uniformed guard nods once. Unfortunately, it's not a *Please-let-me-be-of-assistance* nod, but rather an *I'm-about-to-shoo-you-peasants-out* nod, and then I notice the sign behind him. It distinctly reads *Land and Records* and it directs visitors to the far stairs.

"Never mind," I say, pointing to the sign. "I can see that it's up on the second floor."

He stops nodding and also gestures toward the stairs.

We locate the office, which I hope will prove to be friendlier territory. Within the room stands a lone man behind a long counter. He wears no uniform. Once inside, Ki lets me do the talking.

"We are here to research the names of landowners," I tell him, "not only for the home where we live, but also for a few of our neighbors."

"Then you've come to the right place," he says with a comforting wave of his hand.

I breathe a sigh of relief. "Wonderful."

"Tell me where you live," he asks.

In outlying parts of Cambodia, and also within the dump, there are few formal addresses. While there may be official coordinates recorded somewhere, most homes would be known and described by either their occupants' names or by a physical description of the land and building itself.

"We live in the dump at Stung Meanchey," I say, to begin.

"The dump?" he says, shooting back a look that's hard to read. "Is there a sale going on there?"

I have no clue what he means so I ignore his comment and move forward. "We live on the northeast side, where the ground is higher, above where the water puddles into the marsh on the south, several hundred yards from where the water pipe enters beside the building with the bright blue roof."

I then pass him the list of renters we found in Sopeap's home. "These are the renters. I can describe each dwelling."

He studies the paper before taking a sudden interest in who might be asking. He scans me up and down first, and then Ki Lim.

"Wait here, please," he says sternly, as though we have done something wrong, before he steps away into another office. We hear voices, two people talking, and I lock my eyes on Ki, wondering if we should bolt this instant—though I have absolutely no idea why. Ki returns a shrug.

When the man steps back to the counter, he holds a second paper that he places on the hard surface next to mine. They are identical, his also in Sopeap's distinctive handwriting. "She brought this in nearly a month ago, and then she's returned twice since with additional information that was required," he says. "I remember her well. She was the sick woman—I have her name right here . . ."

"Sick?" I say.

"Yes, not doing well at all."

"Here it is—Sopeap Sin," he confirms.

"Yes," I say, "she is the Rent Collector. Did she say where she was going?"

He shrugs. "I'm sorry, she didn't—and I don't know about her business in collecting rent. I just know her business here was as a landowner."

It takes my brain a minute to play catch-up. "Did you say *landowner?*"

"Yes," he says, tapping his finger on the list sitting on the counter. "Well, until she sold them, that is. Technically, she is now no longer the owner."

I came to find answers, but instead the questions are piling up. Why would she keep the fact that she owned the properties a secret? More important, if she owned a dozen such properties, why would she live at the dump?

"Excuse me," I say. "Can you give me the names of the new owners?"

"Yes, it's public record. Except these transfers are so recent, the documents have not yet been recorded. It's in a different file. Please wait."

He steps away into the same office and again I hear voices. He is shuffling papers as he returns. "Ownership of the twelve listed properties," he says, "transferred to a single person. However, it will be fifteen days before everything is official." He scribbles down the name and city address of our new rent collector, then hands it over.

I stare at the name—*Chenda Lai Sin.*

We are just about to leave when he remembers something. Flipping through his file, he says, "That's right. There was one property not on your list." He digs deeper through his folder until he finds the paper he seeks.

"Here it is," he says. He reads a coordinate, but when I shrug that it means nothing to me, he steps to a long drawer and extracts an aerial plat. I have never seen such a bird's-eye view of the dump, and it's fascinating. It takes me a minute, but I soon identify several landmarks. He points to the home in question. It is Sopeap's home. It wouldn't have been on her list because she didn't need to collect her own rent. The man picks up his papers, lowers his reading glasses, and then finds the listing once again.

"Yes," he says. "This last property was different. In fifteen days, when the documents are recorded, this property will be owned by . . . let's see, Ki Lim and Sang Ly."

The home of the new landowner lies on the outskirts of the city, far enough away that I take a moto to get there. There was a time when I would have worried about trekking off such a distance alone, but no longer. I was concerned about spending the fare, but Ki reminded me that it appears we will no longer have a rent payment. Ki did add that if I find Sopeap—*our* Sopeap—he would like me to offer his humble apology and gratitude.

Now as I stand in front, with my finger on the doorbell of the surrounding gate, I'm hesitant to press the button. I have a hunch who might live here, but I can't be certain. What do I say? How do I start? Without answers, I take a breath and push.

I hear a distant buzz, and then the door to the home, several feet inside the gate, swings open. A well-dressed, middle-aged woman steps out to see who is calling. The way she looks me over, I'm certain she must think I'm a beggar, but I raise my chin and wait for her to approach.

"Yes?" she calls out. "How may I help you?" still keeping her distance.

The beginning is always a critical part of the story.

"Good morning," I reply as confidently as I'm able. "My name is Sang Ly and I am looking for the family of a girl who worked in the city as a housekeeper, many years ago, before the revolution. Her name was . . ." And then I purposely draw out my pause, to study the woman's reaction, to know if I may have the right home.

She leans forward, then actually takes a step closer. Her expression of indifference blends with uncertainty. Her eyes narrow. Her weight shifts. Her chin drops ever so slightly as her mind dusts off memories from a more difficult time. And then, I actually watch her mouth form a sound, a girl's name I have not yet spoken. Even before I finish my question, I already have my answer.

"Her name," I repeat, "was Sopeap Sin. Did you know her?"

She turns back and glances behind, as if someone else at home may have overheard, before pushing a button that releases the latch of the gate that separates us. Then, with a pleading wave of her hand, she beckons me to enter.

"Please," she says, "come in."

She points to a parlor just inside the home's main entrance, and we enter and sit. It is obvious that she wants to be polite, but at the same time she must want to know this instant who I am and what news I bring of their long-lost loved one. Before I can say more, she scoots nearer and confides, "I had a sister named Sopeap, but contact was lost with her during the revolution. Please tell me, do you have information about her? Is she still alive?"

"Before I continue," I say, "I want to be sure that we are discussing the same person. Did your sister work as a housekeeper when the revolution began?"

"Yes," she answers in a tone now reverent yet still begging for answers.

"Did she work for a teacher?"

"A teacher? Yes."

"And the teacher's husband, did he work for the government?"

"Yes, he did." With each answer the anticipation in her voice builds, as do the tears that now well in her eyes. Her hand reaches out and clutches mine.

"Do you know if the teacher was named Soriyan?" I ask.

"Yes, the teacher's name was Soriyan Song. The girl you mention, her housekeeper, Sopeap Sin . . . she is my older sister."

And then, like a crumbling dam that can hold its pressing weight no longer, her story flows out and she is powerless to stop it.

"My name is Rathana," she says. "Sopeap didn't want to go, but Papa encouraged her. He told her she represented the family, that it was important she work hard and always honor our good name. The truth is, we were poor then. Papa couldn't find work, and we desperately needed the money.

"When the revolution took over the country, many families such as ours were separated in the turmoil. Papa was especially heartbroken. We tried to reach Sopeap, but we were in the provinces then, not living near the city, and the Khmer Rouge forced everyone out. When the violence ended, Momma and Papa made their way to the city to look for her. The home where she worked had been burned, all but destroyed. They found work and soon sent for us to join them. We continued to ask, search, and inquire, but were never able to locate Sopeap. We tried working with the new government to find news of her, but unfortunately, we discovered our family wasn't the only one separated by the conflict—there were thousands, perhaps tens of thousands. On occasion we would hear bits and pieces of information that suggested she was still alive—but then, at other times, the news indicated she was dead. It was heart wrenching, especially for Papa—and then the packages began to show up. It gave him such hope."

"Packages?" I ask.

"Yes. It started many years ago. One day we found a box on our doorstep, and when we opened it, to our surprise, it contained money—several thousand *riels*. There was no note, just the carefully bundled stacks of bills. We were certain it was a mistake and we would have happily given it all back, but we didn't know where to send it. And then the next month, it was there again."

"And it has continued?"

"Usually every month. Once in a while, a month would be missed. Then, at a later time, we'd get two in a single month. Papa was convinced that they were from Sopeap, but to me that didn't make sense. If she were alive, she would surely return home. Papa said perhaps she was ashamed for something that had happened during the war—that was the kind of conflict it was. Of course, nobody could really say for certain."

"Did you try to find out who was sending the money?"

"Yes. I have three strong brothers. It took a lot of waiting and many sleepless nights because he would come at the oddest times, even in the middle of the night."

"He?"

"Yes, the person making the deliveries was a young boy, perhaps fourteen or fifteen. We caught him, of course, and he confessed to making the deliveries for a woman, but he claimed that she never told him her name. I didn't believe him. I asked him directly if the money was coming from Sopeap Sin. He didn't flinch, but he said that if we continued to interfere, the packages would stop. He wasn't happy that we'd caught him, and he insisted the woman must never find out."

"But did you ever . . . find her, I mean?"

"The very next month I followed him, quietly and from afar. I had to know if my sister was still alive—for Papa. His health was not good. I followed the boy to the dump at Stung Meanchey. Are you familiar with it?"

"Yes," I say, "I am."

"Following him in the city was easy, but it was more difficult at the dump. It's more dangerous there, and I had to stay close for fear of losing him. I think he must have figured out I was following because he began to weave and crisscross though many paths until I lost him. Still, I returned several times. I would stand back, far away from the people, and I would watch for my sister, Sopeap. On occasion I would see the boy, but never Sopeap. After several months, I determined she wasn't there after all and I quit looking. And then the packages began to arrive by a commercial delivery service, one located in the city."

"I see."

"I followed them as well, but just back to their office. I sat across the street, at a café, nearly every day for almost a month, hoping Sopeap would drop in to mail the package—but she didn't. I never found her there, either."

"I'm sorry."

"So please, tell me," she says as she pauses. "Now that you know my story, I beg of you, do you have news from Sopeap?"

I remember Sopeap—my Sopeap—once saying that heartbreaking news, unlike rice wine, does not get any better with age. I do not drink myself, but at this moment, I think I would try a swallow.

"I am sorry to have to tell you, so many years late, but your sister, Sopeap Sin, the housekeeper, died at the hands of Khmer Rouge soldiers at the beginning of the revolution."

Rathana lowers her head. I follow, feeling guilty for smothering her hope. "Are you certain?" she asks.

I nod my affirmation. "There is more to the story that I would like to tell you," I say. "But before I do, are your brothers at home? I would like everyone to hear, for it is a story of courage, kindness, and loyalty on behalf of your sister that should be told and retold for many generations to come."

"I am sorry," she says, "my three brothers are married with their own families. My husband and I and our three children live here with

Momma to help take care of her. Papa passed away a few years ago."
Then her face brightens. "I can gather everyone tomorrow, if you could
come back." Her eyes tug along with her plea. "It would mean so much
for everyone to hear it for themselves."

"Yes, of course."

And then the front door opens and Rathana and I stand as a
man steps into the room. Behind him shuffles an elderly woman.
"I'm sorry," he announces upon seeing me, "I didn't realize we had
company."

Rathana makes the introductions. "Sang Ly, this is my husband,
Ponleak." He greets me politely and then steps away. The old woman is
about to follow when Rathana calls after her. "Nana?"

She turns and shuffles back. "Nana, there is someone here I'd like
you to meet. This is my new friend, Sang Ly."

I bow and then reach out and clasp her frail and wrinkled hands.
Rathana hesitates, deciding just how much to say. *Always choose words
with great care.* Her hesitation confirms that the woman I am touching
is the mother of the housekeeper, Sopeap Sin.

"It is my honor," I say with genuine sincerity, "to meet you this
day."

"Nana," Rathana says to the old woman, "Sang Ly has a story
that she would like to share with us, a special story, about Sopeap.
She's going to come back tomorrow when the entire family can gather
around. Would you like to hear it?"

The woman's head barely moves, and I'm not sure if she understands until I notice her old eyes quiver. Then she turns and her tiny
feet scrape out of the room.

"Don't let her decaying and uncooperative body fool you," Rathana
says. "Her mind is still keen and curious."

We set a time for my return and then she asks, "Can you tell me how you know so much about my sister?"

"Of course," I reply. "But first, let me ask you about the teacher, the woman for whom your sister worked. Have you seen her since the revolution?"

"Seen her? The teacher? No . . . I mean . . . I was in the province when Sister worked for her, so I never met her. But I'm certain that she would have been killed by the Khmer Rouge. All of the teachers were—anyone educated was put to death. Why do you ask?"

"I believe the teacher your sister worked for is still alive, and I desperately need to find her."

២៨

CHAPTER
TWENTY-EIGHT

On the way back to Stung Meanchey, I visit three additional hospitals. They have never heard of Sopeap or Soriyan. Once home, Ki and I visit Sopeap's home one more time to see if there is anything we may have missed. The only thing out of place that I hadn't noticed previously is a book that is lying open on her desk chair. If one believes the cover, it's the story of a large bird emerging from an even larger fire. Based on Sopeap's previous comments, I think it's the book she was planning to bring on the day I rushed Nisay to the hospital—the book she called her favorite.

Ki sees the cover and notes that it looks like the massive fires that burn at the dump at night, but then he adds, "At the dump the bird would never get away. It would just get burned."

I flip through its pages but see nothing that helps me to know where Sopeap is hiding.

Ki glances around the room one last time. "I don't think this place will survive Nisay." He's trying to be funny, but the city of books reminds me he's right.

After picking up Nisay, we pass Lucky Fat and the boy follows us home. I start a fire to cook dinner, let Lucky Fat entertain Nisay—or is it the other way around?—and while the rice cooks, I continue to read through Sopeap's essays, looking for anything I may have missed.

After carefully reading more than a dozen pages, I think I find a clue. It is an essay I skimmed over previously, one that on the surface seemed to hold no answers. I should have known to look deeper. When I explain that I may have found something, Ki asks me to read it aloud. Lucky Fat is adding his plea. The only one who doesn't care is Nisay. Two out of three isn't bad. Ki shovels rice into Nisay's mouth, anything to keep him quiet, and I begin.

The Old Woman and the Elephant
by Sopeap Sin

The old woman was already weary when the Khmer Rouge soldiers marched her to the work camp at Khum Speu—tired bones, tired mind, tired heart.

She didn't expect to survive long, since others around her—younger, stronger, wiser—were killed or died almost every day. "The educated," the new leaders of the regime announced, "are a stain on the true worker. Cities are evil. Education and learning is useless and selfish. Money and commerce are corrupt. The strength of a nation is in the working man—not the parasites who live off the laborer! Plant rice for the nation to prosper! Only those working in the fields will eat!"

They told her over and over again that she was irrelevant, nothing better than a single grain of rice in a larger communal bowl. "Remove one grain of rice and the bowl is just as full," they would drill into her. "To keep you is no benefit. To destroy you is no loss." It was a holocaust of life but also of common sense and reason.

As a child, the old woman had suffered from nightmares—fiendish, gruesome dreams that had caused her to wake screaming, drenched in sweat and fear. However, no matter how awful they seemed at the time, she always took comfort in a truth her grandmother repeated, "Fear will flee. You will always wake up when morning comes."

In the camp, fear stayed. Everything was backwards there, topsy-turvy, upside down. Truth no longer applied, since the old woman's worst nightmares now played out during the day—when she was awake and her eyes were open.

Only at night would relief come.

Even if an occasional nighttime dream was horrific, it was always better than the alternative that waited for her each time the sun rose.

To a rational woman, someone who valued understanding and wisdom, the Khmer revolution was especially perplexing. She was beaten once for speaking up, and then beaten again two nights later for staying quiet. If she sang the Communist songs at dinner too loudly, she was accused of insulting the group leaders and of wanting to take charge. If she hummed them softly, she was derided for not adequately supporting the new regime. It was a drought of sanity, and with each passing day her own thirst for hope continued to wane.

Reason became so jumbled that after three years, four

months, and sixteen days of living as a single grain of rice, and with no answers in sight, she decided to end her existence. Who in the bowl, she reasoned, would notice?

Not wanting to give Khmer Rouge soldiers the satisfaction of killing an old woman (as if there could be satisfaction in such an act), she awoke early, before the sun, and slipped out of her hut. While others around her slept, she crept noiselessly into the darkness of the surrounding jungle.

To some it may seem that making your way into the jungle undetected was a proper escape. Not in Cambodia—and especially not in the Khum Speu Province. Anyone trekking into the jungle alone and unprotected, especially an old woman, was simply playing jungle-death roulette. It wasn't a question of if she would die, but rather how: land mine or soldier's bullet? Malaria or starvation? Spider bite or poisonous snake? So many interesting possibilities. On that morning, she no longer cared.

She hadn't gone far, just a minute or two into the dense vegetation, when she heard a rustle coming from a stand of trees ahead.

"It's come more quickly than I expected," she said as she closed her eyes and waited for death. But neither man nor animal emerged. And then she heard the rustle again, and once more, she waited. Nothing.

It was still mostly dark. The morning's feathery glow was just beginning to outline shapes and offer dimension. So the old woman patiently stood alone, wondering about the occasional movement and what the morning's unveiling light might bring. By the time she could see clearly, she'd not only grown incredibly curious, she had, in fact, properly considered the uniqueness of her situation. Since she didn't care if she perished—and would be disappointed if she didn't—she saw no harm in moving closer to investigate. And that's when she spied the elephant.

The animal was lying on its side in the thicket, near the base of a rather large banyan tree, occasionally shifting its head as if trying to get more comfortable. The old woman noticed stains of blood marking the animal's side around three piercing bullet holes, each opening a wound that led toward the creature's heart.

She knew about elephants, had learned about them in school, had read essays about them written by her students. Occasionally, her father and their driver had even taken her, as a child, up north to Battambang, where the three, on more than one occasion, had ridden elephants into the jungle with a guide. She understood that though elephants are docile in captivity, wounded wild elephants are among the most fierce and dangerous creatures on all the earth. Today, however, considering that she had come into the jungle to die, she didn't really care. Death by an angry, charging Asian elephant would not have been at the top of her list of ways to die when she had first conceived her plan, but it would be effective, quick, and, arguably, original.

And so she stepped close to the elephant's side and reached out to pat its leathered and worn hide. To her amazement, and perhaps even her disappointment, instead of raising up and charging her to death, the elephant simply lifted its head as if to get a better look before letting out what sounded to the woman like a disappointed sigh.

"I don't know who you were expecting," the woman finally replied, thinking now that this must actually be a dream, but hoping not, as she couldn't bear to wake up to the reality of her life for even one more day. Realizing that she was tired of standing, and that the elephant didn't seem bothered by her presence, the woman slid down against the creature's thick, crinkled skin to rest beside its enormous domed head.

As the two lay silently together, the old woman found herself breathing in unison with the beast's heavy, labored breaths.

Breathe in, breathe out. Breathe in, breathe out.

As she filled her nostrils with the humid morning air, the woman tried to separate the pungent aromas—banyan bark, rotting jungle foliage, elephant dung, blood, loneliness.

She mulled over her extraordinary predicament, letting her hands trace the animal's features and then touch and caress its rough hide. As she did, she felt both her breathing and the animal's becoming less labored.

Breathe in, breathe out. Breathe in, breathe out.

"I am sorry for you, momma elephant," she finally whispered. "I wish there were something I could do."

She waited for the animal to speak, for if this were indeed a dream, then talking elephants would not only be normal, they would be expected.

Breathe in, breathe out. Breathe in, breathe out.

But the animal didn't speak because it wasn't a dream. The creature simply stared back with her sad and teary eyes, perhaps wanting to reply in her own elephant way but being either too exhausted or too near death to make the effort.

Breathe in, breathe out. Breathe in, breathe out.

And that's when the old woman remembered learning that elephants mirror humans in numerous ways—life span, development, family ties, and feelings. Similar to people, they display a range of emotion. They will help one another in adversity, miss an absent loved one when separated, smile when they feel happy, and shed tears when they are sad. And when they are too weak to get up, they die surrounded by their grieving loved ones, just as humans would choose to die. She even remembered reading that when elephants come across other elephant bones on a trail, they will pick them up with their trunks and carry them away to the safety of nearby trees.

"What happened to you, elephant?" the woman finally asked. "Why would the soldiers shoot you?"

Breathe in, breathe out. Breathe in, breathe out.

"Wouldn't they be surprised if they arrived soon to find you lying down in the jungle, chatting with an old woman?" The bizarre notion caused her to chuckle quietly.

Another moment passed as the old woman hesitated, not sure if she should confide her secret. But then, realizing that she was talking to an elephant, she continued, "I want you to know, momma elephant, that I too am tired and that I also came here today to die."

Breathe in, breathe out. Breathe in, breathe out.

The elephant's head shifted as her massive body shuddered, her internal organs beginning to shut down. Still the old woman didn't move, but instead leaned in closer.

"I am sorry you are alone today, momma elephant," she whispered.

No sooner had her words been spoken than she realized that the elephant wasn't alone at all. For she, the old woman, was there by her side, helping the dying creature when comfort and friendship were most needed.

Breathe in, breathe out. Breathe in . . .

And then, the elephant smiled.

. . . breathe out.

The great beast exhaled one last time and it was over.

Nearly an hour passed as the old woman remained beside the elephant, pondering the oddity, wonder, and sacredness of the day.

If she returned to the camp and told them about the creature, she would be hailed as a hero. They'd had only rice gruel to eat for many weeks, and an animal of this size would provide real meat for a very long time. But they would slice up the elephant, cut her into pieces, boil her flesh, and ultimately scatter her bones across the jungle.

The woman stood up from the ground, stretched her muscles, and then spoke to the elephant one last time.

"I came into the jungle this morning thinking only of myself, but now, I dearly need to thank you. I need to thank you, momma elephant, for truly needing me. You see, I haven't been needed for a very, very long time. Today, you've made a difference—at least to me."

She gathered enough leaves and branches to cover the body of the elephant until she was certain it was so well hidden that it would never be found. Then she retraced her early-morning path out of the jungle and back to her hut in the work camp. When the soldiers demanded to know where she had been, she pointed to the jungle path, directly toward the spot where she'd found the elephant, and then she rubbed her stomach and replied, "I didn't feel well. Surely you didn't want me doing my messy business near the huts, did you? You're welcome to go into the jungle and investigate for yourself, if you like that kind of thing."

And then, with a suspicious but convincing smile, she returned to her work to plant rice for the benefit of the new society.

"Is the old woman really Sopeap?" Ki asks. "Is it possible that she actually found an elephant in the jungle?"

"I don't know," I say, frustrated that I'm not able to put my finger on what is so peculiar and bothering about this story. I page back through the writing to confirm a suspicion.

"The woman doesn't have a name," I say. "Doesn't that seem odd?"

Lucky Fat shrugs. "You're the teacher. Is it?"

My brain drops the pieces together one by one. *In stories, everything means something.*

"And wouldn't she be too old to be Sopeap?" I add. "The Khmer revolution occurred in the mid-seventies, so she would have been . . . what? . . . in her mid-thirties at best."

Then I remember the phrase that Sopeap used to describe herself in her letter, and the picture comes together.

"Sopeap isn't the old woman!" I announce, certain of my realization.

"She isn't?"

"No, Sopeap is the elephant."

"The elephant?"

"Yes, and in her story the elephant died almost in sight. Wounded and hidden, but so close, almost anyone could find her—if they just knew where to look."

"What are you saying?"

"I think I know where she might be!"

២៩

CHAPTER
TWENTY-NINE

We stand near the street and wave for a moto. As the driver slows, Ki is still asking questions.

"I'm confused. Why did she leave home again in the first place? I mean, she's lived at Stung Meanchey for years."

"It wouldn't matter if it were a hundred years," I say. "The dump was never her home—no matter how hard she tried to make it so."

"But you don't know exactly where she is?"

"No, not exactly."

"And the book in your bag is going to help you to know?"

"Sort of. It's going to be important once we get there."

"If you don't know where she is, how do we know where *there* is? I mean, how will you actually find her?"

My answer is simple. "I know a momma elephant who is going to lead the way."

The plush area of the Daun Penh district of Phnom Penh, while older, offers stately homes—many rebuilt and restored to the grandeur of their days prior to the revolution, complete with gardens, fountains, and statues. They are estates occupied by the nation's wealthy and important. It's a beautiful and fitting place. We approach the neighborhood, which is guarded by a towering stone wall with two matching iron gates. Thankfully, we arrive by car, courtesy of Rathana and her family.

There is not just one guard shack, but two—one for the entrance and a separate one for anyone leaving. The heavy gates serve to protect the place from outsiders who try to enter. When our car slows, the cars behind us also slow and then stop. A uniformed guard dutifully steps to our window.

From the passenger seat, I turn to Grandma Sin, who is seated behind me in the back. "Is this the place?" I ask.

She lifts up her head, gazes at the homes beyond the gate, and then raises her scrawny and bent fingers toward the second home on the right. Similar to those that surround it, the structure is distinguished and striking. From outside the gate, it looks to be three stories high, with a tiered roof and several open verandas that snake around its levels. I can see grand marble pillars that connect with stone railings, retaining plants, and flowers that both hide and invite.

The guard waits for the driver to speak, and he, in turn, points to me. The guard stoops to see inside, as if I may be some visiting dignitary or royal visitor. I lean toward the window to see his face. He says nothing, but rather raises his bushy eyebrows, as if it were a universal sign that means, "Well, then, who are you and who are you here to see?"

"We are here to speak with the owner of that home," I tell the man, pointing to the home that Grandma Sin has identified.

"What is your business?" he asks. He reminds me of a soldier, and I wonder about the memories that must have flooded Sopeap's head on her return. And then there's the question: What if I'm wrong? Worse, what if I'm right, but the man won't let us pass? What do I say to him that will make any sense? And then I tell a small lie.

"The owner is expecting us. Please call and tell him that we are here to see the old woman."

"What old woman?" the guard asks.

"Just call him. He will know."

Ki sits in the back, next to Grandma Sin. He directs his concern forward. "What if the homeowner doesn't know what you're talking about?"

"He'll know."

"How?"

"He'll know because she is here."

The guard hesitates, then relents, picks up a phone receiver, and pushes a button. I can only hear his end of the conversation.

"Mr. Rangsey? This is Chimm. I have a group of people here asking for you. They say they are here to see the old woman."

There is a long pause. He glances toward me, and then up again to the house.

"Yes, sir," he replies. "I understand. I will tell them."

He hangs up the phone and bends over to the car window. "He will come down to meet you. Please pull through the gate and park your cars just ahead in the empty spaces on the right."

Storm clouds thicken on the horizon, and I wonder if they portend a sign. The man's words imply that Sopeap *is* here, don't they? Why else would he let us in and agree to come down? But what if, instead, he's greeting us because we are here too late?

We are out of the car for what feels like a lifetime before the front door opens and a well-dressed man of about forty steps out of the house. Since I am in front, and the most eager, he presumes I am in charge and extends his hand to me.

"Hello. My name is Heng Rangsey."

"And I am Sang Ly."

"You are here to see the old woman?"

"Yes, we are."

"She told me that she had no one. That she was all alone."

"She was mistaken. It just took a while to find her," I explain.

"Then she was telling the truth, that she once lived in this house before the revolution?"

"Yes."

"I presumed so."

"May we see her?"

"Certainly, but I need to warn you. She is not doing well. She has hardly eaten since she arrived, and she has difficulty speaking—but she has been made comfortable. I've had my housekeeper watching after her."

He motions to the door and we enter. As we do, I can't help but ask, "Did you know her? I mean, before she came?"

"No. I first met her several weeks ago, after she discovered her condition. She seemed fine, and when she explained that she needed to die here, in this particular home, I was understandably reluctant. I told her *no*."

"But she offered you money?"

"Yes, she did. But I refused. I don't need her money. That is not what changed my mind."

"What did, then?"

"She is a teacher. My father was also a teacher, only he wasn't so lucky."

"What do you mean?"

"He was killed by the Khmer Rouge at the beginning of the take-over, as was my older brother. Now please, go up the stairs, across the veranda, and out to the garden roof."

And then he pauses and swallows hard. "When she saw that we had rebuilt the garden roof, she cried like a child. Quite frankly, I haven't been able to get her to rest inside."

I walk up the steps, across an open balcony lined with beautiful plants, then step out into a magnificent garden, only partially blocked by a half roof.

Indeed, I am not prepared for what I see.

Her eyes are closed. Her leathery skin—from spending so much time in the sun of Stung Meanchey—is furrowed and grey. She is heaving slow, deep breaths.

I don't want to wake her, but as I pull a chair close, she opens her eyes, looks up, and seems momentarily confused as to where she might be. She coughs, reaches for a blanket that covers only half her legs, then whispers—but so softly I can't understand what she says. I lean close so that she can repeat it.

"You just won't leave me alone, will you?" she says.

"No. I won't," I tell her. "Not considering that you got it so wrong."

Her pinched features harden with a question of confusion. "Don't worry," I say, "I am here to show you. Now, I have some people I need you to meet."

I motion to Grandma Sin, who is waiting to step close. She shuffles beside Sopeap's bed and then instinctively, like any good mother would, reaches over without saying a word and clasps Sopeap's hands. I am about to explain to Sopeap who the old woman is, but the tears in her eyes tell me that she already knows. *Of course, the packages.* Sopeap would have watched their delivery from afar.

With the old mother close, Sopeap taps her bony finger to her own heart.

"Three holes," she whispers.

Grandma Sin's scratchy voice answers, and I realize it is the first time I have heard her speak. " . . . not your fault. My daughter loved you."

I step back and try to hold my tears, watching two momma elephants nuzzle and reminisce. Then when Grandma Sin shuffles aside, I motion to Rathana, and she moves beside the bed.

"Auntie," she whispers, a common Cambodian title for someone revered, related or not. "I am Rathana, Sopeap's sister. We have not met, but you have made such a difference in our family." She motions to her husband and he steps to her side.

"Auntie, I am Ponleak, Rathana's husband. I am a chemical engineer. I work for an oil company here in Phnom Penh. My parents were able to help me with school because of your kindness and generosity. I will be forever grateful." He reverently bows and then waves forward a teenage boy and a younger girl. "These are two of my children. I have another daughter who is married and living in Seim Reap. We have come here today to honor you."

The children make way for their oldest uncle, a man I met just this morning. He motions for his family to gather close to Sopeap's bed.

"Auntie, my name is Kiri. This is my family. My children have also been able to get a good education. I have a son who is not here. He works in farming. He has an advanced degree in agriculture. But we are most proud of the woman he married—and we even have a grandson." A young mother, whose name I don't remember, holds up a child of two or three. "I wish we'd have had more time to get to know you better," she says, "but regardless, our family will be forever blessed because of your kindness."

Two more families take turns gathering children around *Auntie*, expressing thanks and paying tribute. She is too weak to respond, but it doesn't matter. With the room still full, I work my way around to where I can lean in close, so that I'm certain she can hear me.

"That is your lesson," I tell her, "and there is no other that is more important."

Once everyone has finished and final good-byes have been said, the families file quietly and reverently away, leaving me alone to sit by her side and hold her hand as she continues to heave heavy breaths.

Breathe in, breathe out. Breathe in, breathe out.

As the clouds close in, an evening rain begins to fall. The drops are large, like elephant tears, and as they smack the floor, they break into tiny beads that dance and play across the tiles. The owner of the home, Mr. Rangsey, comes out from inside and together we reach for the corners of Sopeap's bed, ready to pull it in from the edge of the terrace and out of the rain. With all the strength she can muster, she raises her hand to ask that we leave her be. And so Mr. Rangsey excuses himself while I sit with Sopeap and welcome the warm evening shower.

Rain in the dump makes water filthy. Rain in the garden cleanses.

Breathe in, breathe out. Breathe in, breathe out.

The blanket has fallen off, but Sopeap doesn't seem to care. It is only then I notice that one of her brown socks—the baggy, ordinary socks I once criticized—has slipped off of her foot. Her ankles are swollen, but that is not what catches my attention. It is the scars that crisscross her feet, old wounds common to those who gather trash too close to the dump's nighttime fires.

Breathe in, breathe out. Breathe in, breathe out.

If Sopeap is crying, I cannot tell, as the cleansing droplets now run down every furrow of her face. I know that she is dying and that I should run and get the owner or the housekeeper and have them call a doctor. But if I do, they will rush her from the rooftop garden beneath her rescuing rain, and away from her home rebuilt from ashes.

Breathe in, breathe out. Breathe in, breathe out.

To ease her mind and offer comfort, I reach for the story she called her favorite. It is from the author named Hans Andersen. I am not familiar with him, but I plan to change that with a bit more time and Sopeap's gift of books.

I hold her twisted fingers lightly with one hand and turn the book's pages with the other. The pages are getting wet, but it doesn't matter.

Breathe in, breathe out. Breathe in, breathe out.

I read slowly and deliberately, to make sure she can hear and understand every word.

> In the Garden of Paradise bloomed a rosebush. Here, in the first rose, a bird was born.

As my voice reaches Sopeap's ears, her muscles relax, her grip slackens, and any fear that might linger in her heart wanes and flows away in the rain.

I continue.

> His flight was like the flashing of light, his plumage was beauteous, and his song ravishing. But there fell a spark into the nest of the bird, which blazed up forthwith.

Breathe in, breathe out. Breathe in, breathe out.

> The bird perished in the flames; but from the red egg in the nest there fluttered aloft a new one—the one solitary

Phoenix bird. The fable tells that he dwells in Arabia and that every hundred years, he burns himself to death in his nest; but each time a new Phoenix, the only one in the world, rises up from the red egg.

The bird flutters round us, swift as light, beauteous in color, charming in song. When a mother sits by her infant's cradle, he stands on the pillow and, with his wings, forms a glory around the infant's head. He flies through the chamber of content and brings sunshine into it, and the violets on the humble table smell doubly sweet.

Breathe in, breathe out. Breathe in, breathe out.

But the Phoenix is not the bird of Arabia alone. He wings his way in the glimmer of the Northern Lights over the plains of Lapland and flutters among the yellow flowers in the short Greenland summer. Beneath the copper mountains of Fablun and England's coal mines he flies, in the shape of a dusty moth, over the hymnbook that rests on the knees of the pious miner. On a lotus leaf he floats down the sacred waters of the Ganges, and the eye of the Hindoo maid gleams bright when she beholds him.

The Phoenix bird, dost thou not know him? The Bird of Paradise, the holy swan of song! On the car of Thespis he sat in the guise of a chattering raven and flapped his black wings, smeared with the lees of wine; over the sounding harp of Iceland swept the swan's red beak; on Shakespeare's shoulder he sat in the guise of Odin's raven and whispered in the poet's ear, "Immortality!"; and at the minstrels' feast he fluttered through the halls of the Wartburg.

Breathe in, breathe out. Breathe in, breathe out.

The Phoenix bird, dost thou not know him? He sang to thee the Marseillaise and thou kissedst the pen that fell from his wing; he came in the radiance of Paradise, and perchance thou didst turn away from him towards the sparrow who sat with tinsel on his wings.

The Bird of Paradise—renewed each century—born in flame, ending in flame! Thy picture, in a golden frame, hangs in the halls of the rich, but thou thyself often fliest around, lonely and disregarded, a myth—"The Phoenix of Arabia."

Breathe in, breathe out. Breathe in . . .

In Paradise, when thou wert born in the first rose, beneath the Tree of Knowledge, thou receivedst a kiss, and thy right name was given thee—thy name, *Poetry.*

. . . breathe out.

Sopeap lets go of her final breath, flies away with my words that drift distant in the night to the glorious place where family waits—and it is over.

I close the dripping book and place it restfully against her chest. I want to be sad—to wail and lament the passing of my dear teacher and friend, Sopeap Sin—but I do not. Perhaps it is because I don't want the feeling of peace and love that has swept across my life to leave. Instead, I sit back in the rain, letting it also cleanse and wash another, for perhaps an hour, holding Sopeap's hand and pondering the *wonder and sacredness of the day.*

And then, when the time feels right, I pull the blanket over Sopeap's silent body and stand to leave. As I make my way out of the home, I look for the owner or perhaps his housekeeper, to let them know what has happened, and to thank them. They are nowhere, and I presume they have retired to bed for the evening. I will return in the morning to make arrangements for cremation of the body Sopeap has left behind.

As I near the base of the steps, adjacent to the front door, I find Ki asleep in a chair, still waiting. Of all the stories I have read about heroes, and all that I could ever read, of one thing I'm now certain— he is mine. I touch his face and he wakes up. It takes a moment for him to gather his reason, but when he does, he understands what has happened. He rises and folds his arms around me, holding me tight for a very long time.

"Mr. Rangsey said we are welcome to stay the night. He showed me which room."

"Is there time instead to get back to the dump, to get to Sopeap's home?"

"It's late," he says, "but we can make it."

Together, we walk through the dirty streets of Phnom Penh, sometimes in darkness, but it doesn't matter. We walk through Sopeap's renewing, restoring, astonishing, redeeming rain.

mo

CHAPTER
THIRTY

Many have gathered around our old home on the mound. I know most as my neighbors from the dump, but there are also many faces I don't recognize. They are here because Lucky Fat has announced that an important story is about to be told.

When everyone is ready, I step up and inside, just behind where the tarp attaches as it folds onto the roof, so I can stand above the crowd and everyone can hear. At times the events that have occurred in my life over the last several weeks push emotions so close to the surface that it's difficult to speak. Not tonight. Instead I offer a silent plea to Father that my voice will be strong, and then I begin.

"I am here today to tell you of a fable.

"After I finish, some of you may whisper that it is not true. You may say that my words are made up, that my story is nothing but a myth—and you may be right. But as a wise and great teacher once explained so patiently, all good stories—stories that touch your soul, stories that change your nature, stories that cause you to become a better person from their telling—these stories always contain truth.

"Some, including myself, have told a false fable, a story of Sopeap Sin that was a lie. I come tonight to correct your misconceptions and open your eyes.

"I ask now that instead of listening with your ears you listen with your hearts—for Sopeap taught me that hearts comprehend truth.

"Many years ago, the great sky god, Vadavamukha, received word that those living on the earth below in Stung Meanchey had lost their way. They had been consigned by luck, both good and bad, to pick through mountainous piles of other people's trash in an effort to make their living. The long hours, their meager earnings, and the filthy conditions at the dump caused many to lose hope. Even worse, many forgot their true nature.

"'We must help them to see past their filthiness,' said Vadavamukha. And so he counseled with his wife, Queen Reak Ksaksar Devy. They considered many solutions, but each was fraught with problems. Finally, after many days, they agreed they would send down Soriyan, a beautiful princess and also a great teacher in the heavens, to help those at Stung Meanchey. Soriyan was also their daughter.

"And so Princess Soriyan was summoned. However, as the princesses entered the great hall where Vadavamukha and Reak Ksaksar Devy sat, the queen exclaimed, 'This plan will not work. She is too beautiful. If she goes down to the ugliness of Stung Meanchey, her beauty and radiance will blind all who look upon her.'

"Vadavamukha knew his wife was right, and so a great sadness swept across the heavens for the people of Stung Meanchey. But Princess Soriyan stepped forward and exclaimed, 'Do not be sad. The plan *will* work. I will clothe myself in garbage as a disguise, so that I might have the chance to teach the people and restore their hope. For there is no greater gift I can offer than that of hope.'

"Her parents agreed, and so, even though it was difficult for them to send their daughter away, Vadavamukha and Queen Devy clothed Princess Soriyan in filthiness and placed her into a garbage can to obscure her beauty. Then, Vadavamukha hurled the can from the sky toward the earth, where it landed at Stung Meanchey.

"But when it landed, Princess Soriyan struck her head, and she forgot who she was and why she had been sent to Stung Meanchey. For many years, she was called Sopeap Sin, as no one knew her true identity—neither she nor the people whom she had come to teach.

"When Vadavamukha and his wife looked down from the heavens and saw what had happened, the queen said, 'We must do something. Our plan is not working. We must go down and save Soriyan and forget about restoring hope to Stung Meanchey.' But the king wisely answered and said, 'Give our daughter time. She will soon remember, and the experience will make her an even greater teacher, for she will also have empathy.' And so they waited.

"Though it was a difficult trial, Princess Soriyan—or Sopeap Sin, as the people knew her—slowly began to remember her heritage and that she was a great teacher. By now she was old, and she realized there wasn't time to teach all the people living at Stung Meanchey before she would be called back home. But being the wise teacher that she was, she wrote down her most important lessons in the form of simple stories that the people could understand, and she called on others to both write and tell stories, stories filled with truth—though sometimes hidden—to offer direction to anyone with patience and a heart ready to listen.

"To this day, if we look carefully around Stung Meanchey, if we search for stories that teach truth and goodness, stories with lessons that can soften and change our hearts—we will discover hope."

In quiet moments the feeling returns, the same one that washed over me the night Sopeap passed away, the night Ki and I walked back to Stung Meanchey in the rain.

In spite of my learning many new words since, I've never found a proper way to describe this feeling, except to say it is the same as waking up in a place you know is polluted and stained but instead finding it covered in a cleansing blanket of white, a layer that does more than mask. When you dig down, all your filthiness, uncertainty, and fear have vanished and instead you are encircled by pure and overwhelming love.

The moments are infrequent in a hectic life that is still a constant storm of struggle, and yet when they occur, these moments are anchors. They keep me facing in the right direction. I still awake every morning to a dump that is smoky, but through the smoke, I've seen some of the most amazing sunsets.

Still, one thing remains certain—Grandfather spoke the truth. The day Ki found Sopeap's book, the same day he was robbed, the day that felt so miserable and terrible and discouraging—it was indeed *a very lucky day.*

Now I'm going to teach a young boy how to write his name.

ACKNOWLEDGMENTS

I sincerely thank the following for their contributions and support:

The many great writers of classical literature whose work I've referenced or quoted in *The Rent Collector*. In a handful of cases, for the sake of pacing and tone, I've modified their original work. There is a reasonable chance that all are horrified, but their work is in the public domain, and, of course, they are dead and I'm not. Perhaps by the time we meet up, they will have forgiven me.

Joni Buehner, who offered permission to include her amazing poem, *Love Forever*.

Earl Madsen, my associate and business partner, who was instrumental in the success of my first book, *Letters for Emily*. Earl passed away unexpectedly just before Christmas in 2009. His wry humor is still missed. It was at his funeral that I decided to get off my butt and write another book.

The many editors and readers who helped correct my mistakes

and improve the story: Emily Watts, Ken Neff, Richard Peterson, Rosemary Lind, Wendy Ulrich, and, of course, my wife, Alicyn.

JoAn D. Criddle, whose book *To Destroy You Is No Loss* served as a resource to accurately portray Sopeap's experience with the Khmer Rouge.

My son, Trevor, whose documentary film and love of Cambodia provided the basis for my setting, story, and characters.

Sang Ly, Ki Lim, and their children. They touched our lives in ways never expected.

My parents, who always offered shining examples of patience, encouragement, and love.

My amazing children.

Last, but never least, Alicyn. While I am often a skeptic (realist), she is our believer. The combination has worked out pretty well.

DISCUSSION QUESTIONS

See www.TheRentCollectorBook.com for more questions and additional information, including author comments on many of the discussion topics.

1. In the opening pages of *The Rent Collector*, Sang Ly's grandfather promises that it will be a very lucky day. What role do you think luck plays in our lives? How does the idea of luck reconcile with the novel's epigraph, the quote from Buddha on the opening page?

2. After reading *Sarann* (the Cambodian *Cinderella*), Sopeap and Sang Ly discuss how story plots repeat, reinforcing the same lessons. Sopeap calls resurfacing plots "perplexing" and then asks, "Is our DNA to blame for this inherent desire to hope? Is it simply another survival mechanism? Is that why we love Sarann or Cinderella? Or is there more to it?" How would you answer? What are possible explanations for the phenomenon?

3. Sang Ly says that living at the dump is a life where "the hope

of tomorrow is traded to satisfy the hunger of today." How might this statement also apply to those with modern homes, late-model cars, plentiful food, and general material abundance?

4. Sang Ly mentions that Lucky Fat has an "uncanny knack of finding money lost amongst the garbage." Do you suppose someone may have been helping him by placing money for him to find? If so, who?

5. Speaking of her clock, Sang Ly says, "Sometimes broken things deserve to be repaired." What might she be referring to more than the clock?

6. The shelters at Stung Meanchey are built to protect the resting pickers from the sun. What other purposes do they serve? What "shelters" do we build in our own lives? How would you react if the "shelters" in your life were constantly being torn down?

7. At first, Ki is reluctant to welcome change, specifically to see Sang Ly learn to read. He says, "I know that we don't have a lot here, but at least we know where we stand." What do you think he means? When have you found it hard to accept change?

8. Sopeap tells Sang Ly: "To understand literature, you read it with your head, but you interpret it with your heart. The two are forced to work together—and, quite frankly, they often don't get along." Do you agree? Can you think of examples?

9. *Koah Kchol,* or scraping, is an ancient remedy Sang Ly says has been practiced in her family for generations. Do you have your own family remedies that have been passed down? What are they, and do they work?

10. Sang Ly and Sopeap discuss dreams. Have you ever had a

dream that changed your attitude, decisions, or outlook? Was it a subconscious occurrence or something more?

11. In a moment of reflection, Sang Ly admits that she doesn't mean to be a skeptic, to lack hope, or to harbor fear. However, she notes that experience has been her diligent teacher. She asks, *"Grandfather, where is the balance between humbly accepting our life's trials and pleading toward heaven for help, begging for a better tomorrow?"* How would you answer her question?

12. Sang Ly speaks often to her deceased grandfather, but not to her father, until after her meeting with the Healer. Why did her attitude change? How might the same principle apply to relationships in our own lives?

13. Sopeap always wears thick brown socks, no matter the weather. As Sopeap lies dying, Sang Ly notices that the socks have slipped, exposing scars on Sopeap's ankles. How would you presume Sopeap got these scars? How might Sopeap's scars (or rather their source) have influenced her appreciation for the story of the rising Phoenix? In what ways does Sopeap rise from her own ashes, literally and figuratively?

14. The story ends with Sang Ly retelling the myth of Vadavamukha and the coming of Sopeap to Stung Meanchey. By the time you reached the final version in the book's closing pages, had you remembered the original version in the book's opening pages? How had the myth changed? How had Sopeap changed? How had Sang Ly changed?

15. When the story closes, Sang Ly and her family are still living at Stung Meanchey. Are you satisfied with the ending, that they remain at the dump? Why or why not?

AUTHOR'S NOTE

Though *The Rent Collector* is a work of fiction, Stung Meanchey, the setting where it takes place, is real.

In 2009, the capital city's monstrous municipal waste dump was permanently closed by the Cambodian government. An alternative dump was opened several miles to the west of the city. No homes are allowed at the new dump, so many of those who lived and worked at Stung Meanchey now pick through trash in the city, hoping to find enough to recycle and thereby feed their families and keep them together.

I was first introduced to Stung Meanchey, and the people who live there, through my son's documentary, *River of Victory*. (To see what life is actually like living in a garbage dump, please visit *www .RiverOfVictory.com*.) In the film, he followed the struggle of Sang Ly's family at the dump and her desperate journey to visit the Healer, a visit she hoped would save her son.

Using the documentary as a starting point, I tried to write a novel that accurately reflected the setting, conditions, character traits, and important historical facts. Then, going beyond that, I wanted to imagine what might happen if the gift of literacy were given to a family in those circumstances. The scenario I envisioned plays out in the fictional elements of *The Rent Collector.*

I have included photos, taken from the mentioned documentary, to offer the reader a fuller flavor and understanding of Stung Meanchey and its residents. The pictures are not an attempt to portray *my* characters and *their* particular story as factual.

I'm reminded that Ernest Hemingway is reported to have said, "All good books have one thing in common, they are truer than if they had really happened."

I believe he has a point.

Ki Lim, Sang Ly, and Nisay

Picking trash at the dump

Working the trucks

Fires make the task more dangerous

Home

Bath time

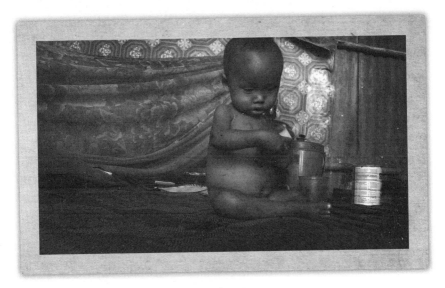

Nisay

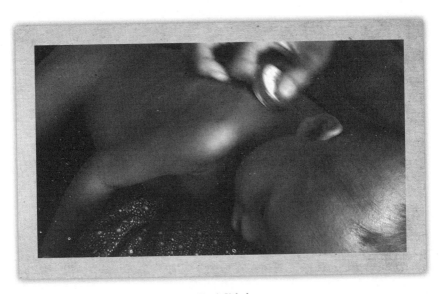

Koah Kchol

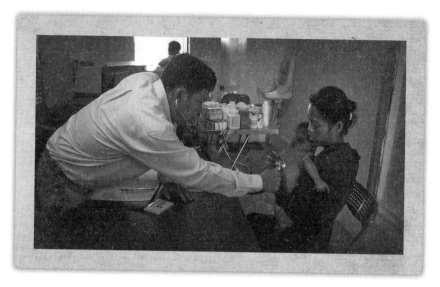

Foreign doctor

Sang Ly picks alone

Lucky Fat

Teva Mao

Snail hunt

Leech bite

Arriving at the province

Uncle's house

The old woman

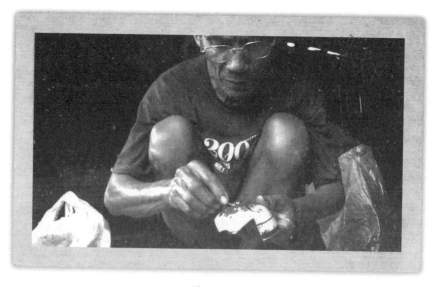

The Healer

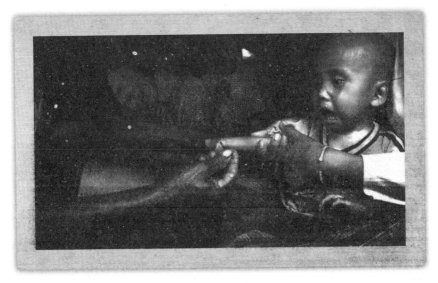

The Healer's treatment

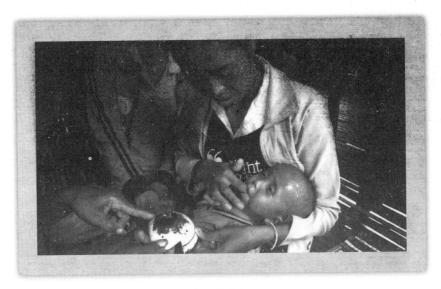

Sang Ly helps

Happy now

Nisay is finally well

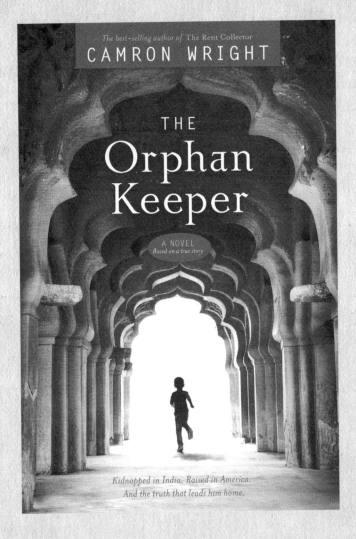